NURSING HOME

by

Ira Eaton

BeachHouse Books
Chesterfield, MO 63006-7151
(636) 394-4950

Copyrights

Acknowledgment

The author wishes to express appreciation to Dr. Bud Banis, and his wife, Lois for their endless patience and assistance in preparing this manuscript.

originally published by Science & Humanities Pre, 1997

BeachHouse Books Edition published 2010

ISBN 9781596300651

PO Box 7151

Chesterfield, MO 63006-7151

(636) 394-4950

www.beachhousebooks.com

This book is dedicated with love

to Sheila,

the center of my universe.

NURSING HOME

CHAPTER 1

Tywalla Lindley sat up groggily in the back seat of the grimy 1948 Buick. It took her a moment to orient herself. When she realized what was happening she immediately leapt out of the car and told the driver to get away. Fast. To her alarm, which would turn to hysteria, she realized that the McIlvane Manor Nursing Home was on fire. A serious roaring fire. And she was in charge. If anybody got hurt, it would be her fault.

Running desperately to the front door, she could hear screams from within and the sound of people beating on the solid front door — the door she had locked and to which she, in her panic, couldn't find the keys. They must have fallen from her skirt, which she had obligingly removed so that the two men in the now-departed Buick could have their way with her.

Tywalla, a big swarthy woman, beat, shook, and kicked the door in sobbing frustration, but to no avail. Soon the door became too hot to touch. The screaming from inside stopped.

When the firemen finally arrived Tywalla Lindley was reduced to a incoherent, blubbering blob. She was seen kneeling and praying on the front sidewalk as the firemen carried out the bodies of the trapped, helpless people. Thirty-four people died in that fire. There had been others before them who perished in similar circumstances. There would be others to follow.

In the confusion, Tywalla got up and dazedly walked away in the general direction of her rooming house. The firemen and police were so busy with the fire scene that she went unnoticed. Tywalla told herself that she never would have gone outside with those men had she known that anything like this was going to happen. She had gone outside with men before and nothing had gone wrong. If only she hadn't helped kill that quart of gin, she wouldn't have fallen asleep. She tried to deal with her guilt and shame by blaming the owners of the nursing home for leaving her there alone. She should have had help. Furthermore, she reasoned, it was God's will.

Some of those people were better off dead. These slim rationalizations weren't strong enough to work for long.

Six months later, on Christmas Day, 1954, Tywalla Lindley took the remainder of her unemployment money and bought soda pop, candy, and small, cheap favors and made her way to a shabby, nearby nursing home. She was full of the spirit of Christmas and giving. There was a fixed smile on her face that didn't seem quite genuine, but no one at the home was looking a gift horse in the mouth. The patients were delighted with this unscheduled Santa Claus and thanked Tywalla many times for her generosity.

Tywalla lingered at the old home long after the excitement of her visit had subsided. It was as though she hoped that something would happen to rekindle the momentary warmth she felt from being center stage. It didn't. The party was over.

Tywalla stepped out into the cold December day at sunset and returned to her lonely, squalid room and killed herself. Her final pitiful gesture couldn't erase the horror of the fire. She tried, but she was unable to drink the screams of the people she had doomed out of her dreams. Ironically, the city of St. Louis had her cremated.

The fire at the McIlvane Manor Nursing Home was given front page newspaper coverage across the nation for one day. It held up as newsworthy in the local St. Louis papers for three days afterwards. The remains of the building were soon leveled so that the tragedy might sooner be forgotten.

Originally, McIlvane Manor was built as a classy, European-style hotel for the 1904 World's Fair in St. Louis. It was an exclusive establishment where celebrities and people of means chose to stay.

The fortunes of the three story hotel began to change in 1950 when a rich and opportunistic gambler bought it from the owner, who was dying of cancer and could no longer maintain its quality standards. The gambler, with the collusion of the local police, soon transformed the hotel into a garish brothel and gambling house that still masqueraded as a hotel. It managed to flourish for a few years until its owner went broke and was found shot to death in an alley. It then sat for over a year, unattended and decaying from neglect.

The building was bought in 1952 by a "retired" chiropractor who, some years earlier, had his license lifted for performing abortions. He and his eccentric wife were becoming well known for buying distressed properties in and around the St. Louis area and transforming them into nursing homes. Rules and standards for nursing homes were so lax during this period that one could get a license for any building and be pretty much free to run it as one's conscience dictated.

The conscience of "Dr." and Mrs. Raymond Calhoun dictated that they run it as an abomination, a business from which the greedy couple could milk every possible cent. To be fair, the building was in sad shape when they bought it. So sad that other buyers were turned away at the Calhoun opening bid of six thousand dollars. Other prospective buyers were factoring in the cost of doing a quality restoration job. The Calhoun plan called for no such restoration. Patching and painting was as far as they ever went. Instant slums were their style. In the period between its closing and the auction, the hotel had deteriorated greatly, as any abandoned structure will. It had become a haven for the city's derelicts and had sustained a number of small fires, had broken pipes, shattered windows, and heavy water damage from leaking roofs. The air conditioning system was completely destroyed, having been scavenged by a local contractor who needed many of its expensive components.

The once noble hotel could have been restored to its former elegant self had it fallen into the hands of someone with style and imagination. The Calhouns, in their usual style, brought in old, used and, in some cases, discarded furniture and patched the old place up enough so they were able to rent beds to desperate people — those who needed help but had no other place to go.

There were still some windows out and there were no screens at all. The flies were everywhere during the summer and they always seemed to linger far into the winter. The roaches were a constant; they knew no season. Those who recalled the place said there was always a fly on some defenseless old person's nose or a vile roach skittering across the floor. The unholy smell of the place could be detected as you approached the building from the sidewalk. Never mind what it was like inside.

It was a wonder there wasn't an outcry from public spirited citizens or people with some vestige of humanitarianism about them. But there wasn't. The building still looked respectable from the vantage point of passersby on Lindell Boulevard so no complaints were ever heard from the citizenry. Besides, people said a nursing home was a far superior use of the building than the cat house it had been before. Maybe it wasn't surprising because people also tended to accept the existing racial conditions in the United States and the shocking state of the country's mental hospitals. There were just some things that the average person was unable to face. Anyway, Korea was enough for most people to worry about.

After the fire, a few state and local politicians made some noises about nursing home reform. It was weak and short lived however. People weren't ready to hear it.

The sleazy, opportunistic Calhouns made out like bandits on the fire. They collected twenty eight thousand dollars in insurance claims—no one sued them—and sold the desirable, double lot to a local building contractor. The property was located in the very fashionable 4500 block of Lindell Boulevard and was prime for development of any kind.

The contractor built a well-designed ultramodern nursing home on the site. He sold it before it was completed to a Chicago based nursing home company that proudly opened it in 1955 under the name of Sunset Meadows.

The Mayor and other local politicians attended the ribbon cutting. Every speechmaker present hailed the opening as a "new day" in the care of the elderly. People felt good about it. Korea was over and the economy was beginning to boom. The phrase, "I like Ike," was on everybody's lips and the promise of an era of prosperity was on the horizon. At least on that day, many people in the area felt that the elderly were going to share in this prosperity.

CHAPTER 2

Gina Marie Oldani could remember her father very clearly, even though he had died of cirrhosis of the liver when she was ten years old. That he should die such an ignominious death didn't surprise those who knew him. His friends weren't surprised because Angelo Oldani drank at least a case of beer every day. He had for the last twenty-five years of his life. He was forty-nine when he died in 1948.

While his friends weren't shocked at his premature demise, they were nevertheless saddened. Angelo was a very popular man. He was a two-hundred-sixty pound laughing, joking Italian who never disappointed a friend. Tales of his daring feats were often discussed by the rank and file of the St. Louis Police Department where he had been an instructor in their School of Judo. To his fellow officers, Angelo Oldani was a man to be emulated and looked up to. Not to his family.

At home, when he was there, a different personality emerged; surly, dominating, and authoritarian were the words Gina would later use to describe her father. It took a professional therapist to bring her to voice this realization many years later. Admissions of that sort don't come easily to most people. Many repress those feelings all their lives. Although there were times when he was cheerful and loving, times when he would hug and kiss her, she was generally very guarded around him. With Angelo Oldani, children were to be seen and not heard; there was absolutely no place for disagreement or discussion about any issue. It was his house, he provided the living and was never questioned by his faithful wife and daughter.

He left his wife Louise with very few material goods and no insurance. He did leave her a $100-a-month mortgage on their modest two bedroom home on Daggett Street, part of the Italian enclave of St. Louis known as Dago Hill. Louise was faced with raising her beloved ten-year-old daughter in spite of the fact she had no work skills or experience. Angelo had never permitted her to work.

The Police Department, because of the high esteem placed on the memory of Angelo, provided Louise with a $350.00 a month job as a secretary. Never mind that she couldn't type; she'd learn. The pay was more than other beginning secretaries were paid but everyone in the Police Department felt good about it.

The loss of her husband was bittersweet for Louise. She had been out of love with him for several years but had grown comfortable in their little home. She had dreaded his occasional drunken, clumsy lovemaking attempts over the past six years. His breath had reeked of stale beer and cigar smoke and he had become incapable of maintaining an erection. They never discussed this problem. The only thing that made life bearable was Gina, the light of her life. Louise didn't necessarily have plans for her daughter's future or for that matter even hope that she would live a life different or somehow better than the one that Louise had come to know. It was enough that she loved Gina fiercely, and that love made her life glow. She would somehow provide a good living and of course a good Catholic education.

Gina's loyalty remained to her father and to the church's teaching which said to honor thy mother and father. This made it impossible for her to think or talk of him as anything but a wonderful man and father until much later in her life when realism would temper her beliefs. Many people exceed their reality in death. So it was with Angelo Oldani.

In the years following Angelo's death, a wonderful close relationship between Louise and Gina developed. Gina was a picture perfect child, bright, pretty, and always respectful and courteous to her teachers. She treated all people with kindness. Now that she was free of the fear and domination of Angelo, Louise also began to flower. She discovered that she was indeed a person with ability and a respected point of view. When she was married, she played the role that was taught her by her parents and the one expected by her husband. She was a subservient housewife who never spent a penny nor went out in public without her husband's permission. She grew quickly with the newly-gained sense of independence and the responsibility of being head of the household.

Louise quickly gained the admiration and respect of all her coworkers at the Police Department. She became proficient at typing and shorthand but beyond that she became the person to whom everybody turned for advice and wise counsel. She had not magically gained all this wisdom since Angelo's death. She had developed it over the course of her life the way other people do. The only difference was that it was no longer repressed. She did, however, resist the advances of the several men who attempted to press their favors upon her. Her old-fashioned value system and her inexplicable devotion to the memory of her late husband simply wouldn't allow flirtation. Neither would her fears that all men were essentially like Angelo. She figured she could get along without another one like him.

By the year 1954, Gina was sixteen years old and an Italian beauty. She had dark hair and flashing eyes with a bright, ready smile and a slender, supple body that invariably turned the heads of boys and men of all ages. She attended St. Mary's, an all-girl Catholic High School on Lindell Boulevard, which was a fifteen minute bus ride from their home on the "Hill". She was a straight "A" student and popular with the other girls at St. Mary's.

Gina hurried home each evening so she could work until six o'clock at Ambregolli's Bakery where she was paid fifty cents an hour. She was very proud to help her mother to that extent. Gina was developing, with guidance from her mother, not only a kind and pleasing personality but a quick and intuitive mind as well. Louise and Gina spent countless hours discussing matters ranging from politics and philosophy to religion and history. They both loved these private, intimate discussions and both of them preferred the company of each other to going out for entertainment with friends. There was never a harsh word or disagreement between them because they loved one another more than themselves. Life was good and neither wanted it to change.

Louise's only living relative was her brother, Vincent Gambrino. Uncle Vinnie, as Gina called him, was two years older than Louise and had amassed a fortune. Nobody knew exactly how great the fortune was or the details of how he had become rich. It was believed that he had ownership in a number of bars and restaurants in New York, Chicago and St. Louis, but Vincent Gambrino was not a man whom you questioned about his personal business.

Vincent lived on a twenty acre estate some forty miles north of St. Louis on a high bluff overlooking the Mississippi River. The mansion was thirty-four rooms with a tennis court and large Olympic-size swimming pool. Objects of art were everywhere. Renoirs, Picassos and sculpture by Rodan were carefully placed throughout the vast house by professional decorators. The house was of museum quality but it was never admired by the public and only rarely by invited visitors. Vincent Gambrino was a very private man.

He was a stranger to the Oldani household until Angelo's death when he appeared at his sister's door five days after the funeral. He confessed that he was unable to visit and be a good uncle and family member because Angelo had told him early on that he didn't want to be associated with him in any way. Louise, of course, knew this was how Angelo wanted it and she was so afraid to cross him that she had gone along. She was deeply ashamed of her behavior and prayed regularly for God to forgive her. They both wept at the lost years and hugged each other for several minutes.

Amends were made and both were relieved that their relationship as brother and sister could resume.

In the days following the cathartic reunion, Vincent became a regular visitor. He fell in love with the beautiful and innocent Gina and wished to shower her with gifts, travel and money. He pleaded with Louise for them to join him in his luxurious mansion where he would show them both a side of life they'd only dreamt about and seen depicted in the movies.

Louise's newly emerging pride and independence as well as her need to jealously guard the close-knit ties with Gina caused her to consistently and forcefully reject her brother's pleading. He finally relented on the condition that he be allowed to visit frequently and that they spend some time with him at his home. This arrangement was to prove satisfactory.

Louise and Gina spent the month of July at Vincent's palatial home during the summer of Gina's seventeenth year. Louise took a week's vacation but had to return to work for the last three weeks of the month. She steadfastly refused to let her brother provide her with any sort of financial assistance or help of any kind. He wanted to have his chauffeur drive her to and from work but she insisted that driving her 1940 Plymouth coupe would do nicely, thank you.

Quite naturally, Louise was tempted frequently to take advantage of some of the outrageously extravagant offers Vincent was always making. Especially tempting were the plans he would lay out for travel both in the United States and abroad. She knew this would be educational and broadening for Gina. She also knew that one day she would capitulate to at least one trip–maybe to New York where Vincent routinely went once a month anyhow. Louise's recalcitrant position of declining gifts from her wealthy brother was puzzling to Gina. Nevertheless, she was steadfastly supportive of her mother whose judgment in her eyes was always sound.

In an earlier conversation Gina had asked her mother why Uncle Vinnie had suddenly materialized after her father's death. She knew there was an uncle named Vincent Gambrino living nearby but knew no details until he finally emerged. Her mother, as always, told her the truth of the matter and how ashamed it made her to have turned her back on her only living relative for all those years. This was yet another instance where her father had denied her something that was rightfully hers. She adored her uncle. He was everything a girl dreamed about when they think about an ideal father. He was Ozzie Nelson and Santa Claus rolled into one smiling, doting package.

In addition to the mind-boggling acquisitions of art, cars, imported furniture, rich tapestry and oriental rugs in every room, Vincent had a library that was first rate. You would rarely catch him reading a book, but Louise and Gina absolutely loved the limitless range of his library. They spent every spare moment reading books ranging from best sellers to classics. Louise marveled at the way Gina would understand and sometimes expand on highly abstract ideas and theories found in some of the books. There was no question about it; this was a very bright child, still naive, but bright as a shiny new penny.

CHAPTER 3

Louise and Gina returned to their home on Daggett Street in early August and were very happy to resume their regular comfortable life. The visit to Uncle Vinnie's had been wonderful, to be sure, but coming home to the little, familiar bungalow was like seeing a dear old friend after a prolonged absence.

The days at her uncle's home had opened new vistas in Gina's understanding of life and what it was about. Her life had always been full of activity, but it was school, work, reading and the close relationship with her mother that had taken her time and energy. She never thought of it, but her existence had been very sheltered, almost cloistered. Her mother had never bought a television set and they didn't receive either the *St. Louis Post-Dispatch* or the *Globe-Democrat*, which were the two leading newspapers in town. This made Gina's realization of what was currently happening in the world limited. She was gaining information and knowledge at a good and steady rate but it was controlled by the Sisters of St. Mary's High School and her mother.

Gina was excited about returning to her senior year at St. Mary's. She had become full of optimism about the future and gained confidence in her abilities to do good work and to get along with people. She scarcely knew what a sour relationship was because she treated everyone nicely and with respect, and people responded to her in kind. The times that she witnessed conflicts between people frightened her and momentarily froze her with a feeling of intense confusion and tension.

School began on September 4, 1956, after the Labor Day weekend, and in spite of temperatures reaching 100 degrees and humidity that resembled what our fighting forces faced on Bataan and Corregidor in World War II, the mood at St. Mary's was happy and upbeat. Gina and Louise had settled back into their comfortable routine and were happy in spite of the oppressive heat which they endured without the benefits of air conditioning. They were beginning to discuss going to New York City with Uncle Vinnie during the week of Christmas vacation. This was very exciting to both of them and they read all they could about that wondrous city and even began planning an itinerary. They wanted to maximize their enjoyment in the short time they would be there.

Thanksgiving dinner was to be held at Uncle Vinnie's. Louise and Gina drove up early that morning and planned to return home that evening despite Vincent's insistence that they stay over. A light snow fall had begun as they set out and, along with the bracing 30-degree temperature, gave them assurance that the prolonged and unusually warm autumn was behind them and the new, glorious winter season was now to be enjoyed. They were lighthearted and giddy on their car ride and spontaneously broke into a medley of familiar Christmas carols as they watched the snow and viewed the Mississippi River which ran parallel to the highway. When they reached the mansion they were let in by Eugene the butler. Their olfactory senses came alive with the wonderful smells from the kitchen. The chef was preparing a traditional Thanksgiving feast of not one, but a brace of turkeys, sweet potatoes, dressing (both cornbread and oyster), homemade dinner rolls, corn, fresh cranberries, and pumpkin pie made from scratch. The anticipation of the meal which wasn't to be served for three more hours was so intense that Vincent rang for the maid and requested that she serve coffee, milk and sweet-rolls to abate their appetites.

As they leisurely finished the light brunch the topic of the trip to New York was broached by Louise. Vincent was ecstatic that they wanted to go. He knew he would show them the city like no one had ever seen it before. The rest of the day was full of animated conversation about the trip, full of questions by Gina and Louise and speeches by Vincent. He talked about not only the historic and marvelous things to see in New York but cautions about the lurking danger there as well. Nothing he could say about the seamy side of the great city could dull their enthusiasm. It was a wonderful day for them all, but particularly for Vincent, whose heart was bursting with joy at the thought of finally being able to share his wealth with his beloved sister and niece.

Dinner was served by two maids in uniform and closely watched by the Italian chef, who personally carved the turkeys. Louise made a comment about the extravagance and overabundance of food which was sloughed off by Vincent in his usual cavalier manner. He replied that life was meant to be enjoyed and that nothing was too good for his family. Louise joined Vincent in a glass of champagne and they toasted their pending trip. Gina, who was allowed her first small glass of wine, asked that they give thanks for having been brought together and allowed the chance to love one another. Tears formed in both adults' eyes and the three of them hugged and patted each other warmly.

The trip home was more sedate than the drive had been that morning. They were comfortably full with a feeling of contentment. The snow had ceased and had left an accumulation of two inches but it had not stuck to the road so driving was no problem even though dusk was upon them. The chef had wrapped leftover turkey, expertly carved, and samples of the other food from the sumptuous meal. They couldn't bear to think of eating more that night but both knew they would enjoy it the next day. Thoughts of New York filled their minds. God was good.

The next day, Friday, both Louise and Gina "slept in" until eight o'clock. This was sinfully late for them but it was enjoyable. It was snowing again and this time it looked like it meant business. They breakfasted lightly and casually, still feeling the effects of the Thanksgiving feast the day before. Cereal and orange juice for Gina, toast and coffee for

14

Louise. They recounted the events of the holiday when Gina made mention of her first glass of wine.

Louise looked surprised and asked, "What wine? I don't remember you drinking any wine"

Gina was puzzled by this but didn't protest. She took it as a sign that maybe her mother didn't want her to drink wine and had suppressed the experience because it was painful. At any rate, she vowed to herself that she would never drink in front of her mother again because she didn't want to cause her one ounce of concern. Later puzzlement over this small incident furrowed Louise's brow. She didn't want Gina to know that she was bothered over such a silly memory lapse.

CHAPTER 4

Louise Gambrino Oldani was feeling exhilarated on an otherwise glum, gray December day. She was thrilled about leaving for New York the next day. She told her friends and coworkers that she was doing it principally for Gina's sake but she knew in her heart that she was bursting with anticipation. She, like Gina, had never been to New York or on an airplane.

Louise was glad to have the stimulus of planning the vacation, going shopping with Gina and making all the preparations for the trip. It took her mind off a slight, nagging feeling that maybe she was getting older or beginning "the change". Lately she was noticing a slight tendency to tire easily and some difficulty with concentration. Sometimes while reading she would find herself staring at the page and daydreaming about nothing in particular.

She was, after all, now in her fifty-second year and had no history of poor health. Louise was five feet five inches tall and weighed one hundred and forty pounds which, with her frame, was only ten pounds heavy. She tended to dress down preferring to wear her slightly graying hair pulled back and tied in a bun. This, together with her habit of wearing severely cut, proper dresses and practical, rather than stylish, shoes, made her look like a sixty-year-old librarian. If she had gone to a beauty salon and a skillful beautician were to have her way, she would have been one the most striking "before and after" examples on record. It was as though she wanted to disguise a very attractive person. The old fashioned wireless glasses she wore completed the disguise. In spite of all these affectations, men could still recognize the potential hiding beneath this shallow facade. Louise didn't wish to do anything to encourage anyone of the opposite sex to be the least bit attracted to her. Maybe she would think about that after Gina was no longer a responsibility. She hoped and prayed that day would never come. She hoped that she and Gina would live together in their little house on Daggett Street forever.

Vincent Gambrino, like his sister, was excitedly looking forward to the New York trip only for different reasons. His feelings stemmed from the fact that he was going to have the chance to spend time with his niece and to make her happy. He was picking out the clothes he would wear with the usual care he exercised in such matters. Vincent was not a tall handsome man at five feet seven and one hundred seventy pounds. He was never seen in public in anything other than a dark blue or gray business suit with matching silk tie and expensive white shirt. His shirts were imported from Italy and had his initials over the right breast; he had them made with no breast pockets for reasons known only to him. He had close-cropped, wiry gray hair with a very low hairline. His forehead was scarcely two fingers wide from the top of his eyebrows, making for an ape-like effect which was added to by close-set brown eyes and a nose that was flat and splattered across his face. Given all his features separately, Vincent Gambrino would have summed up to be a very homely man, but somehow the total effect was, although not handsome, comfortable and easy to like. When he smiled, which was often, a hint of gold flashed from both sides of his mouth where he had "dentistry of distinction" performed over the years. His hands were consistently manicured with shiny, clear lacquer applied at all times. His hands were short and stubby and made the oversized diamond ring on his left hand look bigger than it actually was. Several people had told him that he closely resembled a young Greek tycoon named Aristotle Onassis who was beginning to make a name for himself in the shipping industry. Since he had never met Mr. Onassis or seen a picture of him he didn't know whether to be flattered or insulted. Close inspection and comparison by an impartial panel would have given Gambrino a definite edge in looks over the Greek.

Vincent Gambrino wasn't at all self-conscious about his looks. He was a man who achieved through cunning and persistence, not charm and intellect. He was proud of that. In the past eight years he had moderated his personal habits on orders from his doctor. He moderated his smoking and stopped drinking to excess. He began watching his diet somewhat and attempted to get regular exercise. He suffered a slight heart attack six months before Louise's husband died and believed that he would die himself if he didn't watch it. He religiously took his medicine and kept the knowledge of his bad heart from Louise and Gina.

Promptly at 8:00 a.m. on December 24th a gleaming black Cadillac limousine silently pulled up at the Oldani house. It looked very much out of place in the working class neighborhood, and all the people up and down the street peeked out, hoping to catch a glimpse of the rich, important person who was riding in the back seat. Was it the governor? What business would such a person have here on Daggett Street?

The chauffeur carried the luggage and deposited it in the trunk and they were on their way, going north on Kingshighway toward the airport by 8:10, giving them just enough time to catch their 9:45 flight.

Checking the luggage, getting the boarding passes and finding the proper departing gate would have proved impossible for the inexperienced women but it was no problem whatsoever with the worldly, knowledgeable brother and uncle taking complete charge. As he knew he'd do.

The three of them were seated in first class on a spanking new TWA 707. The takeoff was breath taking and a bit unnerving for the ladies. Vincent laughed at their wide-eyed innocence. Gina couldn't imagine or understand how something as big and as heavy as a 707 could take off and fly. "How can it stay up?" she asked. Her mother and uncle were unable to give a satisfactory explanation for the phenomenon.

The beautiful, attentive stewardess asked if they wanted to order anything to drink. She advised them that an early lunch would be served. Coffee for the adults and a Coke for Gina were ordered by the man without consultation of the other members of the party. Gina and Louise spent most of the flight craning their necks looking at the clouds and marveling over the whole experience. The flight was uneventful and landed at LaGuardia airport on time.

A chauffeur, in livery, met them at the gate and escorted them to the baggage claim area where a large smiling man with a thick foreign accent picked up and carted their luggage to the waiting limo, a replica of the one which took them to the airport in St. Louis. Vincent tipped the porter five dollars and was thanked profusely.

The sun was shining brightly and the temperature was an unseasonable forty eight degrees as the limo quietly and expertly whispered its way through the heavy holiday traffic to the Waldorf-Astoria Hotel where two adjoining suites awaited.

After checking in and receiving a brief tour of the Waldorf, the threesome went out onto Fifth Avenue for their first look at New York City. Vincent insisted that they take a horse drawn carriage ride through Central Park which was an enormously popular decision. After the ride they dined, *alfresco*, on hot dogs with sauerkraut and sodas. The sidewalk vendor had a bank of roasting chestnuts on his cart that smelled marvelous. The rest of the day was spent window shopping, and they were back in the hotel by five o'clock — a wonderful start to their dream vacation.

That evening Vincent ordered dinner from room service, feeling that he shouldn't overstimulate his guests on their first night in New York City. This was a wise choice because Louise was very tired even though she had napped for two hours. She seemed to be sluggish upon awakening and remained that way until retiring early at nine-thirty.

Breakfast arrived at their suite promptly at seven o'clock, complete with flowers from Vincent. When the room service waiter knocked on the door, Louise sat up, blinked, and said "Oh my, I had forgotten where we were." She shrugged and thought to herself that this sort of thing happens to everybody who isn't accustomed to traveling. She felt well rested and told herself to be gay and full of energy so as to not spoil a minute of this vacation for Gina.

During their breakfast, which was twice the amount of food that either could eat, Vincent called and announced that he would be knocking on the door in one hour to take them sightseeing. In precisely sixty two minutes he was there to escort them to the waiting limousine.

Every minute of the next six days was filled with some new sight, smell or taste. Gina and Louise simply could not get over the endless range of restaurants, the wonderful architecture and especially the people. The city was bustling all day, all night, everyday and every night; the crowds and traffic were constant, never ending. Their activity was never-ending as well. They went to three Broadway shows. They would have gone to four, but Louise begged off, saying she was a little under the weather, probably caught a slight bug or something. Gina served her mother dinner in bed that night but Louise ate none of it, falling asleep before taking the first bite. Gina smiled and thought that all the excitement was overwhelming her mother.

Louise woke up with a splitting headache. She said it was one like she had never had before but that she would take some aspirin and it was sure to go away. She didn't want to spoil their last day in New York.

The weather had changed dramatically since they'd arrived. It was now eighteen degrees, windy with sleet and snow and very disagreeable. None of the three were strangers to raw weather, but this cold seemed almost intolerable, especially to Louise. Vincent made sure the limousine was always stationed directly outside any door they exited so that the time spent in the elements was kept to an absolute minimum.

The whirlwind of events that had surrounded the past week continued to stimulate and excite Gina. During the early planning of the trip she was sure her mother would be as enthusiastic as she was, but Louise seemed somehow not attached to all that was going on around her. There was a dreamy vagueness surrounding her that was not behavior that either Vincent or Gina had ever seen before. Gina was concerned enough about it to ask her uncle what he thought. He assured Gina that it was probably their exhausting schedule mixed with a touch of the flu. Vincent didn't know if he thoroughly believed his own explanation and made a mental note to have his sister seen by his doctor when they returned home. Gina was relieved and that was his goal for the moment.

The days in New York had been busily orchestrated by Vincent with respect to the wishes of his guests. They had seen the wonderful Christmas show at Radio City Music Hall featuring the Rockettes and a stage full of live animals, including camels and an elephant. Tours of Chinatown, the Staten Island Ferry with a close up view of the Statue of Liberty, the elevator that zoomed up through the bowels of the Empire State Building at sixty miles per hour (or so the guide said), the complete tour of the United Nations Building and luckily catching sight of Dag Hammarskjold, the elegant stores along Fifth Avenue and the quaint shops on the side streets were all crammed into their week. Each day they ate lunch and dinner at a different swanky restaurant; it seemed that at least one famous personality was dining at the same place. It pleased Vincent to point them out, and it always made him beam to see Gina's face light up with pleasure.

On the flight home, as Louise slept, Vincent asked Gina which was her favorite part of the trip. Gina pondered this for a moment and said that each and every moment would be something she would remember and cherish the rest of her life. But of all the sights and sounds, the fact that some six million people were buzzing around on that little island, day in and day out, and that it just didn't sink from the weight of it all was the biggest revelation. She kissed her Uncle Vinnie and told him she loved him and that he was the kindest man that had ever lived. Vincent Gambrino would have been willing to die for this lovely, innocent child.

Louise was groggy when it was time to deplane, so Gina and Vincent each took an arm and helped her to the waiting Cadillac. As soon as the luggage was put in the trunk they were off, arriving at the Daggett Street house thirty five minutes later. Louise thanked her brother for his many kindnesses and went straight to bed, not even bothering to say goodnight to Gina.

CHAPTER 5

Gina and Louise spent New Year's Eve quietly and without anything more than cursory observation. It was an old family tradition to drink a glass of wine at midnight, and Louise was determined to observe that custom although she was tired and would rather have gone to bed. Gina was mildly surprised when her mother reminded her that they would drink a toast together to welcome in 1958. She cautiously reminded Louise of her reaction to Gina's first glass of wine at Thanksgiving. Louise retorted that the incident was petty and merely a misunderstanding. Gina quickly dropped the subject. Louise fell asleep at nine o'clock in her easy chair. Gina wrestled with whether or not to awaken her but finally reasoned that her mother would be disappointed if she slept through their little celebration.

She gently shook Louise's shoulder and said, "Mother, wake up. It's 11:45 and I know you don't want to miss the electric moment when 1958 arrives."

Louise was slow to come around and was groggy and half-lidded for several minutes.

When she spoke it was to call Angelo and ask if he wanted anything.

Gina was shocked and knelt down by Louise. "Mother, you were just talking to Daddy. You must have been having a dream about him."

Louise smiled weakly, "Yes, I must have been. Goodnight darling. I'm going to bed

Gina slept very little that night. It was two degrees below zero and the wind was howling, making the little house colder than normal. It was alarm over her mother's behavior that kept Gina tossing and turning, not the weather, although the wind added an eerie dimension to the first hours of 1958. Gina had never contemplated what life might be like if her mother was incapacitated or, God forbid, that she would pass away. She had never known her mother to be anything but alert, bright, and completely in control of all her faculties. She prayed over and over for her to be her old self in the morning. Her prayers were not to be answered. January first dawned sunny with the temperature below zero and not expected to exceed five above. Gina fixed coffee and orange juice and baked the blue berry muffins that were Louise's favorites, but on this morning she refused them and took only one cup of coffee and then returned to bed for a nap.

Louise stayed in bed until six o'clock that evening when Gina urged her to get up and eat some of the spaghetti, garlic bread and salad which were lifelong favorites. Louise wasn't at all her animated, conversational self at dinner and only dabbled at her food. Gina couldn't hide her concern any longer.

"Mama, I think we should call Uncle Vinnie and make an appointment for you with his doctor. I'm afraid you have the flu or something. You've lost your appetite and you don't have the usual amount of energy."

"I'm okay, honey. It's just that I'm not used to the traveling. I guess it wore me out. I'll be fine after I return to work tomorrow and get back into my routine."

"Please, Mama, a check up won't hurt." Gina was pleading. "I just read an article which said we all should have one at least once a year. Please, Mama, do it for me."

"All right, sweetheart. You know I can't refuse you anything."

The next day, January 2nd, was a Friday and a work day for Louise, but school didn't resume for Gina until the following Monday. Gina awoke early and fixed a large breakfast of bacon, eggs and toast, but Louise ate almost nothing.

24

When Louise returned from work that day her mood was different. She seemed to be livelier. She had stopped at the drug store and purchased six books of crossword puzzles which was unusual because she rarely had shown any interest in them before. Gina, however, saw this as a very positive sign that everything was going to be okay.

Over their dinner of fried fish, slaw and baked potatoes Gina remarked with enthusiasm, "I called Uncle Vinnie today and he gave me the number of Dr. Zarinsky, the wonderful doctor he's always talking about. Your appointment is for Tuesday at ten a.m. at his office on West Pine."

Louise looked at Gina incredulously. "What appointment? I'm not sick and certainly don't need to pay some expensive doctor to tell me so. How could you have taken it upon yourself to do such a thing?"

Anger from her mother directed at her was such a rare thing that it stunned Gina for a moment. When she gathered herself together she said in a low and apologetic voice, "I'm sorry Mama, but don't you remember last night when you said it would be okay to make you an appointment for a check-up? You said you couldn't refuse me anything."

"Oh yes, I remember. I'm sorry, darling. Things seem to slip my mind sometimes these days. Guess I'm getting old. I'm going to work some crossword puzzles now."

Vincent picked Louise up at 9:30 on Tuesday morning. The cold snap had moderated somewhat and it was now twenty degrees and cloudy. Vincent and Louise chatted idly about the weather on the way to the medical building on West Pine Boulevard. Vincent was acutely aware that his sister didn't quite seem to "be with it," and he was anxious to find out what was the matter so he could get her back on track.

Dr. Zarinsky's office was typical of the offices in the building. The waiting room would comfortably seat a dozen people. There were *Life* and *Look* magazines as well as *National Geographic* distributed around, all of which were limp from use. They all looked tired and well-read with dog-eared corners and torn pages, probably put there by children who were restless.

Promptly at ten a tall, slender and very handsome man in his mid forties burst through the door with a large smile and grasped Vincent's hand pumping it unmercifully.

"Vincent! How nice to see you. You look good. Following your doctor's advice, eh?"

"Hello Edward. Yes, I'm feeling well. This is my sister, Louise, who isn't feeling quite up to par lately. She says she is fine and probably is, but a checkup can't hurt. Right?"

Edward Zarinsky, a graduate of St. Louis University Medical School and a highly respected physician in the community, looked like someone central casting had sent over to play his role. He wore a lab coat with his name monogrammed on it and had a stethoscope around his neck. He appraised Louise with kind, warm eyes and extended his hand. "I'm very glad to meet you, ma'am." He smiled and remarked that it was a very lucky thing that she bore only slight resemblance to her brother. All three laughed heartily at this because it was obvious that the two men had the kind of close friendship that made that sort of joke acceptable. Dr. Zarinsky wasn't in the habit of stepping over the bounds of propriety.

The receptionist and nurse who assisted Edward Zarinsky knew that this patient was special because he never went to greet anybody personally, always preferring to let the receptionist lead them to one of the examining rooms. She would act accordingly and be solicitous of Mrs. Oldani's every whim.

Louise dutifully followed Dr. Zarinsky to his office and took the comfortable chair he offered. Vincent had diplomatically offered to wait in the lounge, thereby not requiring his physician and friend the obligation of suggesting it.

Louise and Dr. Zarinsky emerged thirty minutes later, both smiling.

26

Vincent asked, "Well, what's the verdict, Doc? Will she live?"

"Yes, I believe so. It looks like she has some kind of post viral syndrome that I've seen before and can cause all the symptoms she's experiencing. It usually makes people mildly depressed, listless, and carries with it a lessening of appetite and attendant weight loss. Makes it hard to function properly, but I think with rest and the prescription I'm writing, she'll be back to her old self in a week or so."

The two men's eyes met for an instant. Vincent thought he detected a tinge of uncertainty. "Send me the bill, Ed."

"Have I ever failed, Vincent?"

CHAPTER 6

Dr. Zarinsky's diagnosis of post viral syndrome gave Louise much needed relief. It meant that whatever was bothering her had a name, that it could be treated with rest and medicine and that it would go away. She took to obsessing about it to anyone who would listen, especially Gina. This new behavior was very trying to those around her. She would ask the same questions over and over and when the person to whom she was talking would tire of answering, she would supply the answers herself. Her trouble began looking like some form of mental illness.

It had been ten days since the appointment with Dr. Zarinsky. Louise's condition worsened. She had trouble sleeping and eating, and she was forming a curious need to always be with somebody. She required constant reassurance that her affliction was common and curable. She would grow immensely frustrated because she was prone to lose or misplace things. Her memory, especially the short term kind, was deteriorating. She worked the crossword puzzles whenever she could. Gina realized later that this was a self-prescribed diversion both calculated to keep her mind off her troubles and to validate that her mind was still good and that she could think clearly.

On Friday, January 23, she came home from work early and went to bed. Gina arrived at four p.m., surprised to see the car in its little garage because her mother didn't ordinarily get home until 5:30. Entering the house she found an official looking letter on Police Department stationery lying open on the floor. Gina's concern and curiosity got the best of her and she read:

Dear Mrs. Oldani,

In recent weeks it has become apparent to both me and your other co-workers that your poor health has disabled you to the point that you are unable to perform your duties at the level that our department requires.

It is for this reason, and I believe it to be in your best interest, that I must ask you to take a leave of absence until such time as your health permits you to return and perform at the excellent level we know you're capable of.

Our prayers are with you for a speedy recovery. We look forward to your return.

Sincerely,
Captain Joseph

E. O'Hara

Vincent, after hearing the story from Gina, arranged to have Louise admitted to Barnes Hospital where Ed Zarinsky was on staff.

Dr. Zarinsky, now alarmed and no longer believing that Louise's condition was minimal, ordered every type of test he could think of as well as asking a psychiatrist to see her. Gina spent every day and night at the hospital. Vincent saw to it that she could sleep in the adjoining bed. At the end of three days Dr. Zarinsky called Vincent and Gina to his office for a conference.

He was very kind but got right to the point. "I'm sorry to have to tell you that Mrs. Oldani has a brain tumor. It looks operable if we do it right away. I can't tell you what she'll be like afterward or even if she'll live. I'm certain that she won't live for more than thirty days if we don't operate."

After the initial shock, Gina and Vincent began asking the horde of questions that most loving, devastated families ask. Dr. Zarinsky had played his part in this scenario far more times than he would have liked.

He explained that the tumor appeared to be the infiltrating type; neither layman ever got a completely clear explanation of how infiltrating was different from malignant or, for that matter, if it was different at all. He pointed out the outlines of the vile, detestable dark spot on the x-ray and told them how they would excise the major portion of it but some would have to remain or they would damage her brain too severely. He went on to say, in the most fatherly tones, that this operation would improve the quality of life for a period of time but life expectancy would not be lengthened by more than six months or so.

"You mean she is going to die?" Gina wailed. "Does it have to happen? Could she maybe cheat the Gods?"

"What are the odds she'll pull through, Ed?" Vincent asked in a very hushed tone.

"One out of a hundred is the most optimistic I can be. I'm terribly sorry."

Gina was so shaken by the news that Vincent asked Dr. Zarinsky to prescribe a sedative so she could sleep. The pill acted quickly because Gina was so dazed and exhausted. It was as though she were ready to leave this world of brutal reality. Vincent was back at the hospital at 8:30 the next morning and found Gina dressed and sitting holding her mother's hand. After some small talk, she and her uncle went to the hospital coffee shop to discuss the unbelievable, tragic decision that they must make.

Their discussion lasted for over an hour with each of them alternately arguing for, and then against, the operation. They came to the decision to operate. One chance in a hundred is better than no chance at all.

The operation was scheduled in two days and was to be performed by Dr. Gerald Hastings, a noted surgeon and close friend of Ed Zarinsky's. Louise accepted the news well; at least she was brave for all to see. It was very difficult to know exactly what her feelings and thoughts were because they had become so distorted by the "thing". Gina was unable to utter the word tumor so she and Louise referred to it as the "thing."

Both Gina and Louise were in a more optimistic mood the day of the operation. Surely God would not take this woman, who was virtually a Saint, in her prime of life. They both felt confident that the doctors wouldn't go to all this trouble if they didn't believe that everything would be all right. Doctors are highly trained, have all the up-to-date equipment and years of experience. Surely they wouldn't let this bad dream end tragically.

At eleven the nurses came in to prepare Louise for the operation which was scheduled for one o'clock. On their cart were scissors, a razor, shaving cream, and a hypodermic needle with a vial of medicine beside it. Gina kissed her mother and went to the lounge to pray, large tears welling up in her eyes.

The operation lasted two hours, and the doctors said it was a success. Gina was overjoyed not knowing what success meant exactly. She felt a rush of joy and relief that her mother had survived someone opening up her skull and cutting around on her brain. Maybe this case would be that magical one out of a hundred after all.

Gina was pleasantly surprised to find Louise awake and cognizant the next morning. She was cheerful and said she felt no pain. Gina was relieved that her mother was recognized her immediately and that her power of speech, although slightly slurred, was intact. The two began making plans for the return to their home, both agreeing that the first order of business was to purchase a good quality wig.

Louise was allowed to go home five days after the operation. This was sooner than Gina had expected, but she was glad. She was tiring of the hospital and felt that the sooner they were home, the sooner the rehabilitation process could begin. She had lost more weight than Gina would have guessed. She weighed 120 pounds the day she was discharged. In spite of all she had been through, as she was taken to the waiting limousine in a wheel chair, she looked for all the world a rich, happy woman without a care, accompanied by a beautiful young woman who could have been anything from her daughter to possibly a very much younger sister.

Her mother, although awake and alert, was confused and disoriented. She would say the same things over and over — perseveration, the doctors called it. She also had become very keyed up and became compulsive about walking around. It was as though walking was her job and she had to perform well to demonstrate that she could still function. The wig make her look normal, but Gina was shocked to see that her hair, just a stubble now, was growing back solid white. Gina had grossly underestimated the amount of patience and skill required to care for her mother. The need to walk had now progressed into obsessive pacing that would go on for eight or ten hours a day. This puzzling behavior persisted in spite of Gina bundling her up warmly and taking her on two forty-five minute walks around the neighborhood every day.

Louise's appetite was poor except that she would eat two bananas each day. She had heard Dr. Zarinsky mention she needed potassium and since she knew that bananas were rich in potassium, she religiously adhered to the two-banana-per-day regimen. She would take her vitamins, but only when Gina served them; Louise could never remember when she had last taken one. She could not sleep unless Gina was in the same bed. Even then, four hours a night was tops. The strain was beginning to tell.

Louise's mental capabilities were deteriorating rapidly. She had been home for ten days with Gina by her side constantly. Vincent dropped by every other day or so and suggested that Gina hire a nurse to look after Louise so Gina could get some rest and go back to school. He told her that he thought she was looking tired. Gina was unable to agree to that. She realized that she was bone weary, but her love and sense of loyalty simply would not permit her to leave her mother in the care of another person, no matter how well trained that person might be. Vincent admired his niece but knew that the situation was not going to get any better. In fact, it was his belief that the day was rapidly approaching when it would be impossible for Gina to adequately take care of his sister. He would keep a close eye on things and would know what to do when that time came. He had already made arrangements for that sad eventuality, realizing that convincing Gina was going to be a problem.

CHAPTER 7

Valentine's Day was blustery and cold. The remnants of the last snow storm were still everywhere and together with the gray skies made for a bleak, winter day. Vincent Gambrino was called to the phone by his butler who said it was Miss Gina and that she sounded distraught. He took the phone quickly, nerve ends tingling and heart beat increasing, knowing that the news he was about to receive would not be good. He was right.

"Oh, Uncle Vinnie," Gina wailed, "I don't know what to do. This morning I told Mama to wait in her room while I took a shower and when I got out she was gone. I ran all over the neighborhood but I couldn't find her anywhere. Some neighbors up the street saw her wandering around and took her inside and called me. Uncle Vinnie, Mama doesn't know where she is and sometimes doesn't know who she is." Gina began sobbing.

"There, there sweetheart, Uncle Vinnie will be right over. You try to take it easy 'til I get there. Good-bye sugar."

On the ride over to Daggett Street Vincent rehearsed what he would say to Gina. He knew it was important to convince her that he knew best and that placing Louise in a nursing home was the best thing to do. He would explain how they were experienced and trained to treat people who were afflicted like Louise and it would be in this environment where she would stand the best chance of getting well. A nursing home was, after all, like a hospital and hopefully her stay would be temporary. Vincent had to go over this script several times so that he could come to believe it himself.

Gina's response to the proposal was more impassioned than Vincent had predicted. He mused at how aggressive and strong Gina could be when she really believed in something, a departure from her usual sweet, agreeable personality.

"A nursing home? No, please, Uncle Vinnie! That's not the answer. That's a place where old people go to die. Mother's not old. She's going to get better. She has to. Let me try to take care of her. I was just upset by her running away today. I won't let that happen again. We'll be okay now."

Gina was teary-eyed looking exhausted and older than her eighteen years. She was beside herself, but her uncle was not accustomed to losing arguments and did not intend to lose this one, although his heart ached to see his niece so upset.

He put his arm around her and suggested she fix them some hot cocoa. He knew that it was important to divert her attention so he could start over and not have to defend his position while she was pumped up and at the height of her objections. She would be more open to reason when she was relaxed and calmed down.

He used all the standard ploys. Gina needed to be in school; Louise would get well quicker; the present arrangement would soon wear Gina down and before she knew it she would begin to resent her mother and might even start to lose her patience. This one hit home. Gina hated it, but she had come to realize lately that she was starting to feel sorry for herself because of the intolerable burden she was forced to bear. She prayed for these feelings to go away, but they lay in the back of her consciousness, haunting her and making her feel disloyal and selfish.

Vincent saw that he had touched a nerve, so he threw in the *pièce de résistance* that he knew would clinch the decision.

"Gina, if your mother were capable of reasoning right now she would definitely agree with me. You know that in your heart. You can visit her every day for as long as you like, and with professional care she'll respond quicker and above all she'll be safer. We won't have to worry about things happening like they did today."

Gina began crying again. She felt that this was a direct reflection on her efforts to take care of her mother and a wave of guilt and feeling of inadequacy engulfed her as Vincent knew it would.

"Gina, honey, you have done a magnificent, gallant job. You have held on for much longer than I ever believed anybody could. But we have to consider what is best for Louise now. When she improves to any appreciable degree we can always bring her home. At this time we must make the best decisions we can for her because she can't make them herself." Vincent felt like an undertaker trying to make a family buy a more expensive service than they could afford.

Having many years experience at negotiating and convincing people to see things his way, Vincent was aware that Gina was weakening. He knew that he must nail down a commitment from her now, because leaving the matter unresolved would force him back to the beginning. He came to convince Gina to put her mother in a nursing home and he would leave with nothing less. He also realized that he wanted Gina all to himself.

"Gina, Dr. Zarinsky told me after the operation that this might become necessary so I asked him to recommend the best nursing home in town in case we needed one. He has reserved a private room at Sunset Meadows, a brand new home on Lindell just three blocks east of your school. I didn't want you to have any more to worry about than you already have. I want you to come live with me during this period."

"You can spend whatever time you wish with your mother, both before and after school. I'll supply a car and driver—hey, maybe you could learn to drive. I'll buy you a brand new car of your choice! What do you say?"

Gina had quit crying. She was silent for what seemed like a long time as she thought about this dilemma. Finally she said with reluctance, "Maybe we should give it a try."

Vincent smiled and hugged his niece. He had won again.

CHAPTER 8

Sunset Meadows Nursing Home was a one-year-old facility built by a local construction company and then bought by an out-of-state corporation. The people who actually owned stock in the corporation remained faceless and nameless.

The home was operated by a company who had this same arrangement with dozens of homes across the country. At least that was what their advertising said. Nobody seemed to know for sure who the owners were. The building was attractive from the outside, looking like a small hospital, with a circular driveway in front and a well land-scaped lawn. The front lobby was small with a reception area and a sign-in sheet on a little Queen Anne table. The Administrator's office was behind the receptionist's desk. There was soothing music playing softly but you couldn't tell where it was coming from.

The rest of the facility was cut off from this reception area by two large doors. When you opened them, you could see the nurses' station and three halls running off from it like spokes on a wheel. There were twenty double rooms with adjoining bathrooms on each spoke, making the total occupancy one hundred and twenty. There was a large dining room with a modern, clean looking kitchen attached to it. Everything in the kitchen was stainless steel.

It was eleven o'clock in the morning when the limo pulled up to the front door with Louise, Vincent and Gina in the rear seat. Gina was dreading going in so much that she felt nauseous. She wished she had come to visit and inspect this place ahead of time so she could give her mother assur-ance that it was a good place and that everything would be alright. She had found herself mouthing these platitudes without knowing whether she believed it or not. The three were greeted by Mr. Sylvester Silvey who proudly announced that he was the administrator of Sunset Meadows and that he was very pleased to welcome them.

"So this is Mrs. Louise Oldani," he said. "Well, I've heard a lot of very nice things about you and we're going to do everything possible to make your stay here pleasant. Let me get a staff member to take you to your room where you can make yourself comfortable while I chat briefly with your daughter and brother." With that he looked at the smiling receptionist who immediately buzzed someone and asked that they come up front to show Mrs. Oldani to room 201. It was obvious that this routine had been well practiced.

A very large, smiling lady came through the doors and was introduced by Mr. Silvey as Mrs. Kathryn Larson, Registered Nurse and Director of Nursing. She was in uniform with a starched lab coat and wore an odd-looking cap from the nursing school she attended, probably some twenty years ago. Mrs. Larson, like Mr. Silvey and the receptionist, who had not been introduced, was smiling grandly. She launched on a welcoming speech and began asking Louise rapid-fire questions about her likes and dislikes, interspersing predictions about how much she was going to like it at Sunset Meadows. She talked in a condescending way that was more for the benefit of the family than the patient and reminded Gina of the style some people used with little children, like the syrupy woman on Romper Room. She wanted to say, "This is an adult, a dignified lady who is to be treated with respect. She's recovering from surgery now but other than that, she is normal." Later that day, as Gina thought about the admission, she became angry with herself for not speaking up. She mildly resented the attitude shown to her mother. This was a little surprising because she was accustomed to holding her peace and not questioning the behavior of adults. Both the training of the nuns at school and life with her father had ingrained this attitude very thoroughly, but she realized she must defend her mother who had become unable to protect herself.

As Louise was being shown through the double doors by Mrs. Larson, she began to passively object, saying that she didn't want to go and that she wanted to stay with her daughter. Gina tensed and began a move to comfort her mother but was braced by her uncle who put his arm around her and purred that everything would by alright and that they shouldn't interfere.

"These people know what they're doing, and it's necessary for Louise to become accustomed to the place without us holding her hand. Sunset Meadows is her new home, at least for now, and we must let the professional staff attend to her needs. I know how difficult it is for you honey. Just relax and have faith in Mr. Silvey here. He'll make sure she gets the best of care. Right, Mr. Silvey?"

Sylvester Silvey agreed enthusiastically as he showed Gina and Vincent into his office, offering them both comfortable leather chairs. This was the time when he was at his best. He launched into his five minute speech of being the reassuring, committed professional who would personally see to every need of his guests because their welfare was utmost in his daily consideration. Actually, his utmost consideration at the moment was the joyous news he had received from the home office in Chicago that he would be transferred to Sarasota, Florida. In two weeks he would open yet another facility which the company had purchased, and he could get away from the horrid winters in St. Louis and the monotonous problems of keeping this boring nursing home on its feet.

Sylvester Silvey was an advance man used by the Marigold Corporation to get facilities opened, staffed, and most importantly, filled with patients. He was very good at the job of getting a home under way, but he wasn't a man for the long haul. He would tend to hire people without questioning their past too carefully and was definitely inclined to make everyone, staff, families and residents alike, glowing promises that he could not keep. He had become very comfortable with this style, knowing that he would move on to a new location every three months or so, thereby leaving a dubious legacy to whomever followed. He was carefully plotting his career course, dreaming of the day when paying these dues would lead to an upper level job in the central office which had been promised. This would come to him if his field performance was satisfactory. He was able to summon the strength to put on a show of caring and concern when necessary, but he had arrived at the point where he abhorred working with families. He delegated all of the staff problems he could to his charge nurse whom he promised to make the administrator when he left.

So, with the news of his release from dreary St. Louis and the opportunity to climb one more step up the corporate ladder via the land of palm trees and sunshine, he was greatly pumped up and delighted with himself. He was able to be highly verbal and solicitous to this man, who was obviously a person of means, and this dazed child who was having difficulty separating from her mother.

"I want to give you every assurance that Mrs. Oldani will have topflight care and attention. If ever you have any questions or concerns about her treatment here, don't hesitate to call or visit with Mrs. Larson. She's very dedicated and will be most responsive I'm sure. We try our very best to make your loved one comfortable, and if you're not pleased and happy, then I'm not pleased and happy. Let me assure you that when I'm unhappy then people here jump until I am happy. Heh, heh."

The implication that he looked after every detail and insisted on optimal performance was a part of his spiel that he especially liked. He had said it so often that he actually believed it himself, except on those occasions when someone called his bluff and he revealed himself to be the moral tower of Jell-O that he truly was. He had long ago resigned himself to being a person who avoided confrontation. He was smart enough to surround himself with aggressive people like fat Nurse Larson, whom he both feared and despised, but who would by their very nature browbeat the rest of the staff into doing a more-or-less acceptable job.

By promising her the administrator's job and complete control of the facility, he was able to buy her loyalty and compliance, in spite of the lack of respect she had for weasels of his stripe. They both understood their relationship very well; he had responsibility and control but didn't want it. He preferred a more lofty, above-the-fray, position. She loved command and the grass roots, front-line action and longed to be the administrator. She thought she would change that to superintendent. She always had a fear that a large company like this one might find out about that unpleasant business a few years back in that raunchy little nursing home in Arkansas. With each passing day the possibility of exposure for her role in those multiple deaths became more remote. Poor investigation of the work records of prospective employees allowed the workforce to change jobs with impunity.

Sylvester Silvey droned on about the concepts of quality nursing care. Simultaneously he got Vincent to sign a number of documents that made him the responsible party for the payment of the nursing home's costs which amounted to $1500.00 per month for a single room. Laundry, medicine and incidental supplies were to be billed separately. A double room would have been $750.00 but Vincent preferred to pay double so that Gina could have privacy during her visits.

Gina, having been sheltered from financial considerations, was shocked to learn of the high cost. She was experienced enough to realize that there was no way a normal family could begin to pay these prices. Where did a regular family place their people? Her heart ached as she realized that they probably didn't place them anywhere; they took care of them at home the way that she should be doing.

42

Events were swirling and going so fast that Gina couldn't get a grip on things. At one point life was fine, topped by a wonderful, dream vacation to New York, then her mother became progressively more ill and had to have the operation. Now her mother was so confused and disoriented that she required twenty-four hour care in a strange place called Sunset Meadows. The irony of a name for a nursing home which conjures up a beautiful retirement scene was lost on her for the moment, but would become painfully clear later. She was doing things and making decisions that her viscera told her were wrong, but she felt it necessary to bow to the intelligence and experience of her uncle and Dr. Zarinsky. After all, Uncle Vinnie loved his sister as much as Gina did, didn't he? She was sure he would only do what was in her best interest. To all of this she thought the answer was yes, but why was she constantly nagged with guilt and questions and the feeling that nothing she could say or do would have any effect on this bombardment of bad luck?

All during the latter part of Mr. Silvey's indoctrination, Gina's mind was toiling with this confusion and the desire to be with her mother. Finally she stood and said, "Gentlemen, excuse me please, but I think I should be with Mother to comfort her. She's very scared and unsure you know."

Sylvester Silvey, somewhat irritated that this girl didn't wish to hear his "A" material, was nevertheless always sensitive to the necessity of adjusting his own needs to the needs of people who could have an impact on his career. He quickly rang for his receptionist and said, "By all means, young lady. I was about to suggest that very thing. Camille, would you kindly show Miss Oldani to her mother's room? Thank you."

As soon as Gina left the room, Vincent, who had been patient with Mr. Silvey only because he thought it was comforting for Gina to hear the many assurances he was giving, interrupted what he considered to be verbal diarrhea and said, "Mr. Silvey, I'm sure you will make good in all your promises, and I feel assured you will treat my sister in a

43

manner consistent with the respect you would give your own mother. I want it further understood that her daughter can visit any time she likes for as long as she likes and may, on occasion, stay overnight."

"But," Silvey protested, "we have visiting hours and staying overnight by nonresidents is against the rules."

"Mr. Silvey, I evidently am not making myself clear. If you don't do as I wish I will simply buy this God- damned place and then we will play by my rules—without you." Vincent was glaring. "Now, do you understand?"

"Yes sir, I do." Sylvester hated when people saw through his charade of being the man who calls the shots. Thank God he would soon leave this all behind him. That night, as he sat alone in his small apartment drinking his customary daily pint of gin he would fantasize about how he talked up to that pushy little wop and showed him the door. While he enjoyed the fantasy, he knew such behavior was beyond his capability. He had tried to be assertive many times in his life but was never able to bring it off. He soon rationalized that it was only smart and diplomatic to avoid conflict with a man like Gambrino. He looked like the type who probably had Mafia connections and his big chauffeur looked more like a body guard than a mere driver. Yes, it was definitely wise that he was able to curb his emotions and not confront such a man. After all, he was a business man who's goal was to fill up a nursing home so the home office would pin a gold star on his personnel jacket. Yes, discretion is always the better part of valor, he silently mused while filling his glass with gin.

When Camille opened the big double doors to the main nursing home area, Gina was greeted by a very foul odor. There were a half dozen ladies sitting in an assortment of rocking chairs and wheel chairs, and one of them had obviously soiled herself. Gina's eyes met Camille's. She quickly looked away in embarrassment and quickened her step to room 201. Gina was aware that there was no hustle and bustle here like in the hospital. In fact, she didn't see a single staff person on the way to her mother's room. Louise was sitting alone staring at space when Gina arrived. She didn't even look up when Gina entered the rather stark room. It had two single, hospital-type beds, two three-drawer dressers, and two padded chairs. That was it. The floors were tile and clean, looking like the rest of the floors she had seen, and she was glad to see a nurse's call button attached to each bed. There was a small bathroom with lavatory — Gina wondered where her mother would take a bath — and one closet, presumably for the roommates to share.

Gina pulled the other chair up close to Louise and put her arm around her. "Well, Mother, how do you feel about Sunset Meadows so far?" Questions like this one and the general tone of the conversation that Gina shared with her mother these days were alien and highly unsatisfactory to her. The give and take was gone. Their communication was limited to Gina talking, questioning and probing, and Louise answering in monotone, if at all. Gone were the days when they chatted and sparred and laughed together. Their relationship had been one of mutual respect where each one took joy and pleasure in the company of the other. They were best friends. Now the relationship was, instead of two equal human beings sharing and reinforcing each other, one where a healthy strong person subjugated herself entirely to the needs of her stricken partner. Gina knew this was unhealthy for both her mother and her, but couldn't come up with any alternative except for her mother to get well.

"Oh Gina, it's you. I was afraid you weren't coming back. Where am I? Is this a hospital?" There was fear and panic in Louise's voice.

Gina patiently repeated what she had said, probably a dozen times before, "We're at Sunset Meadows Nursing Home. It's three blocks east of St. Mary's on Lindell Boulevard. Dr. Zarinsky thought it would be best for you to come here for a while until you're better and can return home to live with me like we used to. Won't that be a grand day?"

45

"Honey, don't leave me here. I don't want to stay here. Why do I have to be here? Don't leave me alone, please Gina."

Gina broke into uncontrollable sobs and hugged her mother tightly, unable to utter any consoling words. Part of her problem with offering Louise any encouragement was that she didn't feel encouraged herself. Why indeed did her mother have to come to a place like this? It seemed so cold and barren. She had visualized smiling content people who sang songs and did needlework and enjoyed the company of one another. When you saw advertisements for retirement homes that is the picture that's always presented. A place to spend the golden years when you reaped the rewards of a lifetime of work. She had certainly not seen anything approaching that picture so far. She was so upset and racked with guilt that she sat, immobilized, resembling her mother in posture and expression.

Vincent found them sitting this way when he entered the room. He knew that the next few minutes were crucial and he wanted to handle the separation just right, but there seemed to be no good way to do it—except to do it.

"Well Gina," he began, "it's time for us to be getting home now. Your mother is in excellent hands. I've had a nice chat with Mr. Silvey who will take extra good care of her. It will naturally take her a little time to get used to everything here but I know that everything will work out fine."

Gina dutifully hugged and kissed her mother and said, "I love you Mother and I'll be back bright and early tomorrow to be with you." Gina, aided by her uncle, got up and walked out in a daze. She had a feeling that her body was doing something independent of her mind—as though this was all a dream and that she wasn't really here and this wasn't really happening. As they passed the little circle of ladies in the vestibule she noticed that the foul odor had not gone away. In fact it had intensified. All the ladies in the group looked the way her mother did, sad, lost and forlorn.

46

Gina, in spite of herself, began sobbing again as they left through the big double doors.

CHAPTER 9

Gina, true to her word, was back at the nursing home at 8:00 the next morning. Louise was still in her housecoat, sitting alone in her room with her complete breakfast before her. An over-the-bed table had been provided since she wouldn't go to the dining room. It was easier to simply serve her tray in her room, nobody offered to help her or saw to it that she ate. Gina affixed a napkin under her chin and began feeding her and talking in a soothing way. Louise was very glad to see her, but there was an undercurrent of unexpressed anger that Gina knew stemmed from her being left to face this place alone. After Louise had finished some of her now-cold breakfast, Gina selected clothes for the day. She suggested that Louise get dressed so they could take a walk on the sunny forty-degree day.

Before going outside they walked up and down the halls on an unsupervised tour of the building. Gina thought it was a good idea to orient her mother as much as possible to her new surroundings since it was obvious that no one else was going to.

They passed people, both men and women, in various stages of dress and undress. One lady was completely naked in a room with the door wide open and no staff person in sight. Gina shuddered to think that her mother might be exposed to such an indignity.

The smell of stale urine, while not overpowering, was nevertheless pervasive and unpleasant. There were no puddles visible on the floors, so Gina was puzzled about where it was coming from. She reasoned that over a period of time it just crept into everything and that there was simply nothing you could do about it. Why, then, didn't the hospital smell this way? They must know something that Sunset

Meadows had yet to discover about eradication of odors and good housekeeping.

After their walk up and down Lindell Boulevard, Gina and Louise returned to room 201 which was now made up and tidy. The nursing home had a policy of letting guests eat lunch for fifty cents, so Gina told the lady at the nursing station that she would have lunch with her mother in the dining room. Gina wanted Louise to meet and socialize with other patients as much as possible. Lunch turned out to be a most unpleasant experience, at least for Gina. The dining room seated about eighty people, and since there were over one hundred patients' names on the roster board, Gina assumed that the other twenty or so people ate in their rooms for some reason. Lunch was to be served at noon, so they arrived some five minutes early to get the lay of the land. The dining room was half full when they walked in. Louise maintained the placid, blank look that was always on her face, but Gina blinked and got a kind of eerie feeling. All the old folks were either sitting or shuffling in, but not one patient was speaking to another patient. Some were staring at their silverware which consisted of a tablespoon and a teaspoon, others were mumbling to themselves, but no one was giving anyone else eye contact nor acknowledging the existence of another person in any way. Gina was stunned and saddened by this phenomenon. She had counted on the existence of a number of smiling, compassionate patients who could chat, play cards and be friendly and supportive to her mother. She saw no one who seemed capable until a beautiful gray haired lady with large earrings and glowing cosmetics came rolling in who looked and held herself like royalty. She was dressed very neatly in a stylish dress, and her hair had been recently done. She was smiling, saying hello to people like a politician working the room. She caught Gina's eye and pulled her chair up to their table and said, "Well, well, this most be the new patient Louise. Hello, Louise. I'm Harriet Wormsley. I'm the mother of Delmar

Higgins, State Senator. He was by my first husband, James Marshall Higgins. What's your name young lady?"

Slightly taken aback Gina replied, "Hello Mrs. Wormsley. I'm Gina Oldani. This is my mother Louise Oldani."

Louise smiled and said a very nice and social hello. Some of her deeply ingrained and long-held skills would surface when the need arose. Louise was a very proud lady and could summon the strength to be appropriate in spite of her confusion. The desire to appear normal and not embarrass her daughter brought out her best effort, which pleased Gina immensely because she was seeing signs that her mother was giving up the struggle to get well. Gina had not given in to the inevitability of total senility or even death where her mother was concerned.

Harriet Wormsley smiled and said how nice it was to have Mrs. Oldani at Sunset Meadows. She had seen her come the day before in the limousine and remarked at how that was the most elegant entrance she had seen anybody make in the two years she had been there. They all enjoyed a smile and a titter over that remark. She went on to say, "I've never seen one come in a Cadillac but I've seen a heap of 'em leave in one." She laughed at this by herself. It made Gina tense, and she avoided the glance of her mother. "Yes, I always like to see new patients come in. I'll bet you and I will be friends Louise," Harriet continued.

"You're a lot younger than me, Louise. I'm ninety-two years old. I was living by myself until I came here. Fell and broke my hip. Can't walk no more. I came willingly because I couldn't take care of myself any longer, and I refuse to be a burden to my son. It's not so bad. You'll like it, Louise, if you let yourself." Saying that, she smiled sweetly and patted Louise's hand which was a sign that she knew things were tough but not so tough as to be impossible. Louise smiled and Gina wanted to kiss this wonderful lady who had appeared out of nowhere. Gina thought, "Now this is more like it, I wonder if there are any more around here like her?"

Gina instinctively wanted to work on forming some kind of bond with Harriet. She began, "You certainly look to be in good health and you seem to know everything that goes on here Mrs. Wormsley."

"Call me Wormy, honey. Everybody else does. Called my late husband that too. Guess he is wormy by now." She laughed at her own joke. Gina smiled in spite of herself as did Louise who put her hand over her mouth and said, "Oh."

"You're right, cutie. I do a lot of observing and listening—and the stories I could tell you," gesturing with a limp wrist wave, "but I have to go now and have lunch with my friends. Bye, see you around."

They bid her good-bye and watched her manipulate her chair over to a table which had three other ladies waiting. They all looked alert and greeted Harriet with a smile and seemed to be the only table at which conversation was taking place.

The food came out of the kitchen at 12:15 on a three tiered stainless steel cart. A tiny black woman was pushing it and she was almost obscured by the enormous cart. From a certain angle it looked like the cart was self-propelled. The little woman was perspiring slightly and was hurrying and rushing as fast as she could. She would push the cart up to a table, take the trays off one at a time and set them in front of the patients. She knew all the patients by name and had something to say to each of them that was generally encouraging and cute but always with a tinge of kindergarten teacher to child flavor. "Come on now honey. I want you to eat everything today." "Be my good girl, sugar." "No dessert 'til you eats it all, darlin'." Nobody seemed to mind. Another black lady in a white uniform came out of the kitchen pushing a cart serving the far side of the dining room. Today's menu, which was posted outside the dining room, was

51

roast beef, mashed potatoes, lima beans, rolls and butter, with Jell-O for dessert. When Louise and Gina were finally served it had been altered to meat loaf, mashed potatoes and gravy, peas, bread and butter and pudding. In spite of these differences the meal still seemed balanced and the portions, although somewhat small, appeared adequate. A selection of coffee, milk or water was available.

The serving lady brightened up as she put the uncovered plates in front of Louise and Gina saying, "So, you're my new patient. I heard you came in a limousine. My, my, ain't we fancy. Well, this ain't the Holiday Inn but I'm going to do the best by you I can. Are you her daughter?" Gina nodded affirmatively.

"You sure are a pretty thing. I bet you mama was real pretty when she were young too cause, she's still pretty. Don't you worry you pretty self none, yo mama gon' be all right here." With that she rushed off to the next table. Gina didn't know what to make of her, having never been exposed to Negroes except sometimes on the bus going downtown. She liked this woman though and was comforted by the way she took an interest in all the people.

The food was cooked to death and had no taste. It wasn't as good as the food in the hospital had been, which Gina thought was generally tasteless. Adding salt would have helped but there wasn't any on the table or on the tray. The blandness of the food made it even more difficult to get Louise to eat.

It was easy to understand why a person would say, "I've had enough of that," or "I think I'll just eat my dessert and have coffee." Louise's weight was continuing to drop alarmingly—down to 110 pounds when she was admitted. Gina resolved to bring some bananas, salt and other things that her mother had always been fond of in an effort to stimulate her appetite.

Gina found the whole meal experience very unsatisfactory. The dining room had a pungent odor which seemed to

52

be a mixture of food smells, disinfectant and urine. She now realized that the urine smell was coming from some of the people's clothes because occasionally someone would pass by close enough for the odor to be overpowering.

Gina sat observing the dining room scene after she had finished. Some people gobbled their food and left the dining hall immediately, others dawdled, and some played with their food. Most of the people seemed to take no notice of what was going on around them; when they walked out of the dining room their eyes, for the most part, were cast downward, never looking up or from side to side. Nobody smiled or nodded hello. It was as though they were in a vacant-eyed trance. Robot-like.

Gina sadly concluded that her mother must look like that to the rest of the world, but when Gina looked at Louise she saw the bright, loving and thoughtful person she had always known and loved. She would not accept any scenario other than believing that this appalling condition and strange living situation were only temporary until her mother improved. She clung to that hope tenaciously.

Gina read to her mother that afternoon, went for countless "walks" with her and shared dinner, which was watery tomato soup, crackers, grilled cheese sandwiches and a small square of Jell-O. Once again the little black lady, who announced that her name was Latishia, went through the same routine of serving and chattering. This time Gina found it less entertaining than before. She, too, was like a robot. Wind her up and watch her do her stuff. Gina now detected a lack of sincerity about the woman in the way she busily went through the motions of her routine. Patients weren't responding to her directions and urgings. Rather, they seemed bored by it all and ignored Latishia. Gina understood. She, by now, was so bored and depressed by all of this that she felt like screaming.

The driver came at 8:00 o'clock to pick up Gina. Louise became agitated and pleaded with Gina to stay but the evening nurse overheard their conversation and walked into the room saying, "There, there, Mrs. Oldani. Your daughter is tired and has to go home to get her rest. You need to go to bed too. Tomorrow's another day." She then turned to Gina and said, "Don't give in to her. If you do we'll have this hassle every time you leave. She'll get spoiled."

Gina's blood raced and she felt dizzy. "Would you please step outside?" she commanded.

The frumpy L.P.N., whose pin bore the name of Mrs. Thelma Terwilliger, smiled, showing uneven tobacco stained teeth, and complied with an attitude of tired resignation.

Gina fought for composure but at the same time felt an exhilaration that was foreign. "Mrs. Terwilliger," she began, "my mother has had brain surgery recently and is still suffering from it. She is not a child who will get spoiled nor is she an animal who doesn't mind being talked about as though she were not present. If I am aware of your treating her with anything except the respect she is due, I will be forced to report it to your superior." Gina was trembling with indignation.

Mrs. Terwilliger looked at Gina with contempt and snarled as she walked away "Jesus Christ, just what I need, a know-it-all brat."

On the ride to the riverside mansion Gina brooded in the dark back seat about the frustration of what seemed like an intolerable world. Why had God chosen to put so much misery on her? How much could she stand? She was surprised at her earlier aggressiveness with the nasty Mrs. Terwilliger but at the same time proud of her honest and righteous reaction.

She was more surprised to realize that she had to consciously throttle herself because as Mrs. Terwilliger had walked away with that "get in the last word" shot, Gina very nearly pursued her with the purpose of slapping her face. The very thought, never mind the inclination, had never occurred to Gina before. Maybe this is what they mean when they talk about people cracking under pressure. She could not get her mind off of Sunset Meadows. "Oh, poor Mama," she thought, weeping softly. She wept out of frustration for the predicament that old people experienced within the system of nursing homes. She had read where the Japanese honor their elders and hold them in the highest esteem. They respect the old and infirm and take advantage of their experience and wisdom. This tradition of venerating would make the placing of a family member in a nursing home by a Japanese family an unthinkable act which would result in serious loss of face. Gina felt this sense of shame, yet everyone around her was counseling her with different advice.

No one, not the nuns at St. Mary's, her uncle, or Dr. Zarinsky, had suggested that there was any choice but a nursing home. It might be different if her mother were willing and able to make the decision like Harriet Wormsley had done. Mrs. Wormsley was content, even happy, to be where she was because it was her idea and choice. She was like a big duck in a small pond. She held court and indeed found more stimulation at Sunset Meadows than she probably did living alone in an apartment. It might be different if the facility itself weren't so cold and institutional. The care didn't seem to go beyond simply taking care of the patients physical needs and the quality and dedication of even that was low.

It suddenly occurred to Gina that one of the reasons everybody there was so depressed and robot-like was the stupefying boredom that abounds. The days were all the same. There was never anything to look forward to except meals, and they were as boring and bland as everything else. Gina sat wondering what could be done that might alleviate the boredom. Just then the driver pulled up to the front door. As it opened, it revealed a smiling Uncle Vinnie, standing there with his red smoking jacket, black slacks and ever present white shirt and black tie. This was as causally dressed as Gina had ever seen him.

He hugged her and invited her to join him in his study where she would have milk and homemade chocolate chip cookies while he enjoyed his daily cognac and the one cigar a day he now allowed himself. The study was large, as were all the rooms in this exquisite place, with dark, rich walnut paneling, soft leather furniture, and a gallery of original paintings that alone must have been worth a fortune.

Gina was obviously tense and worried as she sat down in front of the roaring fireplace. Vincent gallantly pushed a large leather ottoman up for her that matched the chair he had offered.

He said, "Slip off your shoes and relax, sweetheart," as the butler brought in the silver tray with her snack and sat it down on the table next to her chair. "That will be all, Eugene."

The very proper butler bowed ever so slightly and said, "Very good, sir." No doubt about it, Uncle Vinnie lived like the rich barons Gina had read about.

They both sat quietly for a moment as Vincent went through the ritual of sniffing his large cigar, then snipped the tip off of it with a little silver instrument designed for that purpose only. He lit the cigar with a large expensive lighter. As soon as this ceremony was complete he took a sip of the cognac and sighed, "There, that's better."

Gina self-consciously made an effort to enjoy the snack he had provided but only nibbled courteously, not really feeling very hungry. She chose to keep her shoes on.

"Well, sweetheart, how did it go today?" he queried.

An unplanned flood of emotion that Gina wanted to squelch came rushing out. "Oh, Uncle Vinnie, I know Sunset Meadows is supposed to be one of the best nursing homes in St. Louis, but if it is, I'd hate to see the worst. Everything about it is so dehumanizing. Everyone is treated like a number instead of a person. The building is nice enough but it's full of unpleasant odors and there is nothing for the patients to do. Some of them had visitors for a brief while and a few of them were reading but the large majority of people there are either in bed because they're too sick to get up or they are shuffling around like they are lost and don't know what to do. The one exception I met is a Mrs. Harriet Wormsley who is very cheerful and content. It would be different if they were all like her. The whole place is so depressing that I can't stand it and neither can Mother, although she didn't say so."

Gina sighed audibly as Vincent leaned forward in the manner of a person who was genuinely interested and concerned. Actually, he wasn't surprised at her reaction to the nursing home. In fact, he was sure everything she was saying was valid, but he knew his sister's days on this earth were numbered, and he wanted to keep her deterioration as remote from himself as possible. Death scared him, and the less he had to think about it the better he liked it. He was unable to admit this human weakness to Gina, just as he was unable to share his innermost feelings with anyone. That's the way he had always been, he reasoned, and it was too late to change now. He was genuinely impressed with the way Gina was able to articulate her feelings and thought to himself that, if she were a man, she'd make a hell of a lawyer. This beautiful, innocent child stirred feelings of love inside him that he thought he was incapable of having. He wanted to iron out all of the problems in her life and give her the advantages in life that only princesses could expect. If Louise would hurry up and die Gina would be his to mold as he saw fit. He knew he could make her love him like a father once the torment of her mother was past.

Gina continued, "Uncle Vinnie, we've got to do something besides leaving Mother in that place. She's very unhappy and doesn't belong there. It's not like the hospital where everyone was nice and attentive and caring. They have over one hundred patients and I never saw a doctor and, except for the kitchen workers and maids, I only counted four nurse's aides. That's not enough to do all the necessary work. A great many of the people there are spooky - senile they call it. How can mother get better in such an environment? She's going to continue to go down hill quickly unless we can do something to help her."

"What do you suggest, my dear?" he said, as fatherly as possible.

Gina thought for a moment and then brightened and said, "We could bring her here and hire nurses to care for her. That way we could really control her activities and encourage her to get better everyday. The cost would probably be less as well."

Vincent leaned back in his luxurious chair and puffed pensively on his smelly, imported cigar. He had to admit that Gina made a very good case. So good that he was backed into a corner and knew it. God, he thought, what a clear thinker and what observational skills this child has. He had dealt with many rich, powerful people in his life and only a few of them were able to distill the crap out of a problem and get to a solution as quickly as this eighteen-year-old girl.

Gina was looking straight into her uncle's eyes, knowing that he was the only person on earth who could make the hurt she was feeling go away. She put her right hand under her leg so that he couldn't see her crossed fingers.

The answer she got wasn't what she wanted to hear. "We both want what is best for Louise," he said in kindly, measured tones. "She's my sister and your mother and we both love her and want her to get well. Tell you what, tomorrow I'll get Dr. Zarinsky to go to the nursing home with me. I'll tell him all you've said and have him reevaluate the situation. I hate to go against such a fine doctor's advise but maybe he'll change his mind and you'll have your way. We're both tired right now and emotionally charged up. I learned a long time ago not to make important decisions under those conditions. It would be best for all of us right now to settle down and get our lives back on a steady, predictable course. I want you to go back to school tomorrow and resume your studies. You can visit your mother until six o'clock in the evening after school at which time I'll have a driver bring you here for dinner. I've had a special room decorated for you with the stuff from your room at the Daggett house. We brought all of your clothes and things as well. On Saturday I am personally going to begin your driving lessons so you can soon have that car I promised you. How does that sound?"

"Uncle Vinnie," Gina's eyes were now focused on some imaginary object on the floor as she tried to deal with her disappointment. "I'm very grateful for everything you've done, and I know you have Mama's and my best interest at heart. I'll do as you say, but I hope you can understand that Mother's welfare is all I can think about. I'll try my best at school but my heart won't be in it."

Vincent stood up and opened his arms to give Gina a hug. He whispered, "You're a wonderful, loving daughter Gina. I'd give anything if you had been born to me." He meant it.

As Gina turned to go upstairs to her room she felt very tired and defeated but managed to smile and say good night.

When she was out of sight Vincent went to the liquor cabinet and poured himself another stiff cognac. He was bothered that the problem of manipulating this situation the way he wanted was getting fouled with emotion. His emotion. It was a factor that he never let cloud his drive for other conquests. Only once before, twenty four years ago, when his marriage of eighteen months ended and his unfaithful wife left with his two- month-old son, was he so personally involved and confused. Well, he wasn't going to let this saga end so unhappily. He drank deeply of the cognac and stared into the dwindling fire.

CHAPTER 10

At 9:00 o'clock the next morning the intercom on Sylvester Silvey's phone buzzed. Through the haze of a hangover he punched the button and said, "Yes?"

His receptionist's voice come through saying, "Mr. Gambrino would like to speak to you on line two." She did so with a sense of spiteful glee because she knew Mr. Silvey didn't like to be bothered with any problem if he could avoid it, and especially not until after noon when he was "feeling better."

"Why didn't you tell him I'm not available?" Silvey growled. His instincts told him to gather himself and to make an attempt to accommodate his caller, in spite of the irritation—or was it fear?—that he felt.

He carefully pushed the blinking phone button. "Good morning, sir. How are you today?" he chirped.

A gruff business like voice that he recognized as his newest patient's brother said, "I'm fine, thank you. Dr. Zarinsky and I will be at the facility at ten o'clock to visit Mrs. Oldani. I would like to get a tour of the building at that time conducted by yourself. Will that be convenient for you?"

"One moment while I check my schedule, please," he lied in order to give him a moment to think. He was alarmed and threatened that this request was being made. He was aware that even though families paid, and paid well, for the services offered by a nursing home, they seldom, if ever, had the temerity to ask for a tour or to question the operation. Touring a nursing home wasn't something people did for kicks. The only reasons for snooping around by outsiders were an interest in buying, which he had encountered before, or to try to uncover suspected problems. And he's bringing a doctor with him. Silvey felt a surge of nausea but nevertheless answered after a short pause, "Yes sir, I believe I can manage to shift appointments around and meet with you. Is there anything special you would like to see?"

"I'll tell you at ten." The phone went dead.

"That little wop bastard!" Silvey thought. He was seldom challenged because he knew from experience that nursing homes are perceived like schools or churches in that they're there to do a certain job and are managed by "professionals" who know what they're doing. Of course they come under scrutiny from time to time but it is always easy to beat down probing questions. Officials of institutions do it largely by intimidation and the sheer force of their personalities. They hide behind mystique, citing their training and years of experience. They imply that anyone who would dare question their commitment and expertise was not only misguided but clearly stepping on turf that is sacrosanct. Their domains are above the understanding of anyone without proper training. He was reminded how lay people take on a respectful, hushed tone when they enter a church or a school as though any business other than praying or learning was not to be conducted. He had noticed that usually even aggressive people became passive when entering his little kingdom and deferred to his explanation, however trite, that things are the way they are because everything we do is for the good of the patient. People who come to a nursing home put saccharin sweet smiles on their faces like people who have entered a place in which they're not comfortable. They often seem humbled.

The growing knot in his stomach warned him that the people whom he would meet with at 10:00 o'clock were not going to be so easily pacified with his usual bullshit. He nervously rushed out of the safety of his office to find Mrs. Larson to warn her and to implore her to make everything as ship-shape as possible, particularly as it concerned Mrs.

Oldani. He felt a pang of longing to get on a plane to Florida that very minute.

Vincent, with the impeccable Dr. Zarinsky in tow, strode through the front door of Sunset Meadows at precisely ten o'clock. Vincent announced to the smiling receptionist that Dr. Zarinsky, with his black medical bag, would be examining Mrs. Oldani and wished for Mr. Silvey to join them in her room in fifteen minutes. With that they disappeared behind the double doors. Camille rose and knocked softly on the Administrator's door, delivered the message and returned to her post, a look of excitement and expectation on her face.

Silvey was annoyed that they didn't pay him the courtesy of stopping to chat with him first. He had a hospitable pot of coffee and three cups ready, hoping to mollify them in any way he could. He got Mrs. Larson on the intercom and said, "They're here. Be careful."

The next fifteen minutes were nerve racking for Sylvester Silvey. He bolstered himself with a shot of vodka that he kept locked in his desk for such emergencies. He waited at his desk wishing for the day when he would rise above all this and take his place in the "golden circle" of the central office. When that day finally comes, he thought, then all I will have to be concerned with are occupancy levels, cost containments, the looming threat of union activities and kicking other administrators' asses to make a profitable bottom line for the company. A station in life that he coveted and felt was definitely his due.

At 10:12 Ed Zarinsky and Vincent Gambrino were having a hushed and serious conversation outside the closed door of room 201.

"I'm afraid she's going downhill faster than we hoped, Vinnie," Zarinsky said. "She's unable to tell me what day it is, who the President of the United States is and she is unable to answer other orientation questions. She can no longer do simple addition and subtraction. Her general state of health is poor as well. She's not eating — losing too much weight. Her motor skills and reflexes are deteriorating rapidly. You noticed that her speech is halting and slurred and the muscle control, particularly on the right side of her body, is weak. I'm terribly sorry, Vince., There's nothing we can do except make her as comfortable as possible. I'll prescribe something for that and leave it at the nurse's station." He got out his prescription pad and began writing.

"How long does she have, Ed?"

"Hard to say exactly," Zarinsky answered gravely. "The way things are going I'd be surprised if she lives another 90 days." As an afterthought he said, "Vince, come in for a checkup next week. I'm worried about what the stress of all this can do to a guy with a heart condition like yours."

"Sure thing, Ed. Thanks for coming over."

Dr. Zarinsky passed Sylvester Silvey, who was ambling down the hall as instructed, and didn't bother to give him as much as a perfunctory nod.

"Arrogant bastard," Silvey fumed under his breath. Vincent greeted Silvey with a disarming smile and a handshake which gave the nervous man brief relief.

"I'd like to see the activity room, the dining room, the kitchen, and I'd like to meet Mrs. Harriet Wormsley," Vincent said authoritatively and abruptly.

"By all means," Silvey replied as confidently as possible, while wondering what this guy had up his sleeve.

He obediently led his adversary around the facility as instructed and ushered him into his office some thirty minutes later.

"Coffee, Mr. Gambrino?" he offered smiling.

"No thanks," Vincent said as he took a seat in front of the desk while Silvey retreated to his elevated chair in an effort to establish who was who.

"Mr. Silvey, my beloved sister is dying. I want her last days to be as peaceful as possible. I also want her last days to be spent at this nursing home or in the hospital. My niece, her daughter, is very dissatisfied with her mother's placement here. I'm going to ask you to do several things to turn that dissatisfaction into a belief that this is the proper place for her mother. I want her to know that you're doing everything possible for her recovery, which my niece still believes is possible. Here's what I want you to do."

After Vincent had outlined his plan the flustered Sylvester Silvey whined, "Mr. Gambrino, all of your ideas are good ones. I wish we could offer the services you've outlined but it would be impossible both economically and logistically. We have other patients to consider."

"Mr. Silvey," Vincent said poker faced, "I did some figuring on the way over here this morning and I'll bet my estimates are close to factual. You take in monthly gross revenues of close to seventy-five thousand dollars per month. You have a payroll of twenty five thousand, a mortgage of ten thousand, tops. You can serve the food here at a dollar and fifty cents per day per patient and your other fixed costs of insurance, supplies and maintenance run in the neighborhood of another seven thousand per month. This leaves a monthly net cash flow of something close to twenty-eight thousand dollars per month. How can you say it is economically impossible?"

Silvey winced visibly. While the figures weren't exact, they were in the ballpark. In his administrative goals their company had set a bottom line profit, when Sunset Meadows was fully occupied, of twenty-six thousand dollars per month before taxes. He knew that most other homes weren't able to generate this level of income, but Sunset Meadows was a flagship nursing home built with prestige in mind and located in a fashionable neighborhood. It commanded and got a patient per diem rate which was above what other homes could command in this day and time.

He also knew that the formula used by the company to build or buy existing homes was so lucrative that within the foreseeable future the industry was going to be controlled by large companies such as the one he worked for. His awareness of this trend had caused him to try to purchase a home, any home, himself so that he could run it for a while and then sell out to a corporation and retire. He was never able to put a deal together, however, because of his lack of capital and his basic lack of drive. He knew this dream was not to be realized. At any rate he was painfully aware that the man across his desk had done his homework.

"Mr. Gambrino, I don't know where you got your figures but I assure you that Sunset Meadows isn't nearly as profitable as you suspect. Why the startup costs alone will take years to recoup and..."

"Let's cut out the horse shit, Silvey," Vince was now on the edge of his chair glaring. "Do as I say and I'm prepared to give you two thousand dollars in cash right now and to donate ten thousand more to the home for a plaque on the activity room wall dedicated to the memory of my sister, when that becomes appropriate."

With that, Vincent sat back and waited for a reply. He got the one he expected and took his leave. When he was safely seated in the back seat of his limo he smiled ruefully and thought, "Vinnie, my boy, you know what makes this old world spin."

Gina arrived at the nursing home at 3:10 that same afternoon and was greeted by a smiling Camille who informed her that her mother had been moved to another room. When Gina asked why, Camille murmured something about the administrator thinking she would be more comfortable in this new location. Gina went down a different wing than the one where room 201 was located and found room 312. As she walked in she was startled to find a room that resembled both their living room and her mother's bedroom at the Daggett Street house. Pictures, throw rugs, tables, lamps, the easy chair and Louise's bed were all here as if by magic. A new television set, something they didn't have before, was also there. Louise was sitting in her easy chair with none other than Harriet Wormsley at her side. Louise's face lit up when Gina walked in.

Gina went to her mother and gave her a kiss on the check. Louise actually looked content. She took a moment to digest the scene before saying anything. When she did speak a torrent of questions came out. "What's going on? Who did this? Why has mother been moved?"

Mrs. Wormsley held up her hand and said, "Slow down, kiddo, one at a time. Well, Mr. Silvey had a meeting with your uncle this morning and they decided that your mother would be happier if she had some of her things with her. They moved her over here next to me because this room is a little larger than the run of the mill. How do you like it Gina?"

Gina answered by asking, "How do you like it Mama?"

Her mother looked at her with a slightly dreamy quality in her eyes and a small sweet smile and said, "Oh, fine. I like it fine. But I'm tired now and I'd like to take a nap." This was a departure in behavior for Louise. Recently she had been agitated most of the time, needed to walk around eight hours out of the day. She had difficulty sleeping and hadn't taken a nap since before the operation. Maybe it was all catching up with her and she would be able to rest.

Later, after Gina had made her mother comfortable, she knocked on Harriet's door. "Mrs. Wormsley, may I talk with you for a minute?" She asked the question from a respectful distance outside the door to Harriet's private room.

"Sure babe, c'mon in."

To Gina's surprise there sat the regal Mrs. Wormsley smoking a cigarette and having a small glass of wine.

"Well, come in and sit down. You're too young for me to offer a cigarette or drink to so you'll just have to watch. I smoke ten of 'em a day and take four ounces of wine before dinner. Been doin' it ever since I was twenty- one years old. Probably why I've lived so long. Second husband hated it."

She paused as Gina smiled and thought, "What a wonderful character this is."

Mrs. Wormsley continued her chatter saying, "I don't know what that rich uncle of yours told old Silvey this morning but the fur has been flying in this place ever since he was here. People scrubbing, cleaning, waxing. I never saw the like. All you saw around here since 11 o'clock was assholes and elbows." Gina blinked as the graphic picture formed in her mind of people bending over and scrubbing with only their rear ends and elbows showing.

"Don't mind me honey," Harriet said, noticing Gina's reaction. "Most people refer to me as salty. When you get to be my age you have license to put away all pretense of being something you're not. You don't have to say or do anything just because people expect it of you or because you want them to like you. I've finally come to the point in my life when it's okay to tell the truth all the time. I discovered this fact when I was seventy two and I've been a free woman ever since. Really, it's very liberating. I've enjoyed the last twenty years of my life more than any other time. I do miss sex though." She giggled as Gina blushed because they both knew that she had made that remark for shock value.

"Not only are they cleaning the place up, this part of it anyway, but they hired an extra nurse's aide for this wing and a lady who will come everyday and take patients for walks, read to them and the like. Silvey explained to me that a doctor was here to see Louise today and, although they are aware of your desire to take her home, the doctor advised your uncle to keep her here for another month or so. It will make it easier for him to visit and check her every day. He couldn't do that if she went home — got an office just down the street. They're installing a grand new five-seat dining table so Louise can eat with our little group." She paused to puff her cigarette and to take a sip of wine.

68

"I must admit," Gina said, taking advantage of Harriet's winding down, "Mother does seem happier or at least mellower than she was yesterday." At that moment there was a knock on the door. A smiling nurse's aide with her hair in a ponytail and wearing a clean, crisp, white uniform, appeared. She was pushing a small cart filled with pills and all kinds of medicine. She came in saying, "Time for your medicine, Wormy."

"Thanks honey," Harriet replied, "this is Gina. She's Louise's daughter." Harriet quaffed an ounce of milk of magnesia and made a face but quickly chased it with a sip of wine and said, "AAH."

"Oh yes, Louise is such a pretty lady. I just looked in to give her the medicine that the doctor ordered but she was asleep. I'll come back later. Gotta hurry now or I'll get behind schedule. Nice to meet you Gina. Don't let Wormy here pull your leg."

"I'll try not to, Wanda," Gina smiled, as she read her identification badge. "Oh say, Wanda, before you go, what kind of medicine did Dr. Zarinsky prescribe for Mama?"

"Let's see here," Wanda said reading her medicine card. "Here it is. She's taking Librium and multivitamins. Gotta go now." She was gone as suddenly as she appeared and as silently—nurses traditionally wear soft-soled shoes which make no noise.

Gina continued to visit with Mrs. Wormsley until five o'clock when she would go in to wake Louise. She wasn't sure if she would ever become comfortable with calling Harriet 'Wormy'. Not so much because the name itself was unseemly, but because Mrs. Wormsley was an adult and polite youngsters simply did not address their elders by first names or nick names. Gina overheard employees of the nursing home addressing patients by "honey" or "sweetie" or "sugar." This common practice rubbed her the wrong way too. It was her belief that older people are due all the respect and dignity that others can bestow upon them. In regular society people are insulted if you call them by the cutesy names used at Sunset Meadows. She wondered how her Uncle Vinnie would like it if someone called him "honey" unless they were family or enjoyed a long and close relationship with him. He'd hit the ceiling because there is, or should be, an understanding between people that a respectful relationship demands that you call your peers and most certainly your elders by Mr., Mrs., or Miss until they give you permission to do otherwise. This was what rankled Gina. No one gave these employees the permission to call the patients these things that had a belittling aspect to them. "Maybe I'm a prude and a stick in the mud," Gina thought, "but these little things all go together and fit into the Sunset Meadow jigsaw puzzle, the title of which is DISRESPECT." Gina was ready to concede that in a few rare cases there probably had grown a bond between patient and attendant in which a mutual closeness existed that made the use of personal names appropriate. But it was practiced *carte blanche* and, at least to Gina, it simply did not feel right.

Louise was somewhat more difficult to rouse from her sleep than usual but when Gina finally was able to gently coax her awake she smiled her sweet smile and said, "It's really nice to wake up and see those beautiful brown eyes." Gina was thrilled. This was the closest thing to something her mother might have said three months ago before this illness that she had uttered since the operation. "Maybe she will be okay. Maybe this is the best place for her now," Gina thought silently. She had begun the process of making herself believe this and sighed with relief.

Gina helped Louise get specially dressed up for dinner since she was going to be joining what Gina had come to think of as the table of royalty at Sunset Meadows. She put on a colorful dress with complementing earrings, necklace and bracelet. Gina did a quick job of painting Louise's fingernails, applying her rouge and brushing the wig so it looked nice. Gina had taken the dress in the day before but it still didn't look quite right. Louise was now fashion-model

70

thin and her cheeks were becoming hollow. Her complexion was sallow and she just didn't look healthy but the make up put some glow back on her. Gina held the mirror up after all her preparations and said, "There Mama, don't you look pretty?"

Louise just stared at her reflection and didn't answer. She would react that way a lot of the time during dinner. It was as though her mind were preoccupied with something else, something far away. She didn't seem to be in any distress, or bothered by the anxiety that plagued her before, but instead, she seemed oblivious and detached from her surroundings. Dinner was pleasant. The "girls" made a place for Gina and included her in all the conversation which was led and directed by Mrs. Wormsley, of course. Mrs. Wormsley ceremoniously introduced Louise and Gina to her three friends, who were all glad to have their intimate circle joined, particularly since it carried with it a new table, larger than the rest. There was Eula Mae Orondorff, who according to Mrs. Wormsley, was eighty-nine years old and had been at the nursing home for only six months. She gave the age and length of stay of each lady as she introduced her. Inez Casey, 78, eighteen months and Lois Stoneman, 86, three years—and the only one at the table who had been there longer than Mrs. Wormsley.

After the formalities, Harriet retained control of the master of ceremonies job and asked Gina to tell the group about herself, her school and their life together before Sunset Meadows.

Gina got into the spirit of things and was as animated and entertaining as she could be. The ladies responded in kind by smiling, nodding and mouthing an occasional knowing "aah" or "uh hm." They were polite and attentive, but at the same time, curiously like Louise, not quite there. After Gina finished her soliloquy, Harriet wasted no time in giving a rundown on the life and times of the other three in the group.

All three ladies, it turned out, had something in common. They had been married to rich men. Beyond that, two of them, Inez and Lois, had something else in common. Their sons and daughters had urged them to come here. The other lady, Eula Mae, unlike the others, had had a career as a concert pianist and had become so depressed when the ability to play gave way to failing eyesight and arthritis, she attempted suicide. Because of this, a judge ruled her incompetent and had her admitted for her own good. Although she had many relatives, none resisted the order. Gina felt uneasy as Harriet continued to tell the very personal histories of everyone, but she couldn't help noticing that the ladies about whom the stories were being told didn't seem to mind at all.

Dinner that night was a great improvement over the earlier fiasco. This time the table was set with knife, fork and spoon. The two large carts came rolling out of the kitchen as before, but this time a smaller one followed. This cart contained six dinners and was pushed by a large muscular black man who smiled a broad smile as he said, "Good evening ladies, I hope you enjoy your dinner this evening. We have a mound of tuna salad, cottage cheese on lettuce, Harvard beets and peach cobbler for dessert. I will serve you coffee, tea or milk, as you wish."

"God, this is too much," Harriet snickered. "What next? A masseuse and steam bath?" The rest of the patients were served in the usual cavalier method and didn't seem to take note of the "silk stocking" treatment. Gina felt embarrassed about the fuss being made. She knew they were being singled out because her uncle had arranged it. He was always creating special situations when they were vacationing in New York. She loved him for caring and being so considerate and wondered why it required his intervention to get Sunset Meadows to provide the level of care and consideration that she was seeing this day. Why didn't they simply run the home in a way that made the patients feel special and their families happy and content? It didn't look to her

72

like it would be that hard. After dinner Gina invited Mrs. Wormsley to her mother's room for television. "That would be nice but I warn you, I'm going to smoke a cigarette," Harriet cautioned.

"I really don't mind at all," Gina graciously replied. Gina turned on the set. It was the last of the Huntley-Brinkley News Report. Gina sat on the bed, Louise in the easy chair and Harriet in her wheel chair, carrying her smoking material and small ashtray.

Gina was happy to have a positive influence like Harriet around. The three of them halfheartedly turned their attention to the TV set, but nobody was actually tuned in.

Gina said to Harriet, "Your friends are all very nice. They are so pleasant and easy going. I wish they would have talked more, however. I'll bet they have some delightful stories to tell about their lives."

"Yes, they've all led very full lives but each of them is frightened of death. They don't want to talk about it." Harriet paused to light up. "They all three have the same doctor. He gives them those pills. That's what makes them so . . . what did you say . . . easy going? I refuse to take 'em. I'm dopey enough as it is. Besides, I have my wine."

"Pills?" Gina was alert. "What kind of pills are you talking about?" she asked, trying to hide her alarm.

"Oh, you know, those new sedatives, tranquilizers they call them. I don't know the names of the pills but I can tell you one thing for sure, they make you tranquil, all right. You surely noticed the change in Louise here."

Gina was dumbfounded. "Yes", she stammered, "but I thought it was due to the room change and that she was simply adjusting to the home and, God, I don't know what I thought." Gina fell silent as she tried to gather her thoughts. This was an explanation why so many people here were so apathetic, why they didn't react the way you would expect them to. She looked at her mother who was sitting calmly looking at the TV screen without seeing. It made Gina shudder as she remembered George Orwell's book, *1984*, which she had read earlier that year. This kind of mind control reminded her of that creepy, scary book. She remembered that the class discussion was very spirited about the book, with the large majority of the class taking the position that it could never happen.

The teacher, in a kind of wrap up of the discussion, cautioned the class that Adolph Hitler had come very close to pulling it off. She asked the class to consider the situation in Russia today which is a police state with the citizens having very little freedom. She then recalled the last thing the teacher said that day. It didn't come through at the time, but suddenly made enormous sense. She had said that changes came about slowly, almost imperceptibly, rather than suddenly and dramatically. It was like the changing of the leaves in autumn. You know they're green in August, and they turn red and brown by late October, but you can't sit and watch it happen because the transformation is too slow. She made the point that if there is a danger of the Orwellian nightmare happening in the United States, it will be a gradual, imperceptible change. Freedom and liberty would have to erode slowly, bit by bit, if we were ever to lose it. She went on to talk about a Senator named Joseph McCarthy who, for whatever reason, caused a large stir in the country by denouncing all kinds of well known people as being communists. He was rebuffed finally, but for a while many people were alarmed that some people believed him. These memories raced through Gina's mind and frightened her. A paranoid figure like Joe McCarthy here, a generation of people sitting around in nursing homes drugged up there, pretty soon you are talking about the insidious, creeping specter about which the high school teacher warned. "Oh, come on now Gina, nothing like that is going to happen," she attempted to reassure herself.

When she returned to the mansion, the reliable and resourceful Uncle Vinnie was waiting like the night before.

They repaired to the study as they had on the previous night.

"Well, my dear, are you as upset this evening as you were last night?" he began.

"I am concerned about something," she replied, "but I have to tell you that Sunset Meadows is a different place now compared to yesterday. Mrs. Wormsley, the lady I told you about, is now in the room next to Mama's. She believes that it was your visit that somehow encouraged the difference. What did you tell Mr. Silvey?" She was asking in a respectful manner that was full of admiration rather than being an inquisition.

Vincent smiled at the directness and utter brightness of Gina, more than at his ability to intimidate and bribe a wimp like Silvey. "Mr. Silvey and I discussed ways in which Louise could be made more comfortable, it's true. It was obvious that she would have a greater struggle getting better if she were as agitated and unhappy as you had described her. You see honey, it's going to be necessary for her to stay there awhile, so Dr. Zarinsky or his partner can now look in on her daily. I just wanted her to be as comfortable as possible." As he finished the manservant entered the room with the silver tray. Their conversation stopped while he went through the serving of the snack and cognac.

As soon as he left the room Gina eyed her uncle directly and said, "Did you know Dr. Zarinsky was going to drug mother?" Her voice took on a certain coldness that told Vincent to be careful. He wanted, above all else, to gain Gina's total trust.

"After examining Louise yesterday morning," he began with no hesitation, "I was aware that Dr. Zarinsky thought it advisable to prescribe something that would help Louise control her anxiety. Why do you ask, sweetheart?"

"Because the pills make her like a lot of other people there. Almost zombie-like. It scares me."

"I can understand how you feel. But Dr. Zarinsky knows what he's doing. You believe that, don't you?" She nodded, somewhat reluctantly.

"The medicine will just be a temporary measure until Louise is able to settle down on her own. As she adjusts, it will be withdrawn little by little." The phrase "little by little" reminded her of her earlier reflection.

"It's just that I hate to see Mother handicapped any more than she already is. I can certainly assure you that the Librium works. She is feeling no pain. It's too bad that the drug reduces her functioning as a side affect."

Vincent took a calculated risk and said, "Gina, I'll call Dr. Zarinsky first thing in the morning and ask him to discontinue the meditation if you wish."

He was right as usual. He was always at his best when he could put other people on the spot.

"No, let's not do that yet. Let's see how she is tomorrow. Is there a possibility of reducing the dosage?"

"Of course, my dear. Little by little."

CHAPTER 11

Gina was able to concentrate better at school for the next few days. Her mind was making a shift from worrying about the conditions at Sunset Meadows to thinking about what she could do to make life better for her mother and the other patients. She hit upon an idea that had merit. She posted this typed notice on the bulletin board outside the school Library.

NOTICE:

Anyone interested in volunteering one hour of their time each day at the Sunset Meadows Nursing Home just down the street meet me in Room 222 immediately after school Friday.

Gina Oldani

When Friday afternoon finally arrived, nineteen noisy, uniformed, teenage girls filed into room 222. Gina settled them down as quickly as possible and began talking.

"Most of you have heard that my mother is a patient at Sunset Meadows Nursing Home. She had a brain tumor removed recently and her doctor feels she can best recover in that environment where he can keep a closer eye on her than if she were at home. I've got to say that I don't like it, but what can I do? How many of you have ever been in a nursing home?" Two hands.

"What was it like?" Gina directed the question to the two hands.

"Ugh! It stunk. It was depressing. I couldn't wait to leave," said the first hand.

"What was it like for you Anna Mae?" she asked the second hand.

"Well, my experience wasn't as negative as hers. The place my grandmother was in was clean and nice. But I'll tell you this—I never want to go to one"

Most of the people in the room nodded agreement to that.

"I know what you mean," Gina said with a trace of sadness in her voice. "But sometimes things happen that we can't do anything about. I've got an idea that I think can make a lot of old people a lot happier. We'll call it Operation Granddaughter. One of the problems with these nursing homes is that they're so darned boring. There's nothing to do—nothing to look forward to. The patients are so turned off they don't even talk to one another. What we could do is this . . ."

Gina went on to tell them that her uncle had given her money to buy a large assortment of games, cards, bingo with prizes, crossword puzzles, books and magazines to read from, and subscriptions to the daily newspapers. She talked about the need for companionship and someone to walk with or to push a wheel chair. She said she was sure that everyone would find her own way of enriching the lives of the patients. Gina's reading of the group's reaction ranged from curiosity and mild commitment to enthusiasm. She actually had no idea if this would work or not but she was determined to make an all-out effort. She had figured one thing right; she asked her uncle to make the request for this program to Mr. Silvey. No problem there.

Saturday morning was cold and windy. Vincent Gambrino offered the old "in like a lion, out like a lamb" bromide to Gina at breakfast. It was the first of March so the remark was appropriate but she had heard it several times before. Today was the day for Gina's first driving lesson. Vincent was going to personally attend to this matter mainly because he wanted to, but also because he wanted to take every opportunity to interact with Gina. Vincent had a collection of cars, all American made. He chose his 1957 Ford Thunderbird for Gina's lesson. He reasoned that it was small and responsive and a good car in which to learn.

His pre-ride explanations of the workings of a car were generous and easy for Gina to follow. He drove the car around the private road, explaining each move as it was executed.

Gina learned very quickly. She drove around the grounds several times, demonstrating to Vincent's satisfaction that all she needed was some experience and a license and she'd be ready for the road. He would see to it that she got both.

One hour later, at the end of the lesson, Gina pulled the shiny black T-Bird carefully to a halt outside the garage.

"You did very well, honey," Vincent said. "You'll be a pro in no time. How did you like it?"

"It was fun. I think driving is something that every teenager dreams of. It's a great feeling of power, control and freedom. It also gives me a feeling of being grown up." Her eyes were sparkling as she turned off the motor.

"I'm glad you're happy. Well, what kind of car do you want? Name it and it's yours," Vincent said.

"Oh, Uncle Vinnie," Gina blushed, "You're too generous with me. I'm beginning to feel like a spoiled child."

"Gina, I'd give anything I own to make you happy. Now you indulge your old Uncle Vinnie and let him spoil you. You deserve it. I love you, sweetheart."

"I love you too, Uncle Vinnie," she said as she awkwardly hugged him in the small car.

Vincent stood at the front door waving as his driver swung the huge limo carrying Gina to the nursing home around the driveway. She waved back actively. It occurred to Vincent to throw her a kiss like he had seen grandparents do, but he decided it wasn't his style.

Vincent returned to the house feeling happier than he could ever remember. His life had been full of accomplishments in terms of financial success, but it had not been a life full of love. He had caught his only wife in bed with a neighbor just two months after the birth of his son. He shot and killed that man and drove the woman out of his house. She took the child with her and Vincent had not heard from either of them since, although he knew where they were. These days he thought about them only occasionally. For several years following the incident he was constantly bothered by his decision to vanquish them and was often tempted to forgive her so he could have his son back. His deep hurt and false pride would never give in to the temptation. Even now that he was older and mellower, he still wouldn't let himself regret the matter. He had done what an honorable man had to do.

Soon after dealing with the adulterous affair, he put all his strength and energy into becoming successful. He wasn't a highly intelligent man and he knew that. But he was very shrewd and cunning. He often thought that he preferred being the latter rather than the former.

Vincent Gambrino started working in a New York restaurant at the age of sixteen. He had left home because his father was so oppressive and because he didn't like school. He had always known that someday he would be a rich man. He figured the sooner he got on with the moneymaking part, the better.

By the time he was twenty one years old he had learned the restaurant business inside out. He had been everything from bus boy to chef to *maitre de*, and on his twenty-second birthday he opened his own place called "Vincent's". By the

80

time he was fifty years old he had opened a total of thirty restaurants in New York and Chicago. He set his goal at one a year and never deviated. He would find a location, get a restaurant going by managing it himself and then he would lease it to one of his select employees. This formula never failed because he was a good judge of character and because he would visit each place at least once a month and inspect it thoroughly. At age fifty-two he sold all but six of the places to the leasees and, already a rich man, found himself with more money that he had ever dreamed of having.

He wasn't a stingy man. He loved to indulge himself and those around him in all the finer things in life. He "entertained" ladies of the evening at least two nights a week preferring to have his driver pick them up and bring them to him rather than the more conventional mode. He paid top dollar and got only the finest merchandise. Now that Gina was living with him, this practice would have to change. Not discontinue—change. Going to town for his sexual gratification was a small price to pay for the joy of having Gina around. Buying that gratification was far superior to the price a man must pay for getting it through the traditional channels. He could never bring himself to trust a woman or to fall in love after his tragic first attempt. He realized his life had been empty of the commitment and closeness that a good marriage and family can bring, but he was now feeling the caring and concern that his life had been devoid of for all these years. He liked the feelings very much. He had thought he would never get to experience them again—or that he didn't deserve to.

CHAPTER 12

Gina viewed Monday afternoon with considerable trepidation. She knew that getting the residents at Sunset Meadows alert and involved was going to be no easy task. She was aware of the many factors weighing against a successful program; the drugs, the indifference of the staff and management, the inexperience and lack of training of her schoolmates were barriers. Also a problem was the simple fact that at least some of the residents had never been the kind to get involved in anything in their lives. A bunch of disorganized high school girls had little chance of reversing conditions so formidable, but that wasn't sufficient cause for Gina not to try.

The next week was one of the most discouraging of Gina's life. By Friday all of her volunteers had dropped out, each giving a reason of not enough spare time or something equally bland. Gina knew they quit because most of them weren't successful, and they got nothing in the way of positive feedback from either staff or residents. As she had been at first, they were overwhelmed by the feelings of gloom and doom that were pervasive at Sunset Meadows. All of the girls were apologetic about quitting and were truly sorry about Gina's mother. They felt sorry for Gina too, but not sorry enough to want to spend any more of their time and effort on a hopeless and thankless task.

Friday night Gina told her uncle about the frustration of this failure experience. "I know it can work," she said, "because I, myself, can make it work. The people I work with came alive and had begun to enjoy themselves - they were smiling and doing things and I know they looked forward to my coming. I had to plan and work hard to get reactions, but I found a way."

Vincent listened patiently and with empathy and when Gina finished he said, "Gina, you have just experienced one of the oldest stories of why businesses fail. The owner of a business or enterprise is usually a person with skill and ambition, but when it comes to planning their futures and training others with the necessary skills to operate success-fully, they fall short of the mark. You have to know how to select people with the right motivation and drive to bring your plans to fruition. No one can run a business by himself; it takes cooperation and teamwork to get the job done. This simple formula is what has made me rich and successful." He went on to detail to her how he would begin a restau-rant, train the people and then pull away after hand select-ing the most able person to continue a successful operation. He explained how extremely important is was to follow up and monitor the progress of the business. They spent over three hours discussing the simple rules Vincent had out-lined. They projected the principles to several businesses and both agreed that even a nursing home could be run in a humane and caring way and still be profitable. They both agreed with the conclusion that a poorly managed home like Sunset Meadows was due to leadership that was indif-ferent or ignorant — or both. Gina went to bed with her head swimming with all the data she had ingested. Her uncle was a very wise man and she had great respect for his business acumen and knew that she could learn a lot from him.

The next morning Gina took an unconducted tour of the great house. It was called DeLassus Place (pronounced del-ah-soo), having been named after a rich Frenchman who built it some eighty years before. Located on a high bluff overlooking the Mississippi River, it commanded a breath-taking view of the flat Illinois farmland. An observation tower was constructed on the third floor, complete with a powerful telescope, which allowed one to make out the facial expressions of the men who worked on the endless parade of river barges that passed by daily. The entry of the house had a large vestibule with an imported Italian slate floor and featured a commanding horseshoe staircase which met on the second floor landing. The hallways were eight feet wide throughout the house which boasted fourteen large bedrooms and ten bathrooms, in addition to a large ballroom on the third floor. The kitchen was very large and impressive. It had all stainless steel appliances, the way you'd imagine a kitchen would look in the restaurant of a fine hotel. The house was managed by the butler, Eugene, two housekeepers, a chef and the ubiquitous chauffeur. The chef and one of the housekeepers drove to DeLassus Place daily, while Eugene, the chauffeur and the other house-keeper, who were married, lived in two apartments located over one of the carriage houses behind the big house. All these servants were very proper and always dressed in Hollywood-style servants attire. They were smiling and friendly to Gina but never allowed themselves to be conver-sational or to ask questions. They would answer any ques-tions Gina might have, to be sure, but were loathe to offer viewpoints or advise. Gina often wondered why they would want to spend their lives in such servitude.

Vincent joined Gina in the third story observation room where she was peering through the long range lens of the telescope. He was puffing slightly from his walk up the stairs and there was more color to his face than usual.

"Uncle Vinnie," Gina asked her eye still pressed against the telescope, "what is that large conglomeration of old buildings setting outside of Godfrey, Illinois? Is it a prison?"

Vincent smiled slightly and answered "No, it's Godfrey State Hospital. A terrible place I'm told — smelly, overcrowd-ed — not a place you'd want to go. You have to crazy to get in." He chuckled hoping that Gina would be likewise amused. She wasn't.

"It makes me sad to think of how many unhappy people must be inside those fences and walls. I can only imagine how much worse it is than Sunset Meadows," as she said that she began to tear up slightly but swiped away at her eyes and fought back the inclination to cry. "Do you think people go there mentally ill and then get cured and leave?"

Vincent became somber because he knew these questions were connected to her mother's condition. "I don't really know, sweetheart," he answered in his most professional tone. "I've heard there are as many as three thousand patients there and it was only built to house two thousand. That's bound to make an already bad situation worse. It's also a terrible place to work, I imagine, low pay, depressing atmosphere and all."

"Yeah, like a nursing home," Gina thought.

Later that day as Gina walked down the hall to her mother's room she heard a "Psst, honey, come here I want to show you something."

It was the cute little eighty nine year old Eula Mae Orndorff looking like the cat who swallowed the canary. "Know what this is?" she said mischievously. "Come here, close."

Eula Mae's room smelled of urine, a smell that Gina was growing to despise. Eula Mae was holding up a small silvery devise with fine thread woven around it. "No, Mrs. Orndorff, I don't believe I've ever seen anything like that. What is it?" Gina asked, being a willing participant in the game. Eula Mae smiled with satisfaction and said, "I knew you wouldn't know what it is. Few old people and no youngsters know. It's a tattin' shuttle. It's for tattin'. My mother taught me how to do it like her mother before her. Been doin' it all my life, or at least since I was sixteen years old. None of my sisters, there were six of 'em, could ever learn how. Momma was always proud of me for that. Here, want to try it?"

Eula Mae handed the tatting shuttle to Gina. It was a shiny metal device about 2 1/2 inches long in the shape of a boat. It had a wheel in the center and a small hook in one end. Its value and use were still a mystery but Gina was sure she was going to be further educated. Eula Mae was smiling as though she held the secrets of the universe and was about to disclose that information, thereby enlightening the rest of the populace, who until this time, had collectively groveled in darkness.

"Give it back. I'll show you," she directed. She then produced from the collection of stuff in her lap, a long string of embroidery that was very delicate and lovely. She made several deft movements with the thread and the shuttle and began to produce more of the tiny, interwoven lace that was suitable for handkerchiefs, doilies and maybe old-fashioned collars.

"Mrs. Orndorff, that's the prettiest work I've ever seen," Gina said delightfully. "I wonder if I might have a small piece of your tattin' so I can show it to my friends and teachers. I'll bet none of them have ever seen it either."

Mrs. Orndorff smiled contentedly. Her day was made. As Gina was leaving Eula Mae's room, she ran into Harriet Wormsley in the hall. "Well, I see you've gotten the tattin' indoctrination," she smirked.

"Yes, I was very impressed at how someone her age could do such intricate work, "Gina said.

"It is a wonder how the old woman can do it. Poor thing gets so confused. Thinks her family members are still living. She's the last of a family of thirteen. You'd better watch yourself. She'll repeat the tattin' lecture every time she sees you from now on. She'd willingly do it ten times a day if there were enough people around with the patience to listen. She burned me out on it a long time ago. Staying for dinner?"

"Yes, I suppose so. See you then." Gina shook her head as they parted. "Mrs. Wormsley is on top of everything," she thought. Louise was sitting in the easy chair staring blankly at the television set. It was tuned to a program that was called American Bandstand. It was the first time Gina had seen it.

Her mother looked tired and wrung out. She had on the same clothes as the day before. The attendant had obviously not bothered to help her lay out fresh things. She had a stain down her front that appeared to be food from either breakfast or lunch and her fingernails were not clean. Gina flew into a frenzy to make her mother more presentable by dinner time. She was highly upset with the nursing home for being so lackadaisical about her mother's grooming, but more than that she was near hysteria because, for the first time, she realized that her mother was only going to get worse, not better. The complete dependence on others, the progression of loss of speech and muscle control, the weakness and dramatic loss of weight were bad signs, but, nevertheless they were physical in nature. The sight of her once fastidious mother sitting in that chair, wig askew and generally soiled and untidy, was the final sad sign to Gina that her mother was going to lose the battle.

With tears in her eyes, Gina resigned herself to cleaning her up, and changing her clothes. She was trying to instill some pride and fight back into the body whose brain was so butchered and ravaged; it simply could no longer do its complex job. As Gina went about her work she noticed that several items of jewelry and clothing were missing, as well as the expensive winter coat that Uncle Vinnie had bought her. She was completely demoralized. Gina went to the telephone to call her uncle. Within half an hour an ambulance pulled up to the front of Sunset Meadows and took Louise and Gina to nearby Barnes Hospital where a room was waiting. Louise Oldani died that night, mercifully, in her sleep.

Vincent took care of all the funeral arrangements, being careful to make them respectable but not ostentatious. The ceremony was held at St. Ambrose Church on the Hill and was well-attended by neighborhood friends, as well as several people from the police department. Gina was surprised and pleased to see Mrs. Wormsley, escorted by her son Senator Higgins. She knew it was difficult for Mrs. Wormsley to get around and she was appreciative of the kind and soothing words the mother and son offered.

Father Gianelli, who presided over the funeral, had known Louise for a good part of her life and was very generous and flattering in his remarks about her. Even at that, Gina was disappointed at how swiftly and succinctly he summarized the life and times of her sainted mother. There was so much more to the woman than anybody could ever know. Many times after that ceremony Gina wished she would have stood up and told the people gathered there how wonderful her mother really was. When the casket closed Gina thought, "I'll never see her again," and began weeping unashamedly.

Her uncle was by her side to comfort and support her.

CHAPTER 13

The summer after her mother's death went by slowly for Gina. She had graduated third in her high school class in spite of a "B" average in the last semester. Her kind and generous uncle had given her a red 1959 Corvette for graduation. She was very proud of it although it made her somewhat self-conscious because of the attention it drew. She didn't seem to be fully aware that a good deal of the admiration she thought was going to the car was actually being lavished on her. She was now nineteen years old and had matured into a woman of considerable charm and beauty. At five feet eight inches and 120 pounds she was a svelte knockout with flashing brown eyes and a smile that revealed extraordinarily white teeth. The car was something of an eye catcher to be sure, but with Gina at the wheel, you're talking show stopper.

Gina had friends out for tennis and swimming during the summer and once, at the urging of Uncle Vinnie, she had a party which featured barbecue and a live band. Boys literally drooled over Gina, but while she was friendly and dated a few of them, she seemed somewhat aloof and unattainable to her male peers. No one thought of her as a rich stuck-up girl, but rather as more mature than others her age, possibly listening to a different drummer—a more sophisticated drummer of a higher order. At any rate, none of the young men of her acquaintance had yet won her heart.

She spent a lot of time reading and thinking about life and sometimes about how sudden and unfair death could be. She thought about nursing homes and Mrs. Wormsley, whom she had visited twice that summer. She thought about what she wanted to be in life. Uncle Vinnie was putting pressure on her to team up with him and open a restaurant in St. Louis, one like no one had ever seen before. It was an idea which had no appeal, but the choices for women in the career world were rather limited. Gina had decided she wanted to do something that would help other people so she gave a lot of thought to nursing and teaching. After much deliberation she decided that the profession in which she could best serve and make the most impact on others would be social work. A field that studied group and individual behavior and that trained people to assist others who were needy was very appealing. She felt it was just right.

In mid-August she was accepted by a small, yet prestigious, liberal arts college located in Fayette, Missouri called Central College.

Fayette was some 160 miles west of St. Louis. It was a small farming community with no industry except for a small shoe factory that was located there for only one reason, cheap labor. There was no way to get there except by car; no train, plane or bus line had facilities in Fayette, Missouri. It had a population of 3500, most of whom were glad to have the revenue that the college brought in. Some of the "townies" were, nevertheless, slightly contemptuous of anyone associated with the college. Professors who had lived and taught in Fayette for fifteen years were still viewed as outsiders who had scarcely unpacked their bags.

Central College was a community unto itself. Maybe fortress would be a better word. It had a student body of 1200 and a football team that rarely did anything except prove embarrassing. The little college did boast a fine and learned staff however, and many top students had elected to go there since it was founded in 1908.

During her first semester Gina was taken under the wing of the head of the sociology department, Dr. Ward Graham-Herwig. Dr. Graham-Herwig took note of her quick, sharp mind and unique problem-solving ability and wanted to make her his personal protégé, hoping to add her to his staff someday. Almost daily Dr. Graham-Herwig also had vivid fantasies about making love to Gina Oldani.

Dr. Ward Graham-Herwig had grown up in London and went to all the finest schools topping off his education with a Ph.D. from Oxford. After graduation he interned at a large hospital in London for one year and then left rather suddenly under conditions that were never made completely clear.

Soon after that he booked passage to New York where he signed on with Belleview Hospital. Belleview was turning some new ground, especially with the care of psychiatric patients after they left the hospital. Rightly enough the idea was called After Care.

His stay at Belleview was brief and undistinguished and was followed by his appointment to the head of the Social Service Department of Central College, Fayette, Missouri, the total department being comprised of Graham-Herwig and a graduate student assistant.

Dr. Graham-Herwig was seen as a very curious fellow by staff and students alike. It was said of him a thousand times, "He really knows his subject; he just doesn't know how to get it across." Heard that before? Usually when you find a person about whom that is said you find a person who can't get anything across, much less college level material.

Dr. Graham-Herwig was a very frail-appearing man, weighing 135 pounds at 5'9". His skin was pale and sallow. He could have posed for the man who has sand kicked in his face at the beach. Unfortunately there was going to be no "before and after" for Graham-Herwig. He lived alone in a tiny, but neat, apartment on the second floor of one of the many two story houses along Church Street which made up the western perimeter of the 52 acres of Christian atmosphere called Central College.

Dr. Graham-Herwig, or Professor as he liked to be called, dressed carefully every day in a business suit, immaculate and highly-starched shirt and well-shined shoes.

In event of threatening weather he would have rubbers, plastic hat guard, raincoat and umbrella at the ready. His haberdashery was immaculate. There was only one thing that one might question; everything he wore was out of the 1940's. He looked like an anemic Humphrey Bogart. His car, an impeccable 1949 Ford business coupe, was parked in a neighbor's garage and wrapped in sheets. Only a few people had ever seen it at all, but the man who once serviced it at the Shell Service Station said it only had 2400 miles on the speedometer and was like new in every respect.

This man was so odd that a small cult of "Graham-Herwig watchers" formed. These students spent considerable time during evenings of drinking beer and listening to the Kingston Trio, trying to put a finger on who or what this mystery man was really about. Members of the group would unceasingly seek a chance to be with the curious oddball with the clouded background. They would sidle up next to him at the Alsop-Turner Drug Store, where he regularly took bananas and cream with sugar, to discuss any subject he might like to dwell upon. He was always too clever to give himself away, however. He would be polite, give almost his whole attention to his bananas and cream, and then bid the interloper a good day.

Like most cult figures, the image of the skinny, painfully shy, and wholly inadequate figure far outran his actual existence. It became a game to create grand, exotic stories of his conquests and adventures. The stories invariably cast the diminutive, bespectacled fellow into roles not unlike the character created by Ian Fleming, James Bond. In this outrageous parody lay the humor, of course. Comparing Dr. Graham-Herwig to James Bond was like equating John Wayne to Mr. Peepers. The students would ridicule that which they didn't understand or anything that seemed incongruous. The head of the social science department was prime material.

His method of teaching class was also incongruous. He would spend the entire fifty minute session reading from a hand written, spiral notebook on the subject of social work. At the same time, an assignment was given to read seven chapters in the text book. About three times each semester a "test" was given which invariably consisted of seven questions to be answered in essay form. Naturally, when word of this got around, his attendance, if not his popularity swelled, especially among the immature scholars who were not inclined to learn something useful along with getting their degrees. Maybe every college has its laugher; well, Dr. Ward Graham-Herwig was Central's.

Gina became aware of the department head's inadequacy early on and thought long and hard about transferring to a school where she would be properly trained. The charm of the little school and the friendship she had already made allowed her to rationalize the problem away. After all, the material was there, all she would have to do is make sure she learned it on her own. Sometimes, when she was alone thinking about nothing in particular, a worrisome and recurring theme would land on her consciousness. She couldn't, or maybe wouldn't, get it to crystallize and become a thought she could articulate clearly, but with each life experience it tended to be reinforced. It had to do with the tendency of everything in life not living up to it's expectancy and potential. The way things were portrayed in books or on television were more vivid and usually happier than they were in real life. As she reviewed her life she knew she was blessed in many ways to have had a loving mother and many beautiful memories of her childhood. She also realized that for a good many people such was not the case.

It wasn't family life that she thought about. The problem revolved around institutions. Schools, for instance. She had always attended Catholic schools, as her mother wished, and was a good and attentive student. The trouble was with the nuns who taught. They taught by rote and drill and never did anything that would cause the students to have fresh thoughts of their own. Only one nun, Sister Felicia, was different. Gina had adored her and spent as much time with her as possible. Gina remembered thinking that if it had not been for her mother and Sister Felicia encouraging her independent thought and investigation of issues in the world she might have grown up to be a nun herself, a thought which was now totally repugnant.

Then there was Sunset Meadows, the nursing home where her mother had spent her last days. The literature, which Gina still had, about the nursing home was very convincing that it was a place where your loved one would be absolutely comfortable and cared for in every way. Gina had found it to be a cold, indifferent place where the nurses aides, who did all the caring and work, were paid $1.00 an hour and had no training. They came to work and if they did a reasonable job they could stay. If they demanded more sheets or towels or things to work with or made a fuss in any way about the care of the patients, they were fired immediately. That was no problem for management because the list of applicants was long.

Now here she was at Central College, a place rich in history and background that, like Sunset Meadows, produced literature which boasted of a liberal arts education second to none. And what do you get? Dr. Ward Graham-Herwig.

Gina began wondering if everything in the world was this way. Was Harvard? How about the United Nations? Is there a possibility that all the institutions in the world are held up by image makers and in fact run by ordinary or, in most cases, inferior people? Her tally sheet so far in her young life was weighing heavily on the possibility that everything in this world was not what it was cracked up to be. She vowed to herself that whatever she was to become in life she would make every effort to be the best possible.

While at Central College, Gina was a serious student but also partook of the social life, such as it was. In her sophomore year she was elected as Homecoming Queen for which she was truly honored but had to realistically admit that the competition was soft. For some reason, Central College was not overrun with good looking girls. A small academically-oriented school out in the middle of nowhere just didn't pack them in, a fact often lamented by the male populace.

She joined a sorority and had many dates, most of which consisted of a local movie and a coke at the student union after. If a suitor was trying to be extravagant and impressive, he would take her 35 miles down the road to Columbia, home of the University of Missouri, for pizza and beer.

During her summers, Gina and Vincent traveled extensively. They went to Rome, Paris, London and Rio de Janeiro. Her relationship with her uncle had developed into something special that they both cherished. They communicated very well and often sat up far into the night talking; these discussions reminded Gina of similar sessions she had enjoyed with her mother.

Gina had taken extra class loads for her first 3 1/2 years because she wanted to get all the class work out of the way and spend her last semester doing a field experience that she and Dr. Graham-Herwig had planned during her first semester. She would train and work under the guidance of a trained social worker and would do her senior thesis on the experience. Naturally, the ever leering Dr. Graham-Herwig would meet with her occasionally for his input. The site of the field experience Gina had chosen proved unusually hard for Dr. Graham-Herwig to develop. He met with considerable resistance, but Gina was especially keen to train at this particular facility so he persisted until the necessary arrangements were made.

On February 1, 1963, Gina Oldani drove past the guard gate of Godfrey State Hospital to begin her career as a social worker.

CHAPTER 14

Godfrey State Psychiatric Hospital was no less eerie and intimidating up close than it was when viewed from the safety of her Missouri home across the Mississippi River. Gina recalled the conversation with her uncle years ago as she had looked at the hospital from the viewing tower of DeLassus Place. Up close it looked like a forbidding fortress with giant smoke stacks that belched gray smoke into the frigid winter air.

The main hospital, or "old section" as some called it, was built around the turn of the century and was mammoth by any standards. It was over two large city blocks long and had four full floors running its entire length. The old section was bound together by an intricate underground basement network that allowed a person to go the length of the enormous edifice without having to go through any doors.

The hospital had its own bakery, power plant, greenhouse, and even featured a farm where the cows furnished the hospital with milk. This hulking, practically self-sufficient hospital housed some 2900 in-patient psychiatric cases of various diagnosis.

The old section was called old because that's what it became in 1961 when the Illinois Institute of Psychiatry was built in its front yard. The IIP was a modern four story glass building that obscured most of the old section from view on the front side. It looked more like a Monsanto office building than a state facility for the mentally deranged. It brought with it a promise of a new era of enlightenment for the mentally ill. Politicians promised the Illinois taxpayers that the research which would be conducted in this modern facility would bring the science of psychiatry kicking and screaming into the twentieth century. The IIP housed four hundred patients and, in addition to its research function, was a training facility for psychiatrists having an affiliation with the University of Illinois at Champaign-Urbana.

The Institute was air conditioned, unlike the old section which wasn't, and had two- and four-person rooms with adjoining bathrooms. The old building had dormitories with a few "private" rooms which were actually padded cells for violent or unruly patients. All the bathrooms in the old section were of the communal type offering no privacy.

The patients who were able to comprehend what was going on around them viewed being transferred to the Institute with mixed feelings. The modern structure was cleaner and less crowded and you got more attention. But there were troubling rumors of drug experiments being conducted that could make you permanently crazy, impotent or maybe even worse. In spite of the negative possibilities, it was rare for a patient or their family to decline transfer when the staff advised it. There was a perception of prestige and maybe an increased chance of recovery for those who were admitted to the Institute. Like many perceptions, the IIP failed to live up to its promise. The Godfrey State Hospital boasted as full a line of services and therapies as was to be found in any state hospital across the country, with possibly the exception of California, which always seemed to be a pacemaker in the field.

The facility had an industrial therapy department which was an adjunct of its vocational rehabilitation program. The four therapists in industrial therapy worked with the various psychiatric teams, placing acceptable patients in work assignments throughout the hospital plant. Any day of the week there were literally hundreds of patients working in the kitchen, laundry, grounds crew and even clerical positions. While these job assignments were said to be therapy, it was clearly understood by everyone that the jobs, in themselves, would not cure anybody and probably would not teach anybody a new skill that could be used in the outside world upon release. It was believed, however, that anything was better than sitting in the dreary, roach-infested wards of the old building day after day. So an industrial therapy assignment was a way to at least maintain oneself at a functional level and lessened the chance of regression. It has always been a belief, and rightly so, that work is good. It gives a person a feeling of self-worth and purpose. This was the underpinnings of the industrial therapy program and made it the largest single therapy in the hospital. It probably should be mentioned that it was also a source of very cheap labor.

Gina was to report to the Director of Social Services at nine on Monday morning, but she was five minutes late because she got lost in the labyrinth of hallways. At 9:06 she was shown into the office of Miss Loretta Mandeville, M.S.W. Miss Mandeville was on the phone and waved Gina into a chair behind her desk as she wrote down notes, presumably corresponding to what the person on the other end of the line was saying. She had a lit Camel cigarette which was hanging from the corner of her lips, causing her to squint and blink from the smoke drifting into her eyes.

She said, "Yes, Doctor, I'll take care of that," and replaced the receiver onto its cradle. She sat there for a moment looking at the phone and then muttered, "Miserable son of a bitch." She then looked at Gina and said, "Hi, you're Gina Oldani aren't you?

"Yes ma'am, how do you do?" Gina's automatic reply was accompanied with a feeling that she might be swimming in uncharted waters.

"That oatmeal-drooling foreign shrink is keeping a guy in this nut house so he can complete a drug study. The patient is as well as he's going to get and has a job and family to go back to. That kind of stuff pisses me off worse than any of the other craziness that goes on in this place." She took a deep breath. "So . . . you want to be a social worker, eh?"

"Yes ma'am, I do."

"Well, I don't know if you'll want to be one after you've been around this place for a while. One thing's for certain, you'll be the best looking social worker I've ever trained," Loretta said, smiling through the blue haze of smoke and giving Gina an appraising look from head to toe.

Loretta Mandeville, at 51 years of age, was a confirmed lesbian and had long ceased to care who knew it. She made sure she looked the part, with boyish cut hair, dressing in slacks only, and plenty of masculine affectations so there would be no doubt in anybody's mind where she stood. Quite bold for 1963 in the midwest. She even had a tattoo on her left shoulder which she didn't flaunt because, like many men who had one applied in a moment of weakness or drunkenness, she was actually sorry it was there.

She lived with another woman named Linda Griffey, who worked in the activities department at the hospital. Linda was 36, slim and very feminine. This controversial pair were not ostracized from the social fabric of the hospital. On the contrary, they were very popular and invited to all the parties and social functions. They gave at least two parties a year themselves and everybody came. It was always a hoot to take some naive new employee into their bedroom and to innocently ask for an explanation as to why there was only one bed in the whole house. Some people were slow learners, but in their defense, homosexuality was a rarity in Godfrey, Illinois.

With all her rough ways and profanity, her brightness was something that no one could take away from Loretta Mandeville. She also felt a special kind of compassion which was limited to selected human beings. This compassion didn't necessarily flow to those on this earth who she thought were in a position to take care of themselves, most notably doctors and lawyers. Rather, she was for the defenseless underdog. People who were down and had no way to get up were the ones for whom she advocated. It was said that taking on Loretta Mandeville was something like trying to stick a wet noodle in a wild cat's ass. It was to be avoided if at all possible. Her reputation for vindictiveness was well documented.

Gina was taken aback by the veteran social worker and simply didn't know what to make of her. She was introducing Gina to colloquialisms and vulgarity unlike any she had known before. The two sat and chatted for an hour or so, mostly with Loretta gaining information from Gina about her goals and background. Gina left nothing out, including her experience with the nursing home. Loretta particularly keyed in on that, probing for the whole story and grunting her agreement where appropriate.

"Honey, I'm not surprised or shocked to hear about the poor care at a nursing home or that your college advisor is an ineffectual, neurotic asshole. Before you're through here, I'll show you confusion, ineptness and incompetence that will make your head spin. No sense putting that off any longer. Let's take a tour."

The first stop was the canteen where soda pop, smoking material, confections, and all sorts of cheap souvenir items were sold by the hospital auxiliary. It was full of dull-eyed patients, most of whom were purchasing pop, candy or cigarettes. Loretta explained these were the privileged patients who had ground passes. She spoke to each, calling them by name. Most responded appropriately. The canteen was one of the few areas, besides doctors offices and the office of the director of nursing, which was air conditioned. Loretta pointed that fact out with a sneer of contempt.

Next stop, kitchen. It was very large and full of stainless steel equipment which at first glance made it look clean, but closer inspection revealed a dull floor and a smell that made one think the floor, indeed the whole place, had been mopped with a sour mop. When Gina remarked that the area didn't exactly promote appetite, Loretta shrugged and said, "Hey, you ought to see the slop by the time it's trucked up to the wards. I'd lose fifty pounds if they ever committed me here—an idea which is not without its supporters by the way."

There were endless confusing corridors with offices that bore the occupant's name and job classification, *i.e.*, dietary, psychology, etc. Most of them had closed doors, but a few were open, revealing people reading, talking on the phone, or merely trying to look as though they were busy. This busyness was heightened in response to the sound of Gina's and Loretta's footsteps on the hard tile floor.

The gigantic laundry was just off the basement corridor at the rear of the building. Here, the only way to tell the staff from the patients was by the mode of dress. The staff wore white and the patients looked like bums. They had one thing in common though. They all moved in glazed-eyed, slow motion as they performed their boring, repetitive tasks. It was hot in this large area even though the windows were open and it was 20° outside. Gina asked how it was bearable in the summer.

"It's not," Loretta replied.

At this point Loretta stopped and said, "Gina, let's go back to my office. I want to discuss something with you before we visit any of the wards."

When they got back to Loretta's office, they both sat down. Loretta offered Gina a cup of coffee which she declined and lit up what must have been her twentieth cigarette since Gina first encountered her.

"What do you think of the place Gina?"

"Well, its kind of ugly and depressing. It's not the kind of environment I would design if I had the mental health of people in mind, but I suppose things are more cheery on the wards. I guess that's where all the real therapy happens."

"Yeah, sure," Loretta guffawed sarcastically. "Gina, how would you like the chance to really get the patient's view of what it's like to be a patient here? How would you like a worm's eye view of the therapy that probably no other social work trainee has ever had before? How would you like to have empathy and understanding of the plight of a patient at Godfrey State that goes beyond what any other employee here could ever dream of possessing? How would you like to co-author an article in the professional journals that will be talked about for years?" Loretta took a breath and waited for a response.

"Well, Loretta," Gina said using her first name as earlier instructed, "I would like very much to acquire great insight into the patient's life and naturally an article in a professional journal would be appealing, particularly if it adds information to the field. How are you proposing that I come by this knowledge and notoriety?"

"What I propose, Miss Oldani, is that we admit you as a schizophrenic patient, complete with a psychiatric history and symptoms. I want you to go home now and think about it. The hospitalization would last for thirty days maximum, and none of the staff here would know who you really are. I'll meet you tomorrow for breakfast at the Rex Cafe on Route 3 north of Godfrey at 9 o'clock and we can discuss the matter. See you then, sweetie."

Gina, although stunned, obediently got up and headed for the door. She turned as Loretta said, "Oh, by the way, your chances of getting a passing grade in this traineeship are zero if you don't agree to commit." She smiled sweetly and said, "Ta ta."

On the short drive back to DeLassus place Gina's head swirled with confusion. She had to admit that the challenge had tremendous appeal and that Loretta was probably right. Committing yourself for treatment was the only real way to know which parts of the system were good and effective and which parts were malfunctioning and needed modification.

She momentarily took on a Joan of Arc feeling of doing something very noble and useful. But then there was the utter creepiness of the place. Would she be safe? Would

102

they drug her? She wished Loretta hadn't added that cheap threat of the grade. If she decided to do it she would do so for the proper, scientific reasons and not because of her fear of something as meaningless as a failing grade. It was the only thing that Loretta had done that truly diminished her. Gina wondered if it was borne out of desperation to get her to cooperate or if that was just her style.

When she got home Uncle Vinnie was surprised to see her so early, having expectations that she would spend the entire day at the hospital. His expectations were so firm that he had arranged for one of his lady friends from St. Louis to visit at two that afternoon. He hurriedly placed a call canceling that visit, still desiring that his use of prostitutes remain a secret from his niece.

Gina asked him to sit down and explained her day and the proposal that Loretta Mandeville had made. She left out the part of the grade threat because she was ashamed for Loretta.

Vincent exploded, "Is that bitch crazy? No way are you going to do something as incredible as that. I won't allow it. If you insist, I'll call the Superintendent and have you exposed." He was silent for a minute and then added more softly, "Please baby, don't do this. It's not safe. God only knows what could happen to a girl like you in a snake pit like that."

"Uncle Vinnie, you've been the dearest person imaginable to me. I respect you and love you very much, as you well know. I made a promise to myself some time ago that whatever I do with my life I'm going to do with total commitment and effort. Didn't you always say, 'If you're going to be a bear, be a Grizzly'? I agree with your reservations and I realize there will be risks and maybe even danger, but if the hospital isn't good enough for me, how can it be good enough for anybody? I haven't made up my mind completely but I've got to level with you, I see it as an opportunity to maybe do something really useful and important. I'll make my final decision after my discussion with Loretta in the morning." With that she smiled and said, "You wouldn't really turn me in, would you?"

He shook his head sadly from side to side and said, "You're just like me, baby. When you want something you make your own rules in order to get it." He hugged her and then they discussed what being a patient in a state hospital might be like. Vincent took his nitroglycerin tablets that night to calm the palpitations and chest pains brought on by this unexpected and troubling turn of events.

The next morning as Loretta wolfed down pancakes and sausage, she apologized for the tacky threat of the bad grade. She admitted that it was a ploy which was beneath her. She convinced Gina that it must have grown out of her desire to get people to begin to make changes at the hospital. She went on at considerable length about her dreams and hopes for the mentally ill. She was the only person Gina had ever seen eat, smoke, and talk at the same time, with equal fervor given to each activity.

In the end, she convinced Gina of her sincerity and promised to watch out for her welfare as well as she possibly could. She also promised to let her roommate, Linda, in on the scheme as a fail safe mechanism. This, in addition to Gina's uncle, would insure her safety.

Here was the plan. Loretta would call the sheriff's office the day after tomorrow and report a strange acting woman roaming the streets of Godfrey, evidently confused and disoriented. The Sheriff, if Gina played her role properly, would bring her to the admitting ward of the hospital for observation. Gina and Loretta would meet back at the Rex tomorrow morning at which time Loretta would bring in a real live hallucinatory, schizophrenic woman for Gina to get to know and mimic. Loretta cautioned Gina not to bathe or brush her teeth from this moment on and to try and whip up a little body odor for effect. Some cheap, old, smelly clothes would also be a nice touch.

The next morning, as agreed, Loretta appeared at the Rex Cafe. Gina was surprised to see that she was alone.

"The schizophrenic I planned to bring was ill this morning," Loretta explained. "It's not important though. Besides you'll be meeting enough schizophrenics in the next month to last you a lifetime. How are you feeling about our little scheme?"

"I'm committed to the concept of gaining new insights into the treatment of the mentally ill," Gina began seriously. "I can understand how this idea might make that possible to some degree and it certainly is a dramatic way of doing so. Has anyone ever done this before?"

"Not that I know of."

"Tell me some more about what I can expect," Gina said.

"Well, I don't expect you to have any trouble fooling anybody. That's part of the problem; they don't know who's crazy and who isn't. The hospital is loaded with a bunch of dumb-ass foreign doctors who don't know a cat turd from a chocolate Hershey's Kiss. They've come to America to practice, but due to their lack of communication skills with the English language and their generally inferior training they aren't able to make a living. In other words, no one wants them but the nut houses. So, state mental hospitals wind up with inferior leadership and expertise at the top level. I believe that shrinks get into the field for two reasons: they simply want an easy forty-hour-a-week job or they have enormous emotional problems of their own and want to work on ways to treat themselves. The suicide rate for psychiatrists is higher than any other professional group."

Gina said, "I didn't know that." She was impressed with Loretta's ability to verbalize on the topic of mental illness and the problems of the delivery of service in the field. She had noticed in her prior conversations that as Loretta became engrossed in conversation, she became increasingly articulate with the curse words lessening and some of the "butchisms" dropping out as well. Gina concluded that she

105

merely became a person who forgot to maintain the male persona when she was intellectually involved. Gina liked her much better at these times and even though her opinions were harsh and unkind, maybe there was some truth to them. "We shall see," Gina thought.

Loretta continued. "It will be necessary for you to dress appropriately and to appear grungy. Let me see your feet."

"My feet?"

"Yes, it's important."

Gina complied with a puzzled look by slipping off one of her expensive pumps, revealing a careful pedicure with glistening red polish.

"Yeah, just as I thought. Take off the polish from your fingers and toes and cut them short and irregularly. Make sure your nails are dirty and your hair is wild and greasy. Wear sandals even though it's winter. Schizos never come in clean and well-manicured. Their personal hygiene is always the pits, unless they have some kind of cleaning compulsion."

Gina's brow knitted and her head tilted quizzically. Loretta smiled and said, "That's a condition we see occasionally where a patient has an obsessive compulsive drive to wash themselves almost continuously. They'll use bleach and harsh detergents which turns their skin bright red from irritation, but they're unable to stop the behavior."

"Some patients are likewise obsessed with the idea of stepping on a crack in the sidewalk. That's a good little symptom for you to manifest. Take great pains to always step over the cracks. You know the old saying, 'Step on a crack, break your mama's back.' "

Loretta smiled as though the little saying had some secret meaning to her and went on, "You'll be seen within forty-eight hours of admission by a team consisting of a psychiatrist, social worker, nurse, and industrial therapist and maybe a psychologist. This is where I want you to be

106

really sensitive to how you're being treated. What do they say or do that you feel will have relevance to your treatment? How comfortable do they make you feel? The shrink will ask most of the questions; he'll be a foreigner and probably hard to understand. His major objective will be to categorize you, give you a diagnosis so he can prescribe some pills and observe your behavior. Don't take the pills. Their effect on sane people is different than it is on schizophrenics. Usually the effect is heightened, so don't swallow them. Try to appear lethargic and dreamy, answer questions, if you answer at all, out of context and fake being confused and disoriented . . ."

"Sounds like you're describing senility," Gina interrupted.

"I know," Loretta said, appreciating the observation. "There are a lot of similarities. I'm pushing for the idea of getting our older patients out of the hospital and into nursing homes. That's where they belong. Many of the homes are so dreadfully substandard though . . . but that's another problem that we can't deal with now. When you get into the hospital, keep a low profile. Don't do anything to bring attention to yourself. Watch the other patients and pick up some of their symptoms but don't be seen talking to other patients too much. They don't do that—talk to one another, that is. They'll talk to staff but not very much with each other. You'd arouse suspicion if you did. You'll have to dream up a history for yourself. Where you're from, where you worked, etc. Make the town remote, but make it somewhere that you're familiar with. Same with the job, make it menial but something you're familiar with. 'Kay?" Gina nodded.

"It would be best if you reported no family or friends whatsoever. Somebody might get ambitious and try to contact them. I doubt it, but you never know. You're being so good looking kind of throws a curve into the game. That factor might make someone take an extra special interest in you."

"What are you saying, a sexual interest?" Gina asked being rightfully concerned.

"Well, that's possible too, but I was thinking more about the normal human reaction to someone who is beautiful. Hasn't it ever occurred to you that people have always favored you and you were the teacher's pet and everybody's little favorite? It's partly because you're bright and nice, but it's also because people simply have a better perception of a good looking person than they do of someone who, well, someone who looks like me. There are numerous studies in literature which bear this out. Researchers have shown the pictures of the same man with gorgeous women, and then with average looking women, to hundreds of normal people and asked what they believed the man's occupation to be. The same man, when portrayed with the good looking women, were thought to be doctors or executives but were believed to have much lower level occupations when seen with the everyday, glasses-wearing, hips-bulging lady. Also, when teachers are asked to rate kids' abilities before knowing them, guess what happens?"

"The better the looks, the higher the ability rating?" answered Gina.

"Right," Loretta said, lighting another Camel and motioning for the waitress.

"What's yours, sweetie?" the brassy, gum chewing redhead asked.

Loretta replied, "Bacon, eggs over easy, biscuits with gravy and more coffee. Gina?"

"Orange juice and toast."

They both sat silently for a minute, then Loretta began again, "That's all I meant by your good looks throwing some unpredictability into the picture. Sometimes people react and do things before they understand the reasons or drive behind it. Be on your guard at all times. Some of the help at Godfrey are as sick as the patients. Low pay and low job status naturally attract the bottom of the barrel folks. You'll see what I mean. I'm not trying to scare you, only inform. Knowledge is power."

"Tell me some more about schizophrenia. It's the disease that means a split personality, isn't it? Like Dr. Jekyll and Mr. Hyde?" Gina asked because mental illness wasn't covered at college and all she knew was what she had learned from articles and novels. Her understanding was shallow.

"No, not exactly," Loretta said, off on another mini lecture. "Dr. Jekyll and Mr. Hyde was a classic case of multiple personalities which is a rare condition that I have not seen in all my experience. Schizophrenia is a mental illness usually having its onset in early life, somewhere around twenty years of age or so, where the victim begins having auditory and/or visual hallucinations and becomes completely unable to function or get along in society. Working and relating effectively with other people becomes impossible. In fact, schizos usually are very self centered and have no regard or concern for other people at all. There are several types of schizophrenia. For instance, the hebephrenic type where the person is always moving and talking in a manic way or the catatonic type where they move as slow as molasses. In some cases the catatonic will remain in a fixed position for hours at a time. One of the other major schizophrenic types is the paranoid. He's the guy who usually causes the trouble out there in the community. They tend to be the type with the capability to be dangerous to other people. They have this belief that others are out to get them. Suspicion of others and even of institutions like the FBI are prevalent delusions. Many times they act out aggressively toward the people or things that they believe have it in for them. We get the FBI, every now and then, investigating a letter that one of our patients has written to the President of the United States saying threatening things."

"I could go on for the rest of the day, but suffice it to say that it is a very debilitating and crippling illness that at this time seems to have no cure and for which no one knows the cause. It's kind of a 'what comes first, the chicken or the egg' question. We know that the fluid in the spine of the schizophrenic is different from that found in a normal person and that the brain activity is much different between the two groups. We don't know, however, which came first, the differences in chemistry causing the disease, or if someone becomes a schizophrenic and then the brain waves and body chemistry change as a result."

"Is it inherited? Indications are that children raised by crazy parents will learn to think the same way themselves and solve problems in that way. If you could ask a patient only one question in the diagnosing of schizophrenia it might well be, 'Do you have a twin sister or brother who is schizophrenic?' If the answer coming back is a 'yes,' then you can be eighty percent sure that the person you're talking to is schizophrenic as well. There is a question in the field at this time as to whether or not our society makes people more crazy than do the societies of other countries. As far as I'm concerned it's not necessarily so. Schizophrenics are found all over the world, even in remote African villages."

Loretta was on a roll. She continued, "A person who is psychotic isn't necessarily psychotic all the time. Sometimes you'll see patients walking around completely out of it, blubbering. Other times you'll see the same people in the canteen relating pretty well and seeming to be in touch with reality. They have spontaneous remissions, times when they get better for no apparent reason. Regretfully, we don't know how to make these remissions happen, although many of the researchers in the field think that the pills are going to be our salvation. The thinking is that the pills are going to develop to the point where a mentally ill person is going to be able to function like a diabetic. Take your medicine, keep diet and exercise within certain limits and he can live a normal life."

"You haven't mentioned anything about psychiatric therapy and counseling," Gina said. "I pictured a little man with a goatee, a notepad and a couch helping patients work out their conflicts and problems by talking."

110

Loretta smiled and began again, "Recently in Michigan a large scale study was performed to attempt to evaluate how much therapy and rehabilitation actually affect the psychiatric patient. They took one hundred randomly selected inpatients in a psychiatric hospital and gave them intense psychotherapy for a period of one year. They were, at the same time, observing another one hundred psychiatric patients from the same institution who had been matched for sex, age, IQ, and psychiatric diagnosis. At the end of the year the same number of people who received all the therapy and attention were still crazy and institutionalized as were those who received nothing. These results are consistent with other investigations in the field. You don't get any better with therapy than you do without it."

"If it doesn't work, how can they go on practicing it?" Gina asked incredulously.

"Why do you think they call it practice? I guess they're going to keep doing it until they get it right, which, at least in the case of chronic schizophrenics, will probably be never. The classic Freudian model simply does not apply to or work on that population. Psychiatric social workers have attached themselves to a bankrupt idea and don't know how to get shed of it. A guy named B.F. Skinner is writing about a concept he calls behavior modification that has promise. They're doing work down at Anna State Hospital where they take a ward full of long term chronic schizophrenics, people who haven't functioned for years, people who have to be told to bathe, eat and defecate because they won't by themselves. They are able to get them to perform these behaviors through bribery. They believe that people do whatever they do because of either positive or negative rewards. They train them like dogs. Patients still sit around every day on the wards, but every fifteen minutes or so a bell rings and they all get up like robots and go pick up a token. That token buys their way through a turnstile where they can get food or beverages. I know this sounds bizarre, but at least it is proof that the nonfunctioning mentality can be short-circuited and that the worst, chronic patients will still perform for a reward. I'm excited about it. I think that this approach, along with further sophistication of drugs, is where the future lies."

"That's the first positive thing you've said," Gina said, looking Loretta straight in the eye.

"Oh, there's no doubt about it. I'm negative and pessimistic as hell. I've been in this field for twenty five years, I've done graduate work at the Ph.D. level and have been trained and certified as a psychotherapist. In my younger days I was more like you are, full of the belief that there is a silver lining in the mental illness cloud. Over the years I have seen relatively few of our patients walk off into the sunset, happy and functioning on an acceptable level. Psychotherapy might be beneficial to a rich, neurotic person who needs someone to listen to him and give rationalization to his thoughts and behavior. I also believe it is a viable treatment for mild depression, but not much else. By the way, if the shrink begins talking about giving you shock treatments then stop the game immediately. Insist on them letting you call me or Linda and we'll come over and get you discharged."

"Shock treatments I've heard of, but you make them sound dangerous," Gina said wide-eyed.

"I've seen hundreds of people improve for a short period after electro-shock therapy but it's going out of vogue and even being made illegal in some states. It knocks your recent memory out. You couldn't say what you had for breakfast after one, for instance. There's a certain unsettling Frankenstein flavor to the treatment. They strap you onto an examining table at your ankles, midriff and shoulders, because people convulse so violently when the juice is thrown to them that they have been known to fall off and even break their backs."

"Sounds barbaric."

"The doctor puts salve on your temples and then attaches electrodes. He then turns on a measured amount of electric current for just a few seconds. A rubber gag is in the patient's mouth to avoid tongue biting. The patient convulses, the juice is turned off, and he or she is wheeled out and another is brought in, assembly-line fashion. They'll do as many as forty in one morning. If you want to experience shock therapy, we can arrange it."

"I'll pass."

Loretta arched her eyebrow and said dryly, "I think that is in your best interest. Psychiatry has to go through its infancy just as medicine has done. You've heard of bleeding sick people with leeches to get the poison out of them, haven't you?" Gina nodded.

"Psychiatry is just coming out of that period. People who are crazy are locked up by society to get them out of their midst. It's really no different from the prison model, only that its called a hospital and little foreign jerks with white coats walk around so that the masquerade is complete. You're locked up like a prison and you're not leaving until it is believed that you are controlled by the drugs or somehow you have calmed down and are not seen as a danger to yourself or others. But, that's enough."

"Enough?" Gina asked.

"I don't want to bias you any further with my negative ranting. After all, that's the beauty of this whole idea. A sweet, naive child enters the snake pit world of the state mental sanitarium, defenseless and not knowing what to expect or what she may have to do to survive. I'm telling you, I believe we are going to come out of this with a lot of eye-opening data that both the lay and professional community are going to take notice of and react to. My most optimistic hope is that this little project is going to play a role in forwarding the cause for enlightened treatment and research in the field of mental illness. I know that sounds corny, especially coming from me, but I definitely feel it's possible."

Gina nodded and said, "I feel the same way obviously or else I wouldn't be doing it."

"Good, then we're all set?"

Gina answered, "Yes, I'll be on the streets of Godfrey tomorrow morning at ten, looking and acting as schizophrenic as I possibly can."

"O.K. I'll call the Sheriff's office and report you. Good luck, Gina."

"I'm getting the feeling I may need some luck," Gina said, unable to completely shake her concern.

They departed.

CHAPTER 15

February 4, 1963.

Cold rain, mixed with sleet, pelted the top of his patrol car as Harry Lynn Naylor pulled up to the Rex Cafe for his customary heavy breakfast and daily chat with several of the good ol' boys who, for lack of something better to do, congregated daily at the Rex. Topics of local concern were usually the focus, primarily because the interests of the participants didn't go beyond the bounds of Godfrey County Illinois. Gossip, the high school football team, success and failure of local business men, and the relative merits of American cars were generally the centerpieces of conversation and debate among the eight to ten regulars.

Ridiculing one another was also popular and sometimes done in heavy handed fashion that fomented resentment. The victim could ill afford to display anger because it would brand him as one who could dish it out but not take it. Therefore, the only way to get along in this forum was to laugh when court was in session on your case and then to be as ascerbic and cutting with your "joshing" as possible.

This pastime was not unlike one played on some inner city street corners of America. This less subtle game called "the dozens" where participants, primarily black males, hurt and ridicule each other, often until a fight broke out. Occasionally the "dozens" had been directly connected to homicide. The game of dozens produces negative allegations of the victims sexual prowess, his clothes and the most sensitive area, his mamma. The fights usually begin after someone has "signified" that another person's mother had been giving away or selling her sexual favors. A sample of the dozens might go like this: "Hey man, I saw you mamma last night on the corner and I ax'ed Junior what she was doin'."

He said, "Man, what's wrong with you? Even Ray Charles can see that she's sellin' her booty."

The game played daily at the Rex had the element of "let me do it to you before you do it to me" mentality. It was hard to know if the men liked or had any positive regard for each other. After listening to one of their sessions, an observer would suspect that they didn't. However, the nucleus of the group had been meeting like this for years which surely indicated that they were getting something positive out of it.

The waitress, always the target of much sexual innuendo, believed that it was a sort of therapy, a place where the boys could vent some of their hostility, kind of like kicking a dog. She played her role perfectly because, except for one man named George, who was pathetically cheap, the boys tipped generously. George's cheapness was a favorite subject of ridicule and although it made him very uneasy, it did little to alter his behavior. They liked to tell the one about his laying a sizable tip on the table at a restaurant and then scooping it off as the dinner party departed, thinking that no one had observed the larceny. He didn't regret doing it; he did regret that he had been caught. The story would probably haunt him to his grave, especially since he was a prosperous insurance man.

Harry Lynn Naylor had only joined this group some two months earlier and had been thinking that he would drop out and take his coffee elsewhere. He was uncomfortable with the duel of wits, essentially because he was so devoid of the commodity. He realized that he wasn't the brightest person in the world and he took great pains to hide the fact from as many people as possible. What he didn't fully realize was that he did a poor job of concealing his dullness.

Because he was new to the group, he'd thus far been sheltered from abuse and he had been careful not to rattle the cages of the other players in the hopes of not receiving retribution. He knew that eventually he would be fair game and was afraid he wouldn't be able to handle it. He needed to preserve whatever positive self image he had. His life had a way of stripping him of any good feelings he might have about himself.

Harry Lynn was born twenty-eight years ago in tiny Excello, Missouri, and grew up in nearby Macon, Missouri, in north central Missouri. His parents were successful farmers. He lived on the family farm just outside of town with them and an older brother and sister. His parents were Pentecostal and were very fundamentalist in their view of creation and morals. Henry Lynn had inwardly never bought their religious beliefs as far back as he could remember.

More than the beliefs, it was the other people who belonged to their church that he had found ignorant and objectionable. He didn't want to be identified with this group but always kept these feelings to himself because the rest of his family was comfortable with all of it, and he knew he'd be thrashed if he ever dissented.

At age thirteen, Harry Lynn Naylor discovered the wonders of masturbation, which by no small coincidence, was the same time he saw his first eight-page bible. He was to spend a considerable part of the rest of his life fascinated with, and in a way, controlled by pornography.

By the time he was sixteen and a junior at Macon High School, he had a very ritualistic and self styled method of fantasizing. He would buy or steal any and all pornographic material available and spend countless hours looking at it and masturbating—sometimes as often as four times a day. He would cut out the heads of the girls in the high school yearbook or pictures of women in the local newspaper and paste them onto the pictures of large-breasted models who were photographed in seductive poses—some of them spread-eagled. This was his favorite because it was easy to believe that these people, most of whom he knew, were offering themselves to him and were completely under his

117

domination and control, finding him desirable, if not down right irresistible. In reality, of course, no one on earth found Harry Lynn irresistible.

In order to achieve some measure of respectability, Harry Lynn worked very hard on his lessons and managed to make average grades in his courses. He also went out for football and finally made the starting team in his senior year at the inglorious guard position. He was not only a personally unheralded player but the team as a whole was the victim of defeat upon defeat, closing out the season with an eight loss-zero win record. Football, he learned, might have glory, but it was reserved for the guys who scored the touchdowns and for the teams who won their games. At five feet eight inches and one hundred ninety pounds he realistically didn't think that the movie scouts were going to seek him out as a replacement for James Dean. He was always a woman slayer in his fantasies though.

The summer after his senior year he saved up fifteen dollars and took the farm truck to Moberly, Missouri, where there was rumored to be a house of prostitution. He found the Sycamore Hotel and emerged happier than he could ever remember. Sex was finally something that was as good as he imagined it would be and Harry Lynn Naylor had done more than his share of imagining. He continued to frequent the brothel in Moberly for the rest of the summer. At the same time he began to court a local girl named Melinda Tessereau who, for a time, became the almost exclusive object of his sexual fantasies. He obtained every picture of her for his paste-on game that he could find. Finally, after a determined and unimaginative courtship, he was able to persuade her to marry him two years after their graduation from high school. They lived with his parents on the farm for seven dreary years until his uncle, Ben Samuelson, was elected Sheriff of Godfrey County, Illinois, and was persuaded to ask Harry Lynn to come and serve as one of his three deputies.

Melinda had viewed the move to Illinois with trepidation. She had long since become aware of her husband's preoccupation with sex and was uncomfortable serving as the star actress in his many fetishes. She hated herself for the many times he had been able to get her drunk and then photograph her in the bizarre situations and positions that she had never dreamed possible. The only times she had successfully been able to beg off was when he wanted to introduce another man and, God forbid, a dog into the scenario.

Her first introduction to Harry Lynn's involvement with pornography came shortly before their marriage when she was washing his used MG sports car and lifted the rubber trunk mat to clean it. Under the mat were three magazines, all featuring nothing but naked women in provocative poses. Some had their heads cut off, which puzzled her over for years until she found the high school album with the heads of many of her friends cut out. Then it all came together for her how sick Harry Lynn must be.

He told her that the magazines she found weren't his and that he had been keeping them for her brother. Only after his death did Melinda come to learn that Harry Lynn had regularly propositioned nearly every eligible female in her family and had exposed himself to a select few. None of them was ever forthcoming about the ugly incidents because no one wanted to hurt Melinda. Harry Lynn knew this instinctively and had proceeded with abandon.

To Melinda, moving to Illinois meant leaving the support and safety of her family. She was afraid Harry might even become more brazen in an environment where he wasn't so well known. There was already suspicion in Macon that he was the much hunted window peeker. If he would behave like that in Macon what lengths might he go to in a new community?

He placated her fears by promising yet one more time that he had put all those things behind him and they would be making a new start in Godfrey. After all, he would be a law man and would have to set a good example. She wanted to believe him this time.

Their sex life had been more normal since the move. He quit suggesting sex with other men and dogs and the photographic sessions stopped. Melinda felt a certain sense of relief but not to the point where she completely relaxed her guard. Harry Lynn went out by himself quite frequently and many times he didn't get back until 8:00 in the morning. This concerned her.

The bomb went off one Friday night about six months after they and their two children moved into the small rental house in Godfrey. Harry Lynn came home at four in the morning, ashen faced and visibly shaken. For once in his life he told Melinda the true, unvarnished story of what had happened.

Soon after they came to Godfrey he had met a young blond waitress named Kelly who was generously endowed physically and somewhat less well endowed mentally. They had struck up an affair which led to frequent sexual encounters which explained how he had been spending his nights. Kelly became pregnant and, even though they were dangerous and illegal, they decided that an abortion was the best solution.

Harry Lynn, having gained some access to the seedy world of the criminal through his job, had been told that in order to procure the services of an abortionist you must hang around an area in the 4200 Block of Olive Street in St. Louis known as Gaslight Square.

Gaslight Square was an entertainment phenomenon, an imitation of what was happening in New York's Greenwich Village and influenced by the Beatnik fad. It was a street lined on both sides with bars, restaurants, coffee houses, and night clubs of various sizes. In its early days it was a monstrous success. Conservative St. Louis had never seen anything like it. On any given night you could see, in

120

addition to the regular local bands and entertainers, the Smothers Brothers, Phyllis Diller, Lennie Bruce and other blossoming stars of the early sixties.

After two years of success and the chic reputation of being the place where the rich go slumming, it increasingly became the place where the undesirable went slumming. The bars turned sleazy, and rock and roll bands became the vogue instead of the Dixieland bands and gentle folk singers who had held sway before. This trend, along with the appearance of roaming gangs of neighborhood toughs wanting to see and be seen, caused the people with money, who previously frequented the area, to stay away. The deterioration and demise of Gaslight Square was nearly complete when Harry Lynn Naylor strolled the streets and hung out in the bars trying to make connections that would lead him to someone who would perform the abortion.

Success was finally his when, for ten dollars, a cab driver gave him the number of an experienced man. Harry Lynn called the number and made an appointment to meet the abortionist the next evening at the Golden Eagle Bar in Gaslight Square.

The abortionist turned out to be a barber named Bobby Elmore from a suburb called Hazelwood who had done a number of abortions. His fee was three hundred dollars. They'd meet him in a second floor apartment located down the street at 4104 Olive two nights later..

Harry Lynn and Kelly were on time but Bobby was an hour late. "Unavoidably detained," he explained.

Kelly was becoming increasingly desperate and had become almost hysterical because of the wait in the dirty, smelly apartment.

Seeing Kelly, Bobby exclaimed, "My God, how far gone is she?"

"Close to five months," Harry Lynn answered.

"No way man, that's too far along. Abortions are only safe if you get there before the third month. If we do it now in her advanced condition, we'll kill the baby all right, but we may kill the mother too. I'm not willing to risk it." Bobby was shaking his head from side to side almost as though he were saddened.

Truth be told, he was sad because he needed the three hundred dollars desperately. The money would help pay off some gambling debts that were now long overdue and for which he was being threatened with bodily harm.

Harry Lynn finally talked Bobby into going ahead with the abortion by offering him another one hundred dollars to do the job. Bobby Elmore knew the risks were grave, but the extra hundred was all it took to completely assuage his defective conscience.

The results were predictable. Kelly began hemorrhaging immediately following the procedure and Bobby Elmore packed his little kit and fled, leaving Harry Lynn with a dying, hysterical girl. He fought the temptation to flee as well and summoned nobler instincts. He put her in a cab, directing the driver to take her to City Hospital which was about fifteen minutes away. Harry Lynn's nobler instincts proved to have their limits because he didn't accompany Kelly to the hospital but headed for home instead. He hoped that no one had seen him.

The next day Harry Lynn learned that Kelly had been transferred to Barnes Hospital because City Hospital was not able to handle the critical nature of her condition. Thankfully, she lived through the ordeal. although she could never be a mother and would undoubtedly carry psychological scars for the rest of her life. The police were called and the whole story came out.

Bobby Elmore was sent up for three years while Harry Lynn escaped prosecution because of Kelly's testimony that they were only two love-sick, confused kids who didn't understand what they were doing. They were victims of desperation and ignorance for which the jury had sympathy and showed leniency. This traumatic event would have caused most marriages to crumble, but Harry Lynn was so contrite and genuinely sick over the matter that Melinda believed that he had learned his lesson. She decided not to abandon him. Melinda realized that her decision to stay wasn't wholly based on the belief that her strange, unfaithful and lying husband had miraculously turned some corner. Realistically, chances were quite slim that he was now going to become a normal, trustworthy husband and father. Harry Lynn was very contrite and persuasive and promised his wife a new beginning, knowing that Melinda would not be able to turn him down.

He understood that she was wed to ideas and beliefs, more than she was wed to her husband, and he had always capitalized on that knowledge. She believed that failure in a marriage was the worst failure on earth. She believed that they must stay together for the good of the children. She believed that his adulterous behavior and the disgusting sexual demands he made were due to her inability to be a good wife and satisfactory bed partner, although she tried very hard to please him on both counts. She believed that ending the marriage would mean going home to Macon. Facing family and friends would be impossible and besides, she knew of no way she could earn a living.

Harry Lynn behaved like a choir boy for over three months following the abortion fiasco but was unable to sustain his new facade beyond that. He did become less demanding on Melinda and more discreet with his catting around and use of pornography. Life in the Naylors' household settled down to a dullness that was a relief for everyone.

CHAPTER 16

The day was filled with a cold, icy rain. As Harry Lynn was about to open his squad car door to brave the cold rain and enter the Rex Care, a female voice on his radio squawked, "Unidentified woman wandering on Main Street, suspicious nature, please investigate."

Harry Lynn answered immediately, "10-4 Susie, I'll take the call. Car three, over and out." With that he restarted the engine and swung out of the parking lot as quickly as possible wondering whether or not to put on his siren and light. He decided not to because it wasn't advisable to draw undue attention to what probably was a minor matter. He regretted having to make that decision because he really liked going full bore with lights and siren, but he was feeling a strange pressure from his uncle lately; maybe his job performance wasn't up to par. He thought a low profile was best, at least for now.

Harry Lynn loved calls like this one. On his way to town he fantasized about how the woman would look and the delightful possibility that she might become his secret mistress. He could hide her away from the world so she would exist for his pleasure only. The call was titillating to him whereas other police officers would find it a nuisance and a bore, preferring to get their excitement out of more danger-filled situations. Not Harry Lynn; he liked to brag that he was a lover, not a fighter.

The Deputy Sheriff's job suited him completely. He took to the uniform and the side arm immediately and found that he liked to swagger around shopping malls and places where people could see him. Most people smiled and nodded and little kids looked up at him with awe. He knew that all law abiding people liked his presence. It made them feel as though order was established and would prevail. Law abiding people want officers visible all the time. They want to let them know that they appreciate them. They want to buy them a cup of coffee and get to know them personally.

Harry Lynn had never received such positive feedback and respect before in his life and he reveled in it. He was even thinking about a diet to make the uniform fit better. A svelte figure to replace his now portly appearance would surely heighten his appeal with the women folk of Godfrey County. The khaki colored uniform alone, with western style hat, stripes on the trousers and an American flag on the sleeve meant more to Harry Lynn than he could ever express in words. It identified him as one of the good guys—a keeper of law and order and the American dream. When he was wearing the uniform he felt and acted like a completely different person than the farm boy from Macon, Missouri.

Sometimes he thought about how the uniform changed him and believed that the phenomenon of altered self image probably worked on all people who wore a uniform. No doubt the men who fashioned the rules of the Catholic Church understood the principle full well. How many people would become priests if it weren't for the uniform and the trappings that went with it? And what about nuns? Without those ridiculous habits and the protection of their order, how many women would give up their lives to the degree that nuns do? The need for humans to identify with something can be overwhelming. Same principle, he reasoned. They are relieved of the responsibility of becoming a complete well-rounded and functioning person and are issued a uniform denoting membership in their club just like law officers. The dues were sure higher; praying all the time and walking around with your hands folded in a prayer position seemed childish and extreme to Harry Lynn. But he certainly understood the uniform part and the tremendous reinforcement a person received from that. He resolved that he would never take a job the rest of his life that didn't involve a uniform. It transformed him into something he wasn't. It helped to hide his gross inadequacy from the rest of the world.

CHAPTER 17

Sheriff Ben Samuelson watched from the Capital Cafe in downtown Godfrey. The shivering, hurried, people were trying to get inside and out of the inclement weather. All except the young, wild looking and confused girl who was wandering aimlessly without a winter coat and wearing what looked like sandals. Ben had grown up around the Grafton area and was accustomed to seeing patients from the State Hospital. Much earlier in his life he had even worked there for several months as an attendant. He had called the hospital to make sure this was not another run-away. They quickly confirmed that it was not.

Ben was waiting and watching to see how his nephew would handle the situation. He was getting complaints about Harry Lynn showing up all over the county at odd times and in places where he had no business, as well as rumors that he was a notorious skirt chaser. He meant to take these matters up with the boy in the very near future, but first he wanted to see how he would handle this obviously disturbed young lady, who coincidentally was tall, slender and attractive. He didn't have to wait long.

Harry Lynn pulled up alongside Gina and asked her to get into his car. At the sight of her he realized that maybe his fantasy about a mistress might come true. This girl was dirty and disheveled but there was no mistaking her classic good looks. His heart beat faster as she got into the back seat of his car.

Before he could begin to question her or pull away he caught sight of his Uncle Ben striding toward the car. "Shit," he muttered.

"What'cha got here Harry Lynn?"

"Don't know yet Ben. I was about to question her. Got a call over the radio about her."

"Believe I'll join you, if'n you don't mind."

"Sure, get in," Harry Lynn said his heart falling. Time for him to play like a cop instead of having his way with this wild, animalistic girl.

Gina played her role well as the two men questioned her about who she was and where she was going. She was vague, unsure and as off the wall as she could be to them. She soon convinced them that she was a confused disoriented person without visible means of support. She laughed out of context a few times for effect. "Nice touch," she thought.

Harry Lynn took the lead in the interrogation with the Sheriff observing. After five minutes of getting nowhere they decided that it was in her best interest to take her to the State Hospital for observation.

Gina thought it best to protest, at least slightly.

"Oh, please," she pleaded somewhat lamely, "don't take me to one of those awful places."

"So you've been in one before, eh?" Harry Lynn chuckled, feeling that he had uncovered some key information that bolstered the decision to take her to Godfrey State.

Before she could answer, Ben Samuelson said, "Honey, we're gonna have to take you over there for your own good. I don't know how you got here but I couldn't sleep tonight with a pretty thing like you running around loose with no one to take care of you. Now, they'll treat you right at this hospital and protect you until as you can take better care of yourself. Trust me, I know what I'm talkin' about." With that he motioned for his deputy to drive off.

"Crap, he's going with me," Harry Lynn thought.

Ben Samuelson spoke softly and gave Gina reassurance that everything would work out fine for her. He was a fatherly figure and easy to believe. A big man at six foot three and two hundred and fifty pounds, he was both a law man and consummate politician who intended to be reelected to the Sheriff's post once more before seeking higher office. He wasn't about to let the behavior of his errant nephew put those plans in any sort of jeopardy. He was definitely going to turn the screws down on the boy as soon as he delivered this loony girl to that smelly pig sty they called a hospital. Ben silently thanked God that none of his family had ever been admitted. He wouldn't be taking this girl there now if there were any reasonable alternative available. There wasn't. When it came to facilities such as jails and state hospitals he often thought that it seemed more like 1933 than 1963; they were on the road to improvement, but there was a long way to go before acceptability was reached.

As his thoughts drifted during the fifteen minute ride to the hospital, Ben mused to himself about how the archaic system usually worked to his advantage. The county paid him three dollars a day to feed prisoners and his actual cost was just over a dollar. He realized that he definitely fed the prisoners inferior and inadequate food, but worse than that he knew that he put some people into jail unnecessarily and held some people over longer than necessary. He couldn't make money with an empty jail and didn't intend to try.

It was easy for this man, who considered himself essentially moral, to justify in his own mind this system that preyed on its victims. It was the way it had always been, it was a reward for doing a dangerous and sometimes unpleasant job, and the people who were put in jail didn't deserve any better treatment than they received. This rationale allowed Ben to live with himself. He wondered what kind of rip-offs the politicians were getting to keep the state hospital so backward and crowded. That might bear looking into as he planned to be a state legislator someday. His thoughts were interrupted as they pulled into the driveway leading to the admitting office of Godfrey State Hospital. Ben thought glumly that if this confused, yet passive, person in the rear seat were a man he would be in Ben's jail by now.

129

At least somebody would profit from that. Unfortunately, when a person came over here, nobody won, not Ben, not the taxpayers and certainly not the person who was to be admitted. He swore bitterly to himself. "What'd you say, Ben?" Harry Lynn asked.

"Just thinking out loud about how crummy the world can sometimes be," Ben answered.

CHAPTER 18

During the short ride to the hospital Gina's mind was swirling as she tried to settle down and experience what was happening to her in a detached and scientific way. She found it impossible. How could you be objective and calm when it was YOUR body which was being carted off against your will? No matter what else might lie in store, she was certain of one thing. This drive to the state hospital was as real as it could be and she was being treated no differently than anyone else would have been.

A sense of overwhelming uneasiness was flooding her senses and the only comfort she could derive from the situation was the surety that she could put an end to this game anytime she felt like it.

It was difficult to pull out which exact fear was causing her the most worry. It didn't help when the leering deputy adjusted his rear view mirror so that she was directly in his line of view. She had endured leers and stares from males all her life and had not been unduly bothered by them. This creep was somehow especially annoying. She was thankful for the large, older man who at least attempted to reassure her that everything would be O.K. She felt herself needing his understanding and appreciating it.

The fear of the unknown is the worst fear on earth.

This saying came back to her now even though she didn't know to whom to attribute it. She was afraid of being locked up with other people who weren't admitted because they chose to be. She had no idea what the inside of a ward looked like or how the other patients would act. Would she have a roommate or a private room? Fear of the unknown. . .

Loretta Mandeville had briefed her on life in the hospital ward but that was like somebody telling you what a cheeseburger tastes like. You don't really know what it's like until you eat one, and then you can't describe it either.

Loretta herself was a cause for further concern in the back of Gina's mind. The feeling she had for Loretta went beyond any disdain that a heterosexual might feel for a homosexual. There was an uneasy feeling that this woman wasn't above doing harm to another human being. She had an aggressive and intimidating approach to people that Gina had never observed before. There was something sinister about the woman. She shrugged off these negative and fearful reactions to Loretta and the deputy as displacement of her anxiety about entering the hospital.

Gina, as she stepped out of the squad car assisted by the ever-noble Sheriff, was swept away by the feeling that this wasn't really happening and that she wasn't really going through this. Things were going too fast. She hadn't done enough to prepare.

In spite of herself, she silently asked God to help her sustain the courage to see this through. She reminded herself that it was vitally important that the plight of the mentally ill be brought to light and she was going to see to it that conditions, good and bad, at Godfrey State Hospital were exposed. She wondered if her mother would be proud.

Being admitted to a state hospital is probably less than a joyful experience anywhere, so Gina, as she would tell about this escapade later, wasn't too critical of this part. Ben Samuelson merely signed some form and a file was begun with a big red warning on the front which read, " DON'T RELEASE WITHOUT NOTIFYING THE COUNTY SHERIFF." This formality having been done, the kindly sheriff and his chubby, ever-gawking assistant took their leave. Gina fought back the urge to expose herself so she could go with them. Instead, a neat, nice looking lady in her fifties

132

appeared and asked Gina in a kindly way to please come with her.

"Where are we going?" Gina asked.

"We've got to clean you up before anything else can happen. You're a mess. I'll bet you're really pretty when you're cleaned up. My name's Marie, honey, what's yours?"

"Elizabeth Taylor," Gina answered trying to be dead serious.

Marie smiled and said, "O.K. Liz, whatever you say." Just then a large male orderly appeared.

"What we got here, Marie?" he asked, grinning a crooked grin which exposed a missing front tooth.

"Just you escort us over to the admitting ward and mind your knitting. She don't need nobody cowboyin' her just now," Marie said reproachfully. Marie was obviously accustomed to obedience. She got it from the hulking attendant.

The door closed and Marie locked it as they arrived at Gina's new and, thankfully, temporary home. The ward was simply called D1. There were some forty wards in the old section. Each was designated by a letter of the alphabet A through J with a number following the letter which corresponded to the floor it was on. The admitting unit was in the D building on the first floor.

The idea of the admitting ward was to observe patients as they came in, to diagnose them and then to send them to an appropriate place in the hospital or to let them go. This idea, which worked relatively well when the hospital had 1800 patients, didn't work at all with the population at 3000 where it now stood.

There was no place to send patients. All the wards were full. So there was occasionally some trading around, *i.e.*, putting a violent or agitated person on a secure ward that wasn't staffed and equipped to handle those special, aggressive people and sending a more adjusted and sedated person to the agitated person's bed.

The admitting ward, instead of being a relatively low population ward where psychiatric teams could observe a patient, had become just another overcrowded ward with patients sleeping in the day room and three to a two person room. Worst of all it commingled every imaginable kind of diagnostic example.

Gina's first impression made her flinch and blink. She was greeted by two female attendants wrestling a heavy young girl to the floor as they attempted to put leather handcuffs on her. All three combatants were yelling and cursing. Marie told Gina to stay put as she entered the fray. The young girl was subdued in very short order and put behind a locked door where she continued to shout obscenities.

Gina looked frightened, primarily because she was. Marie, who had acquitted herself very well in the scuffle, rejoined Gina and said, "Don't let it worry you none. That sort of thing don't happen near as often as it used to now that we got all them new drugs. Used to be, in the old days, we fought from the beginning of the shift 'til the end. I was a lot younger then. Don't mind an occasional scrap still. You come on now."

She took Gina to a shower room and told her to undress as she turned on the shower and adjusted the water. Gina had undressed in front of people before at school during physical education class but she had never been asked to disrobe in front of someone who would stand by and watch. She hesitated.

"Come on, Miss Elizabeth Taylor. I ain't got all day," Marie commanded.

Gina did as she was told. When Marie inspected Gina's hair she shrunk away at the touch.

"I got to make sure you don't have bugs. Stand still," she ordered.

"O.K. you're clean," she said after a rough inspection. "Wash yourself thoroughly and put on these clothes. I'll send your stuff to the laundry." For a minute Gina was reminded of the stories she had heard about the Nazi concentration camps where the people were deloused and herded around like cattle. This seemed no different.

Gina finished her shower, dried off on the scratchy towel which Marie had provided and began putting on the hospital clothes. They were cheap, old, ill-fitting and smelled of bleach. They did seem clean, however.

A striped blouse, plaid skirt and saddle oxfords with white socks were not exactly what Gina Oldani, lately of DeLassus Place, was accustomed to wearing. She made no indication that she was in anyway displeased. She remembered that her mother had told her that we were tried with adversity so that we could develop strong character. She had the feeling that this place was going to develop her character beyond anyone's wildest imagination.

After the shower she was left alone. No one told her any rules, where she'd sleep or anything else. Marie strode off to the nursing station, flipping her a "See you around, kiddo." She was on her own. She sat down in the day room to collect her thoughts.

She found herself looking at the walls, wondering if a psychiatrist was somehow behind them observing her. She was sure she wasn't going to be able to convince anyone that she belonged here. She became increasingly sure of that as she observed some of her fellow patients. They all looked their roles.

There were old ones and young ones. Skinny and fat. Tall and short. Most of the patients were white. Some were obviously retarded. What were they doing here? Weren't there special places for them?

Most of the people were in motion, either walking around aimlessly or wiggling in their chair. There was a TV which wasn't on. Gina would soon learn that it was broken — had been since anyone could remember. There was a ping pong table without a net and three paddles with no sandpaper and the handles broken on two of them. No little white balls were visible.

Over in the corner were four stacks of mattresses, five high, with a pile of blankets and pillows stacked neatly alongside. Gina realized where she was probably going to spend the night.

The ward didn't actually seem to be grossly over-crowded. Although there were people everywhere you looked, there was space available. Not enough to be alone, but enough so that someone wouldn't be right in your face all the time.

At twelve noon the space problem was going to get worse because all the people who worked out in the hospital plant came in for lunch. Their addition tended to make the ward more intolerable because of the additional noise and the increased smell of roll-your-own cigarettes, which always hung heavy on the place anyhow. None of the patients were allowed matches so there was a constant parade to the nursing station for lights. Some of the people lit their cigarettes off of others. Gina would never understand why this practice was called a cat trick. Most slang expressions were grounded with easily understood and traceable antecedents like when a situation comes to a head, that relates to a pimple. When someone becomes upset and displays anger, they are said to "go off". This expression obviously calls to mind a steam engine that builds up pressure which must be released. But cat trick? The analogy was lost on Gina.

Some of the ladies had smoked so long and frequently that their fingers were stained a nasty shade of yellowish-brown. All of them were wearing state clothes like Gina's. It was obvious that dental care was a low priority because many of the people were edentulous or were missing teeth. At the very least, some of the mouths had stained teeth with white unhealthy gums and crusty tartar in evidence. A veritable colony of halitosis. Most of the women were sporting unattractive hair cuts that looked like they were cut following the outline of a bowl. Gina hoped she wouldn't undergo that.

A good many of the women were overweight to one degree or another. The other portion seemed to be skinny. There were simply no shapely women. The tawdry clothes did nothing to flatter anyone's figure, to be sure, but this crowd couldn't have been helped by a French designer.

A realization swept over Gina as she watched and considered. "These people were all poor to begin with," she reasoned half out loud. "Sure." she thought, "People with means would never end up in a place like this. It's like they say about criminals, the prisons are full of minorities and people from the bottom rung of the social ladder. If you have enough money for a proper defense, by and large, you won't be sent up. Same deal here." Although she hadn't seen many minorities, she was sure she would find the overwhelming percentage of people residing at Godfrey State were from the lowest socio-economic group. She found it curious that there wasn't a disproportionately high percentage of black people as in the prisons.

8:15 P.M. The front door opened as it had done fifty or more times in the hour or so that Gina had been sitting watching the goings-on of D1. People, staff and patients alike, were constantly coming and going. Patients usually were escorted by staff but some were allowed to go about on their own. These were favored with a grounds pass, Gina would later learn.

This time the open door brought two carts with large covered pots and uncovered pitchers of milk which had sloshed all over every thing on the cart. Lunch was about to be served.

The dining room was unlocked. Gina discovered because of the census, which was almost double what was intended for the ward, there were two sittings. No one told her what to do so she remained seated, thinking that surely someone would soon direct her.

No one did. Gina didn't really mind. The lunch scene was appalling. The patients lined up silently; it was as though you would be punished if you talked. Although there was no such rule in evidence, it became obvious that order and quiet were desired — and enforced.

Three patients served — make that slopped — the food while two attendants stood around watching. It was green pea soup, Polish sausage, corn, and something that looked like lemon pudding. Thick slices of crusty white bread from the hospital bakery and warm pitchers of milk from the hospital dairy were served as well. "Not the Tenderloin Room of the Chase Hotel," Gina thought, "but adequate for sustenance." Gina discovered during the dinner meal when she boldly took a vacant seat during the second serving that her first evaluation was far too generous. She was to find that she was unable to fully eat any meal. The food was always carelessly served and it was always cold by the time it arrived and put on plates without dividers so it all ran together. But that wasn't the thing that really bothered Gina. She had experience with indifference. The food at the school cafeteria at Central College was unflavorful, boring, and predictable, but meals were still a time of social encounter to which you looked forward.

Here, there was no interaction among the people. The smells of the food served in the steel plates and bowls and metal cups with spoons only — no knives or forks — was blended with the constant overpowering smell of people who only bathed once a week, people who brushed their teeth, if they had any, infrequently. This affront to the olfactory senses was complemented by the sight of people who literally wolfed their food. They were like hungry animals who were afraid that if they didn't hurry, someone might come and take it away.

One of the ladies sitting across from Gina was blind and another close by was so spastic that sometimes she couldn't hit her mouth. They both had a terrible time and the only help they got was from other patients. The attendants did nothing to assist. A number of little old ladies, who were so stooped over that they couldn't sit up over the table, simply raked the food from the table to their mouths, which were waiting at table height.

The people who seemed to have some modicum of mealtime manners ate quickly without looking up. Gina knew she would never be able to resolve the mealtime problem. She would surely lose weight during her stay if she were required to take meals under these conditions.

As Gina lay on her pallet on the day room floor that night she was sorry she hadn't listened to her own second thoughts about going through with this charade. Why had she fallen for Loretta Mandeville's persuasiveness? She had to admit that her own driving feeling which told her she had to do it because it was her only chance to prove her commitment had been the chief factor which had led her to this impulsive act. She prayed that people would listen to her and believe what she would have to say. How could they not?

There was a sense of unreality as she lay there that first night, listening to the continuous sound of doors slamming and people snoring and farting. She realized she was ill-prepared to be involved in this crazy idea. It was like being pushed under an ice cold shower before you were ready or willing. Loretta had explained a lot of things, but the feelings of hopelessness and helplessness were overwhelming now. Gina thought about trying to talk her way out of this insufferable snake pit, as her uncle had rightly called it, immediately. She began talking to herself, "Not yet, hang on, be strong, learn how the others survive. You can do it." She fell into an uneasy, restless sleep around 4 a.m. with her mother's words echoing in her head, "Anything that doesn't kill you will make you stronger."

She awoke the next day at six, still tired but relieved to see the day light and glad that the creepy night was over. The ever present foul odor of unclean bodies had been complemented with the pungent smell of urine. Two of the ladies in the day room had wet their beds during the night and their mattresses were stacked with the rest. This meant that there was a possibility that Gina could sleep on one of them tonight because they were randomly put back on the stack and would be carelessly put out again at night. She shuddered at the thought.

Gina spent the next five days malingering on D1. During that time she had some of the most intense feelings she ever had to deal with outside of the death of her mother.

On the second day she was approached by an intelligent looking black patient who introduced herself as Miss Karen Lee Ammonette. She looked to be around fifty years old. She was actually thirty-three. "Been rode hard and put away wet too many times," she explained later.

"What you doin' here girl?" Karen Lee asked.

Gina looked her dead in the eye and said, "The Sheriff picked me up and brought me here."

"You ever been in a place like this before? What's your name anyhow?"

"Nancy Lee McCarty," Gina lied. "No, this is my first time."

"You look scared, Nancy, or whatever your name is. You got any cigarettes?"

"No, I don't use them."

"Are you crazy?" Karen Lee asked. "You don't look like you belong here."

"I don' t know," Gina meekly answered. "Are you?"

"Naw, hell no." Karen Lee smiled. "I'm an alcoholic. Been locked up here, in jail, and hospitals all over the country. I get out, mess up, come back for six months to dry out and go through the same thing again. I'm fixin' to leave this unholy place in a couple of weeks. Looking forward to a bottle and a man — although you can get both of 'em here."

"You can?" Gina asked wide eyed.

"Sure, sugar. Stick with me. I'll show you the ropes." There was an openness and camaraderie already forming between the two women. Gina felt better being able to relate to someone in her right mind. She would find out in the days to come that a lot of the women on D1 were nondelusional, oriented and alert.

More each day Gina disregarded Loretta's caution about talking to patients openly. She became aware that no one was watching her or cared anything at all about what she did or didn't do—as long as she didn't make waves and problems for the attendants.

There were others on the ward like Karen Lee who weren't crazy but were there for alcohol problems, difficulties with the law, attempted suicide, and some in whom Gina couldn't clearly ascertain any problems whatsoever other than "their family wanted them put away." The State Hospital was a dumping ground for everybody for whom society didn't have a place. A very sad and perplexing situation.

From the first day Gina was puzzled that she never heard any women complain about the gross mistreatment and barren surroundings. Karen Lee, who had rapidly become her confidant, explained it away by saying that "everybody was too far down and it didn't do no good nohow."

By the fifth day Gina was beginning to be able to feel for and identify with her fellow inmates. As she sat on the ward, dreading meals, dreading bedtime, wondering when in the world someone would come and see her, she knew that her "treatment" was going to be the same as Karen Lee's. Nonexistent.

She wept one day as she thought about all these pitiful people who, sometime before in their lives, had been children who heard about the tooth fairy and had Christmas, Halloween and the Easter Bunny. Surely many of them had experienced all the beautiful things of childhood. Now those children had come to this.

Gina came to understand how no one in this horrible place wanted to see anything beautiful because they didn't want to compare that with the ugliness surrounding themselves. It was heartbreaking that human beings, the creatures on this earth whom God had bestowed with unquestionable dignity, would be reduced to this level of subsistence. Through her tears she also understood how the system made these people into the cattle they had become. Patients were treated like things, like extensions of the chair they were sitting on, with no humanity. Gina remembered the nursing home her mother was in and thought the same thing was true there. Not to the degree it was practiced here, but with the same contempt for human dignity and the same overt belittling of the individual.

CHAPTER 19

On the afternoon of the fifth day of Gina's incarceration she was paid a visit by Loretta Mandeville who came bearing gifts—a Coke and a Hershey bar for which Gina was grateful. Loretta opened the door to the dining room. She had a ring of keys that must have had twenty five different keys on it. Having keys, especially to the attendants and unprofessional staffers, was a badge of honor. It was the principal thing that separated them from the patients. It was common to see one of the lower level employees twirling keys as if to taunt those who had none. It was like a child sing-songing the old saying "Nayh nayh nayh nayh nayh nayh." No one questioned Loretta's motives for being on D1 because she was widely known as a senior administrator and social worker around the hospital who not only met with the superintendent on a regular basis but was a member of his executive committee and, as such, had considerable say about how things went at Godfrey State.

There were also rumoring and snickering among the ward attendants about Loretta's sexuality. When she took Gina into the dining room, knowing looks with eyes toward the ceiling were exchanged by Marie and her coworkers. It was well known that Loretta would pay a visit to any newly admitted patient who was even remotely comely. They were surprised that Gina's arrival hadn't brought her trotting over sooner in that this new girl was the best looking thing to hit the front gates in anyone's memory.

Loretta smiled as Gina hungrily consumed the candy bar and Coke and waited a minute before she began the conversation.

"Well kid, how's it going?" she began, "Is it like you thought it would be?"

"God, no," Gina replied, "It's far worse than I had ever imagined. It's intolerable. Inhuman. It's like some horror film. I can't believe that human beings are treated like this in 1963. 1863, maybe. This place shouldn't be dignified with the name hospital. It's a stinking abomination that holds anybody and everybody that families and society doesn't want but can't put in prison. Prison would probably be better. I feel so sorry for the people here. I. . .I. . ." Gina started crying out of anger and frustration.

"There, there baby," Loretta murmured sympathetically and patted Gina on the hand, wanting to hold her but thinking better of it. "Everything is going to be all right."

Gina blinked back her tears and let Loretta have it, "Going to be all right? How can you sit there and say that? What's going to make it all right? You? Bullshit! You haven't done anything in all your years here and you're not going to start now! You're part of the problem, not part of the solution. I can't believe anybody could sit idly by while other people were forced to live in the conditions I've been observing. You call yourself a social worker? Overseer of a concentration camp would be a better title! You said psychiatry was on its way out of the dark ages. Well I've got news for you. It's so far back in the woods that I doubt it will ever see the light of day."

"Now hold your horses young lady." It was Loretta's turn to vent some of her frustration. The nerve of this upstart questioning her contribution and motivation. If she could have seen this place just a dozen or so years before when there were no tranquilizers she'd have thought abomination! Loretta knew that Gina's accusations were valid and she also knew that she bore some guilt for not being more aggressive in trying to be a change agent. But the older she got the less she tried. The forces of resistance, meaning the legislature and the primadonna medical staff, were satisfied with the status quo. They would even brag about the advances and improvements in the state hospital system anytime they were given a forum. Gina's attack, although

144

justified, nevertheless smarted and made Loretta feel threatened. She therefore did what all threatened people do. She became defensive and gave a heated lecture about her years of selfless dedication and how she had been instrumental in bringing about many positive changes in the institution.

Gina was so upset and overwrought that she was having none of it. Half standing out of her seat now, she was almost shouting, "You're so twisted and sick yourself that you couldn't possibly help others! You need to be under psychiatric care yourself rather than be. . ."

Loretta abruptly got up and almost ran out of the room, giving Gina a last hostile look over her shoulder. Gina went to the doors to the dining room and watched as she hurriedly let herself out.

Marie sauntered up with a toothpick hanging out the right side of her mouth and said, "Not going to give her a little, eh? Good for you."

Gina went back to the day room and sat down to try and sort things out. Loretta had looked angry enough to kill. She was not only frightening in and of herself but Gina was concerned about what she might try to do in terms of retribution. Gina didn't often lose her cool the way she had with Loretta but she had to admit she felt better. To hell with the consequences. Besides her rich and powerful uncle knew where she was. She'd be okay. Loretta could do nothing to harm her. Full speed ahead.

Gina was aware that a part of the anger she spewed at Loretta was coming from some unresolved guilt feelings that she was having of her own. She had begun feeling like a fake. Other patients had been telling her confidential things about themselves that they never would have if they had known who she was and what she was about. She got close to these human beings under the false pretense that she was one of them when she wasn't. They talked to her of the burnt bridges and about how hopeless and helpless they felt without knowing that Gina could leave and they couldn't.

Gina began knowing her fellow patients as human beings, each with his or her own unique individuality and each with something to offer the world. She couldn't understand why they needed to be locked up like this and have their freedom and, in fact their very lives, taken away from them. Her tears were now giving way to anger and resolve.

CHAPTER 20

The morning that Gina left for her bizarre hospitalization Vincent Gambrino was on the phone to his closest friend, Bernard Shaikowitz, who lived in Chicago. Bernie Shaikowitz was the head waiter in Vincent's first restaurant and became the man over thirty years ago, to whom Vinnie "spun off" the first of his fabulously successful places. Bernie and Vinnie became very close, life long friends. They visited often and kept in constant touch over the years. Vinnie was honored when asked to be the Godfather of Bernie's first-born son, Samuel. Vincent took his role seriously and had sent Sam a lavish birthday present every year of his life since he was born twenty-seven years ago. If anything were to happen, Bernie knew he wouldn't have to worry about his family because his friend Vincent would see to things.

Things had gone very well for the Shaikowitz family since Vinnie helped them in getting started those thirty years ago. Bernie was a very wise and opportunistic businessman who had been very fortunate in acquiring a large Chicago cab company, dozens of valuable real estate holdings and a very lucrative insurance business. He was a millionaire. He looked like one and lived like one. Bernie Shaikowitz was very well connected with anyone and everyone in Chicago who was holding power and influence. He only used his connections when absolutely necessary and was always very generous with the favors he did for others. He kept the ratio of debts owed to debts collectible in a very favorable balance.

His pride and joy was his son Sam. Sam was an average looking fellow with an infectious grin and a zest for life. He was being groomed to take over the family enterprises and still lived at home in the sumptuous Shaikowitz mansion. He adored his father and would do anything he asked.

Vincent, after exchanging customary pleasantries, grew serious and said, "Listen Bernie, I'm going to be in Chicago next week and I want to discuss with you a foolish thing my beloved niece has done. I've sworn to her that I wouldn't divulge the secret, but with you it'll be O.K."

"My God, you sound really worried Vinnie. Can't you tell me over the phone? What can I do to help? Come Vinnie. It's me."

"Don't concern yourself, my friend. All is well. She's just caught up in the impetuousness of youth. Wants to change the world. Next week will be soon enough. My best to family."

"Whatever you say, Vinnie. Call and I'll have a limo at the airport."

Vincent was not a man to leave things to chance. It didn't really matter that he had solemnly promised Gina that he wouldn't tell anyone about her ridiculous escapade. He wanted the bases covered so that her safety was guaranteed. His friend Bernie knew how to get things done and would see to Gina's welfare just as Vinnie would insure the best interests of the Shaikowitz family were that to become necessary.

As another measure Vincent called his lawyer, Lawrence K. Daniels, to set up a meeting to discuss Gina's situation. Daniels had drawn up an encompassing will years ago which left everything to Gina. Vinnie always kept him apprised of everything, well almost everything, in his life. Daniel's secretary said that her boss was on vacation in Jamaica and wouldn't be back for a week.

"O.K." Vinnie said, "have him call me when he gets back."

Chapter 21

Melinda Naylor had driven to the home of her mother and father in Macon, Missouri, that morning with a troubled mind and a heavy heart. There was no doubt in her mind what she was going to do. When she unexpectedly arrived with the children, her mother knew something was wrong but she didn't panic and rush things. She had known this day would come and now she was prepared to support her daughter and help in whatever way she could.

Later that afternoon Melinda asked her mother to go for a walk, and she began to unravel her story in relatively unemotional terms. It seemed to Melinda that she was describing a saga in someone else's life. It just wasn't in her life plans for something this incredible to happen to her. But here it was and for just cause, in her opinion, she was going to file for divorce.

The night before, Harry Lynn had been picked up at their house by another man for an evening of beer drinking, an activity which Harry Lynn participated in frequently, so it wasn't unusual. After they left, Melinda went to the trunk of their car because she couldn't find a can of tomato paste she had purchased at the grocery store. She thought it might have spilled out of the bag and been overlooked in the trunk. She was right. The tomato paste was there and so was her husband's cheap briefcase that he always said contained confidential law enforcement business. Melinda's curiosity had been building for some time about the contents of the briefcase and now it got the better of her. She took it into the house and opened it, very surprised that it wasn't locked.

It was full of the rankest type of hard-core pornography. Everything imaginable was there, children involved in sex acts, lesbianism, and graphic photos of men and women in all manner of sexual positions. She was hurrying through the distasteful material when she came upon something that made her blood run cold. It was a series of photographs of Harry Lynn and an older woman in various sexual poses. That was bad enough but Melinda became immediately aware that the action had taken place in her house! The repugnance of the behavior was enough to floor anybody, but the violation of using her home was unbearable.

It was like someone hitting his mother. There were certain taboos that normal people understand without having to be told. You either grew up with certain standards about right and wrong built in or you didn't. This was the last straw for Melinda.

Early warning signs had appeared right after they were married but Melinda had been able to somehow deal with everything, including the horrendous abortion involving Harry Lynn and his girl friend who almost died.

She told her mother about finding the "girlie" magazines under the rubber floor mat in their little MG sports car as she was thoroughly washing the car on the day before their wedding. Harry Lynn had explained it away by saying he was keeping them for her brother. Her mother was horrified as she spoke. She went on to tell her mother about the time when their next door neighbor had knocked on the door and accused Harry Lynn of window peeking on his wife. He had been able to talk his way out of that one too.

As Melinda recounted all of the distasteful things that had occurred over the years, a piece of the puzzle dropped into place that stunned both her and her mother.

Over the years, pictures of females had occasionally turned up with their heads neatly cut out as if someone had used an exacto knife. Harry Lynn's high school yearbook and pictures of her mother had mysteriously disappeared from time to time and now Melinda had solved the mystery. Some of the women posing spread eagled in the magazines she found in the briefcase, which she had brought along for

150

evidence, had their heads cut out in the same way as the pictures of the family and friends had before. He was taping the heads of people he knew, even her own mother, onto the bodies of the revolting models and then doing God knows what. It was all so sick that Melinda wanted to wretch.

After her mother had heard her out, she began telling Melinda of the incredible things that Harry Lynn had been doing throughout their marriage. He had exposed himself to her on more than one occasion and had laughed in an insane, high pitched way as she had run away from him. She made sure she was never alone with him again. He had made improper advances to every woman on their side of the family that he could manage to get alone — sometimes at Thanksgiving and Christmas when the rest of the family was in the next room. It was strange how the family had protected Melinda from the knowledge of this sick and bizarre behavior, particularly in light of the fact that it was hard to find any likable or redeeming qualities in the man. He wasn't sociable or likable and he certainly wasn't a financial success. The whole family would feel enormous relief when they learned of the divorce.

Most people, when told that the split up of a marriage is imminent, say things like, "Oh, I 'm so sorry to hear that." Melinda didn't get much feedback like that in the days to come. More often it was, "Good for you!" or "It's about time," or "I'm glad you finally woke up." Harry Lynn Naylor had a local reputation as detestable pond scum. Now he was pond scum without a wife or family.

As soon as Harry Lynn realized what was happening he drove to Macon and pleaded for forgiveness. He even cried and once again promised to clean up his act. This time it fell on deaf ears. He drove back to their little rented house in Godfrey, confused and feeling very sorry for himself. His denial and rationalization system were so twisted that he was unable to blame himself for anything that had occurred. If he would have been equipped with a winning personality to go with his lack of conscience, he would have been a world- class sociopath. As it was, he was a run-of-the-mill sociopath, the kind that society will deal with in one way or the other. The world-class types usually go on to be politicians or president of the local Rotary or, in some way, talk themselves into leadership positions. They are able to fool some of the people some of the time if they are slick enough to evade jail or a worse fate first.

CHAPTER 22

On her eighth day Gina was finally seen by a psychiatrist. By now she wasn't bothering much to play the crazy role. No one here knew the difference. After all the tales the other patients and some of the attendants had told her about the shrinks, she had no illusions that they would be skillful at exposing her either. The doctor who examined her was a Mexican or Spaniard named Dr. Teodoro Menendez. He was short and stocky with dark black hair, olive complexion and dark, twinkling eyes. He carried with him a chart and was making an entry in it as Gina was brought before him. There was a small desk between them and no other furniture in the small, drab office.

"Well, how are you today?" he began in broken and hard to understand English.

"Fine."

"What brings you here to the hospital?"

"I think it was a 1961 Ford."

He smiled and said, "No, no. I mean what set of conditions or circumstances made it necessary for you to come?"

"I don't know why I'm here. The Sheriff brought me," Gina said.

"I see. What were you doing that he felt it necessary to commit you here?"

Gina would give him nothing. She was flat as a pancake.

Dr. Menendez continued, "What kind of a hospital do you think this is?"

"It's no kind of hospital. It's a pig sty and a prison," Gina shot back with hostility.

Dr. Menendez looked mildly shocked but stayed on task. "Tell me what day it is."

"Tuesday, February 18th, 1963."

"Start at 100, subtract 7, then subtract 7 from that number. Do this until I tell you to stop."

"93, 86, 79, 78, 65, 58 -"

"Okay. Thank you. Now would you take this paper and pencil and draw a picture of yourself?"

Gina drew a stick figure picture of a girl with a big scowl on her face and, as an afterthought, put a butcher knife in the right hand.

The now-frowning doctor then asked if she would like to have a job in the hospital while she was here.

"How much would I get paid? How long will I be here? What kind of job would it be?" Gina asked the questions rapid fire, playing the role of the simpleton, for a reason she couldn't explain. It was okay to free wheel or to be any way you wanted. It made no difference.

"I can't predict how long your stay here will be. It depends on your progress," Dr. Menendez said.

"Progress from what to what?" Gina replied, "What's wrong with me? What are you going to do about it? What will my treatment be? What criteria do I have to meet in order to be released or for you to say I'm well?"

Dr. Menendez smiled and said, "I'm going to prescribe some meditation for you. I believe you have what we call a paranoid personality with antisocial features."

Gina began laughing uncontrollably. Dr. Menendez left the office and D1. She would probably never see him again but she was reminded of him again at the medicine pass. The attendant gave her a 300 milligram tablet of Thorazine, which she was to receive three times daily. She managed to avoid swallowing them by putting them in her cheek as Karen Lee had taught her.

Karen Lee was an enjoyable free spirit and Gina took quite a liking to her. She left the ward each day to go to her job in the laundry and Gina looked forward to her return at the end of the day. Karen Lee had been in and out of Godfrey four times, as well as other institutions, over the years. She also liked Gina and wanted to make her stay as comfortable as possible. She took particular delight telling stories that made Gina laugh. Her stories usually centered around the two things she enjoyed, men and booze. Her stories almost always started something like, "One day when we were drinking home brew (or whisky or gin). . ." and ended with some sort of sexual escapade. She became particularly animated when she described the men she had been with. "Yeah, old Ben had a dick like a wagon tongue and it was always harder than Chinese arithmetic," or "We all called him 'pud' or 'butter dick'. Girl, he was hung so heavy I swear I'd never put that much meat in a pot of beans." After every raunchy story she would lean back and hoot with laughter, making it impossible not to join. Karen Lee was a very good listener and absolutely the most therapeutic person Gina had encountered at Godfrey State. She was very empathetic as Gina talked about the terror she felt at first and continued to feel.

"Yeah, I always felt that way too, at first, but I've put that all behind me now. It was impossible for me to relax for the first two admissions because of the tension of being watched all the time."

"That's exactly how I feel," Gina answered. "You're always kept exhausted because of the tension. You can never rest."

"Tha's right, baby. You got it."

The two were silent for a moment while they sat back and observed the ebb and flow of the other patients as they meandered aimlessly around the ward.

" Karen, since I've been here I've been curious about the low number of Negroes committed here. What's the story?"

"My people prefer to take care of their own. They be superstitious about these places and afraid to come. Besides, the whole white world thinks niggahs is dumb and crazy anyhow, so we just keeps our folks at home. They better off there."

"You said a mouthful there." Gina nodded, "You know I can feel myself actually picking up some of the symptoms you see around here. I smoked a cigarette the other day — more out of boredom than anything else."

"Know what you're talkin' about," Karen Lee said nodding her head just as Gina had done. "Sometimes it seems like a world of seeing things and hearing things that ain't real, you know..."

"Hallucinations," Gina offered.

"Yeah," Karen Lee said, "... this world is so bad that any unreal world that you can make up is better. Most of the people you see trippin' off around here are just doin' so for the hell of it. It's like you smokin' - any stimulation is better than nothin'. And that's what this place offers, nothin'."

"I heard that!" Gina said, borrowing one of Karen Lee's pet sayings. They both laughed at that. Karen was flattered.

The grinding boredom of D1 — no magazines, no TV, no structured activities — took its toll on a person's mental health. Gina realized, after her blowup at Loretta Mandeville and the discourteous way she treated Dr. Menendez, that she was beginning to unravel and that her emotions were getting out of control. She noticed that she was somewhat irrational from time to time. Her voice would become high with a strident quality and she couldn't shake an increasing feeling of suspiciousness for others, particularly the staff. In direct opposition to her negative feelings about her jailers were her feelings of closeness and identification with the patients. It was we and them. She knew that one day soon she would be gone but she would never stop thinking about these pitiful souls. She would be gone but they would not be forgotten.

156

CHAPTER 23

Vincent Gambrino woke up on the morning of February 20th not feeling well. Lately he had been staying close to home and taking life easy, not because he wanted to, but because he just didn't feel like traveling and tending to business like he usually did. He was having angina more frequently than ever before and his use of the medicine to control the pain was on the increase. He had done his best to follow Dr. Zarinsky's orders but it didn't seem to help, and while he didn't consider himself a foolish man he nevertheless could not seriously contemplate his own mortality. "If I'm going to go, I'm going to go," he often said.

With this "eat, drink and be merry" philosophy in mind, he decided that what he needed to feel better was a good old-fashioned piece of ass. On second thought, make that two pieces of ass. If a little bit will do you some good, then a whole lot will do you a whole lot of good.

Shirley Foxworth had been a practicing call girl for two years now and had just celebrated her twenty-fourth birthday. She was every man's fantasy - blonde, buxom, leggy and very classy. She was delighted to receive the call from her "business manager" on that chilly Tuesday morning to go to the mansion on the river. She had been there twice before and had genuinely liked the gentleman client. He was, while demanding and creative, always polite and extremely generous. She had another appointment at five o'clock so this promised to be a profitable day. This always made her business manager, who told her a car would be for her at eleven o'clock, very happy.

Shirley dressed carefully and elegantly because she knew that's what the client liked. When the limousine pulled up at her apartment house in the fashionable Clayton area of St. Louis, she was surprised to see another woman already in the car. The woman was familiar so Shirley got in without hesitation.

"Well, well, Miss Denise Washington, what are you doing here, as if I can't guess," Shirley said with a smirk and arched eyebrow.

"You got it kid," the brassy, floozie woman with wild curly hair and too much makeup, replied. Denise was wearing a red mini skirt with white go-go boots and a cheap looking fox jacket.

"You know, it's girls like you who give us classy people a bad name," Shirley said, only half kidding, and looked out the window in studied boredom as the car pulled into traffic. She didn't begrudge her colleague a living but her joining in today meant that it was going to be a circus, which always made her work longer and harder. The client was paying twice as much and would expect twice the action, whether or not he was up to it. She preferred to work alone because she could control the trick and get the guy off whenever she wanted. Her distaste for an occasional *menage-a-trois* certainly didn't stem from shyness or timidity. She preferred to work alone because she liked to control the customer so she could get in and out with the least amount of hassle. She always remembered her mother saying that we are born and we die and the easier you can get from one place to the other, the better.

At least a part of Shirley's annoyance with having Denise along was the fact that she had balled this old Italian gent twice before and evidently that wasn't good enough for him now—he had to kink it up to get off. It made her momentarily doubt her allure and desirability. Any man who saw Shirley would attest to the fact that these self doubts were totally unwarranted. "Oh well," she philosophically told herself. "It beats working for a living."

Now that she had this talk with herself she was ready to get down to business. On the way to DeLassus Place she and Denise worked up a kind of "script." Shirley would play the classic, mistress of the house who had nothing but disdain for sex but upon catching her man with the maid, a notorious tramp convincingly played by Denise, would get involved as never before and become positively pneumatic. They both laughed and agreed that ought to get the old boy's blood boiling. Shirley said, "If that doesn't do it, I'll go down to the garage and get a jump starter." They laughed again.

The room where the ladies were shown was kept under lock and key. Gina had no idea of its existence. It was a large room with adjoining bathroom and dressing area. There was a large round bed in the center of the room and no other furniture. The walls and ceiling were covered with mirrors and there was a movie screen which could be pulled down for use when the master willed it so.

"Wow," Denise exclaimed, "this beats the hell out of the seedy motels I'm used to."

"Get ready and put your heart into this honey," Shirley said seriously. "This guy pays big bucks for a good show."

The "show" went according to script except for one thing. Vincent Gambrino suffered a fatal heart attack as he tried to perform in Act II.

Shirley and Denise were not prepared for this frightening occurrence because neither of them had experienced anything like it before. They knew that the possibility always existed with these older guys and they had heard stories about it happening to other girls; there were even jokes about it. But now it was really happening to them and they were both shocked and petrified. Shirley, the brighter of the two by far, finally gathered her wits and got the trembling, wailing Denise to calm down. She explained to Denise that it was like the difference in watching someone getting shot on TV and seeing the real thing. When you watched from the comfort of your home and weren't really involved, it was one thing, but to be on the scene of an actual

160

shooting, well, that was a horse of another color. This was real and they were involved. "The important thing is that we get our asses out of here. There's nothing we can do for the old geezer now. We've got to think of ourselves, and besides, I don't think he's going to want the next of kin to know how he went out, do you?"

"No." Denise whimpered.

Shirley and Denise covered him, left him in bed and made a hasty exit—but not before searching Vinnie's smoking jacket. They found three hundred dollars and summoned the chauffeur to take them back to the city. Vincent wasn't found until dinner time.

CHAPTER 24

Gina was unable to justify her stay any longer at the state hospital. It was an easy decision to make, of course, because every fiber of her being begged to leave. Had it not been for her relationship with the patients, and especially Karen Lee Ammonette, she wouldn't have been able to stick it out this long. The fact that Karen Lee was leaving today made the decision easier.

Because of her outburst toward Loretta Mandeville, she doubted whether there would be a collaborative article forthcoming as they had planned. It was now questionable whether Loretta would even recommend that she receive her remaining college credits. So be it. If Gina had to go back to college to earn her final credits in the conventional way, it would be okay. She thought briefly about the sensational article she was going to write about this wretched, ineffective place and how she hoped it would be recognized and printed in a popular magazine.

At one o'clock that afternoon Karen Lee packed her meager belongings into a paper grocery sack and said a sad and tearful farewell to Gina. She gave Gina the phone number of a tavern in nearby Venice, Illinois, where she could be reached. The door closed and she was gone, giving Gina a chilly sense of isolation and aloneness. There may have been a small piece of envy entwined in her feelings as well. No sooner had the door closed than it opened again revealing the substantial figure of a smiling Loretta Mandeville.

"Just the person I wanted to see," Gina said testily. It was time to tell her she was putting an end to the charade.

"I'm not surprised, Gina," Loretta said in an uncommonly kind voice. "Let's go into the dining room and chat. I've brought two Cokes and a bag of peanuts." Gina sat down in the dining room and waited for Loretta to open the Cokes on the other side of the serving counter. Finally, Loretta emerged and sat the Coke and peanuts in front of Gina, smiling and saying, "There you go."

"Thanks," Gina said as she drank deeply from the frosty bottle. After setting the bottle down, she wrinkled her brow and said, "That Coke has a funny aftertaste."

"I think your taster is probably messed up after eating the hospital slop," Loretta said in a friendly way. "I've heard others say it can happen. Have some peanuts. Maybe they'll taste better."

Gina poured herself a handful of the salty peanuts and after munching a few said, "Yes, they taste O.K."

"Well, Gina, your general attitude tells me that you're still angry but you seem to be more in control than the last time I saw you. That's good. You implied that there was something you wished to tell me."

"Yes. I can't see how my staying here any longer is going to help me gain any further insights about being a patient in a state hospital. I'm a quick study; I've learned enough in the last two weeks to do me. I can't stand to have any more fun."

Loretta smiled. "Had it, eh? I was hoping you could tough it out a little longer until you got assigned to a job and got a chance to move around in the hospital culture."

"I don't think I actually need to live it to know what it's like," Gina responded. "I've heard enough stories from the other patients to enable me to give a full and vivid account of the industrial therapy program here." Her voice was tinged with sarcasm. "By the way, Loretta, where do you and I stand in regards to the article that we talked about and my college credit? Both things are important to me but I don't know how you feel about it since I kind of clouded up and rained all over you the other day." Gina took another sip of the half empty Coke.

163

"Well, I have to admit that I was pissed off at that little hissy fit you threw, but I'm over that now. Right now I think its important for you to get yourself out of here and relax and reflect for awhile. You're too angry and excited right now to be making any decisions that would affect the article or your college credit." Loretta said compassionately.

"I guess you're right," Gina said, feeling relieved. "How do I get out? Are you going to tell them?"

"No, my dear," Loretta replied with a cold blooded gleam in her eye. "I'm leaving now. It's your job to talk yourself out." With that she got up and headed for the door. "Ta, ta sweetie. And Gina? Good luck." Loretta stopped at the nurses station before leaving and said to Marie, "You better check on that new girl. I think she's having a psychotic break." With that she was gone.

When Marie got to the dining room she found Gina writhing and screaming on the floor. She called for help and a strait jacket because she knew from experience that these people became extremely strong when they went crazy like this. It took three people to subdue Gina and get her into the padded side room, safely trussed up in the strait jacket. A doctor was called who arrived one hour later to give Gina a shot of Thorazine. He diagnosed her condition as an acute schizophrenic breakdown.

After the excitement had died down and the doctor had left, Marie said to her coworkers, "You know, I believe that everyone who comes here, comes for a reason. It isn't always because they're crazy; sometimes it's the law, sometimes the family. I thought this girl was one of those who was just down on her luck and wound up here because there was no place else to go. I've had several talks with her and she sure seemed normal to me, and I'm not easy to fool after all the time I've spent in this place. Oh well, goes to show you."

The next three days were the most terrifying Gina had ever spent. She experienced Technicolor visual hallucinations of the most unimaginable sort along with voices and wild discordant music going on in her head. In the moments when she was lucid, she thought how ironic it was that she should become crazy at this time and in this place. Had anyone thoroughly researched the possibility that mental illness was contagious? Silly, she thought, but how could you account for this sudden and uncontrollable attack which left her unable to think clearly and flooded her senses with scary visions and noises? Gina had to bear her agony alone. She was locked up alone in the padded side room and had no one to talk with to help straighten out her thinking. She wasn't able to eat during this period nor did she sleep for more than short periods. She was exhausted, dizzy and weak and unable to think anything except delusional thoughts. Thankfully the condition began to lessen after the third day, but the hallucinations gave way to utter terror and concern for her situation. She was worried about her ability to get out of this wretched place. She needed to call Uncle Vinnie to come and free her from this bondage. The foul Loretta Mandeville had meant to leave her without support all along. How odd it was that she experienced her attack just at the time that Loretta was leaving. Was it caused by the stress of hearing she would have to talk herself out of the hospital without Loretta's assistance? She thought not. Gina had always been able to meet problems calmly and rationally before and had absolutely never experienced anything like her "nervous spell"—that's how the people around the hospital referred to psychotic breaks. Gina was finally able to gather her faculties and was beginning to plan her departure from the loathsome Godfrey State Hospital.

CHAPTER 25

Loretta Mandeville sat at her kitchen table tossing off double hookers of straight Jim Beam and ruminating about how sour life had become for her. She was listening to a new folk singer on the hi-fi, Bob Dylan, who was currently very popular with the professional staff she knew. Well, maybe he was the poet of the new generation but his downbeat songs only made her more depressed, so she turned it off just as her lover walked in.

"My, my. Don't we have a long face," Linda said teasingly.

Loretta looked at her thoughtfully for a moment and then said, "With good reason, my sweet. Sit down and let me tell you about it."

Linda took off her coat, poured herself a stiff one out of the half empty Beam bottle and took a chair across the table from Loretta.

"You remember me telling you about that beautiful young student from Central College who was going to do a work study program and her senior thesis with me?"

"Yes," Linda nodded, "I was a little jealous when you first described her. Sounded like somebody who could easily beat my time."

"Linda, I can't deny that I wanted to seduce this girl in the worst way, but she repelled any advance that I made. I guess that's what made me do what I did."

"Oh, oh. What was that?" Linda was now concerned because she knew Loretta to be capable of nearly anything and that she was particularly nasty when she felt anyone, male or female, was rejecting her.

"Well," Loretta began, "I talked her into admitting herself into the hospital as a kind of a research investigation so she could write about the mental hospital experience from first-hand knowledge. After nearly two weeks she became quite angry and unloaded on me, so I figured, screw her, you know? Not only did I decide to not help her get out but I went one step farther. I got my pharmacist buddy to fix me up one of those LSD tablets that everybody is taking. I dissolved it in a Coke and she drank it. She's been in a padded side room for the last three days. She doesn't know what hit her."

"God, that's dangerous, Loretta! It's one thing to take that shit for kicks and go tripping but having someone slip it to you is really bogus. She probably thinks she's gone nuts for real. What if you've permanently damaged her?"

"Tough shit. I don't want to think about it anymore. I'm taking off to Florida for a week's vacation tomorrow morning. Want to come?"

CHAPTER 26

On the fourth morning of her incarceration in the hateful side room Gina was visited by the stern, but kind attendant, Marie. Marie had brought her breakfast of cereal and cold toast which Gina gladly ate because she had taken nothing but liquids for the last three days.

"Well, you seem to be feeling better," Marie said. "I'm glad."

"Yes, thanks" Gina smiled. "I don't know what came over me. Nothing like that has ever happened to me before. It's very creepy to not have control of your mind." She shook her head sadly from side to side for a moment then seemed to brighten up. "But I'm back to normal now. When do you think I can get out of this depressing padded cell?"

"I'll call the doctor and recommend that he okay your coming out as soon as possible. He always goes along with what we say—makes you wonder who's really running this place doesn't it?"

"Yeah," Gina answered glumly.

Just as Marie had predicted, an attendant unlocked the door shortly before noon and let Gina out. She went straight for the bathroom to take a hot shower and to get into clean clothes. Afterwards she felt refreshed—almost reborn—and began thinking about a way out. She knew how and when to do it if she had to. But first she was going to make a sincere best effort to talk her way out.

To her surprise, Marie was able to get Doctor Menendez and the head of the nursing service, Mrs. Cora Jackson, to come over to the ward to talk to Gina that very afternoon. No question about it, Marie knew how to get things done.

The three of them seated themselves in the little side office, Dr. Menendez and Mrs. Jackson behind the desk, of course, and Gina on the other side. Gina told herself that if she ever had an office of any kind she would never hide behind a desk when talking to another person. It set up a power situation and put distance between people that was hard to overcome. A roll-top desk facing the wall would be good so you were forced to face your clients unobstructed. It would be doubly good to roll the top down over the telephone when conversing with others. That would say to them that they would have her full attention and not even the phone would interrupt. Gina was amazed that her mind was dealing with such minutia while her fate was hanging in the balance.

Dr. Menendez, dressed in his customary white lab coat with his name tag prominently displayed, was his bland, smiling self as Gina told them her story. He seemed to listen but didn't react in any substantial way which would indicate his willingness to believe what was being said to him. Mrs. Jackson, on the other hand, was cold and full of probing questions. She interrupted at one point and asked to be excused for a moment. She returned in less than five minutes. After Gina had finished her story about how she became admitted to Godfrey State, Nurse Jackson asked that she step out of the office for a minute while she and the doctor discussed the matter.

As the office door closed behind Gina, Nurse Jackson began offering her unsolicited opinion in rapid fire English which she knew was hard for Dr. Menendez to follow. She liked to do whatever she could to tip the scales of control in her favor.

"I never heard such a preposterous story; I can't believe a word of it. Loretta Mandeville could never do such a thing. She has her faults maybe, but she'd never do anything like this. We won't know for a week because she's on vacation. There was no answer at the Vincent Gambrino residence. I'll try again tomorrow. In the meantime why don't you prescribe a sedative for the child that will help her get some rest. We'll get to the bottom of this soon."

Dr. Menendez merely nodded his head and said, "You tell her," and walked out shaking his head in dismay. In his country the physician was always treated with utmost respect and was always looked up to for advice and for answers to complex questions. While this held true for many Americans, he very frequently ran into aggressive people like Nurse Jackson who liked to assert themselves. He had found that this personality type would grab hold of the control tiller when possible.

Dr. Menendez was basically a passive man and because of that trait he avoided contact with the Jacksons and Mandevilles of the world whenever he could. To his increasing chagrin, he found he was consistently knuckling under to their wishes, mainly because they were so aggressive and verbal. Truthfully, he had to admit, their experience and understanding of the culture were valuable and had to be considered. He would be glad when his tenure at this depressing state hospital was ended so he could establish a private practice and not have to be bothered with state employees who continually overstepped their boundaries by challenging his authority. He cursed under his breath in his native tongue something that would loosely translate as "castrating bitch."

Nurse Jackson, following doctor's orders, told Gina how they would proceed. She maintained her authoritarian attitude. She was as brief and as cold as possible.

Gina felt that she would eventually be able to convince the authorities of Godfrey State that she was not mentally ill and that her admittance was done as part of her college work. But who knew how long this would take? Another chilling thought occurred to her. How would the hospital administration react when they learned an impostor had viewed the system from the inside? They could guess that she would surely write a negative, expose type article about

170

conditions at the hospital. She was sure that every possible roadblock would be thrown up to prevent her from blowing the whistle.

Gina was chilled with a new sense of urgency. She knew she had to break out as soon as possible.

Just as scheduled, at 5:30 that evening the food truck arrived at the front door. The man who pushed it unlocked the door, pushed the truck onto the ward and closed the self locking door behind him. The patients began to gather outside the dining room which was now opened and ready to receive the gaggle of dull-eyed diners. The dietary delivery man unloaded the metal food containers behind the counter and two employees and two patients began dishing it up immediately. The metal plates, cups and single spoons were already set up on the tables and the servers went around and put the food on the plates. The patients were then let in to consume it. They began in the same joyless, robot-like fashion of the thousands of boring meals that had gone before. Everyone was busy and concentrated on the job at hand.

Gina followed the food delivery man to the door, smiling at him and making small talk. He was friendly but in a hurry to get the rest of his load delivered to the other wards. As he opened the door and pushed the large food truck through it, Gina said flirtatiously, "See you tomorrow, sweetie. I'll get the door for you."

The man smiled and winked. "See you tomorrow, baby," he said watching the door shut behind him. He went on his way thinking about how he'd have to look that chick up when she got out.

Gina did indeed close the door but she inserted a small piece of cardboard so that the lock couldn't click. She held the door shut until the man was out of sight and then stepped through the door, closing and locking it behind her. With any kind of luck at all she knew she wouldn't be missed maybe until bedtime. She would have to get clear of

171

the hospital complex as soon as possible. She had no money to call her uncle and no coat. This was a problem because being coatless would call attention to her as the temperature was now down to forty degrees. To her surprise she merely walked right out of the building and soon found herself on the dark country road leading away from the hospital. Godfrey State Hospital was all lit up and somehow managed to look warm and friendly in the otherwise cold and lonely area. Gina turned to get what she hoped was her last look.

CHAPTER 27

Harry Lynn Naylor was in a nasty mood. He had been drinking beer since eleven that morning, and while that alone was normally enough cause for some type of mood change in a person, he had further cause for surliness. The woman he had been drinking with throughout the afternoon had just spurned his sloppy invitation to go to bed with him. Added to this letdown, he was worried about his Uncle Ben's recent change in attitude. In fact, the Sheriff had made it clear that if Harry Lynn didn't clean up his act on a number of fronts, he would be forced to let him go. No more Deputy Sheriff's uniform. That, on top of his wife's leaving him, would be too much to bear. It had become dark outside without his noticing. He got a six-pack-to-go and left the dismal little roadside tavern. He got into his car, lit a cigar, opened a beer and began to drive home, about two cans of beer away by his reckoning.

Traffic was practically nonexistent along the country road. It always was at this time of day; the 5 o'clock rush of people leaving the state hospital had cleared out. His radio was wailing a tune that managed to combine the familiar country and western themes of alcoholism and adultery. Harry Lynn sang along as he drove.

Lately he had become increasingly reflective about himself. He had always been a guy who had simply operated from his instincts and never from a conscious plan or a code of conduct. As a child, and to a lesser degree as an adult, he had been able to put on a convincing show to his parents and others that he believed in God and that the Boy Scouts' values were his values. But he always knew that he didn't really buy any of it. He had read parts of the Bible but found it strange and hard to understand. And how about that story of the guy named Noah? He knew that nobody could round up two kinds of every species of animal and crowd them onto a wooden ark which was only forty cubits long. How could he feed them? To say nothing of the other problems. He simply couldn't accept that stuff on faith. Not much time was spent trying to come to grips with what he really did believe. About anything. He was all visceral. If it felt good, do it. Just as he couldn't understand what the Bible was about, so too did he misunderstood the meaning of life.

But now his behavior was catching up with him more and more. He obviously could no longer manipulate Melinda, and his Uncle Ben was down on his case as well. Harry Lynn approached these problems the way he always had throughout his life. He ruminated about the circumstances that were causing him the discomfort and wondered how he could convince his wife and uncle that their view of him was far too dim. Never did his thought process take him down the road that maybe there were some character flaws that he badly needed to take a look at and try to make some honest efforts at mending his ways. For him it was always the world which was out of step, not him.

His headlights caught a reflection up ahead. It looked like—yes, it was—a woman walking along without a coat. He pulled up alongside without hesitation, rolled down the window, and in the most polite and sober voice he could muster said, "Can I offer you a lift into town, ma'am?"

The lady hesitated but kept walking and said, "No thanks, I'd better walk. Thank you anyhow."

His car was now rolling along beside her as he tried again. "You have nothing to fear. I'm a married man and a Christian. I mean you no harm. I'm afraid you're going to catch your death of cold out there."

Gina had always relied on the vibrations that she got from people. Although she was shivering from the cold and knew that the town was probably at least five miles further,

her vibes on this guy were strictly negative. There was something familiar about him and she was scared and alarmed. She once again told him no thanks and crossed the road so that he couldn't drive along beside her. The car drove off. She was relieved and began to walk faster.

Harry Lynn drove off, but knew that he wasn't through with this lady. He had recognized her as the girl he picked up in town about three weeks ago and took to the state hospital with his uncle. Had it not been for Uncle Ben interfering, he might've gotten some action out of her that day. Well, no matter. Everything that goes around comes around. He was determined now that he was going to get laid today after all. He drove about a half mile ahead and pulled off on a side road. He waited in a ditch, crouched like an animal about to strike its prey. He had his billy club just in case she decided to be difficult.

The moon was shining, although very low in the sky. It was a crystal clear night so Harry Lynn was able to see Gina coming even before he heard her footsteps in the cold, silent evening. His breath was coming in gasps that made little puffs of steam each time he exhaled. He was excited. This was perfect. No one would ever know. He was sure she hadn't recognized him. People always remarked how completely different he looked out of his uniform. Besides, she'd been totally out of it the day he picked her up. No problem with being identified.

As Gina came near, he jumped up out of the weed-filled ditch directly in front of her and said, "Little lady, you're comin' with me like I said." Gina was momentarily frozen with fear at the sight of this man brandishing a club. She started running the other way in a desperate attempt to get away. He was ready for this, however, and caught her in less than ten strides and laid his night stick across the back of her head savagely. Gina fell to the ground, cutting her face, hands, and knees on the cruel chat. She was unconscious when she hit the roadside. The now-frantic Harry Lynn loaded her into the back-seat of his car like a sack of grain and handcuffed her hands behind her back. He drove off, not knowing exactly where he was going to take her, but he snapped open another beer and began anticipating the things he was going to do to his love slave. He believed that the gift of this girl laid in his lap was a sign that his luck was going to change for the better.

Harry Lynn's insight about his sexual obsessiveness and the compulsive drive to satisfy the abnormal urges that went with it was much like the alcoholic's illness. He was never able to admit to himself that he had a problem in the first place, so naturally there was no awareness of the need to do something about it. He never had a close male friend but in his associations with men, he always liked to turn the subject to sex when possible. He usually got the feedback that he wanted. Men thought about sex a lot and got as much of it as they possibly could. He never factored the lie and brag index into what other men said about sex. He took it all at face value. He always figured that most other men were exactly like him, only too shy and repressed to go out and get what they needed. He didn't realize that his preoccupation with fantasy and masturbation and his relentless pursuit of women was extraordinary and abnormal. It was in this way that his obsession with sex was like the alcoholic's drive to drink. And like the alcoholic, he was always disappointed with the actual act — no matter whether it was with a woman or masturbating. He was always depressed afterwards because the actual experience never lived up to his expectations. These letdowns, instead of being a motivation to back off, became renewed impetus to search for newer and more satisfying sexual escapades. The realization that the fantasizing was always far more satisfying than the real thing had not yet registered. He was still about the business of searching for that one person who could make all the dreams become reality for him.

As he drove he was having trouble thinking of a safe place to go. His drunken mind was in turmoil because he wanted this beautiful girl to willingly give herself to him and do his every bidding, yet he was regretting the need to hit her with his night stick. He had never been violent before and he hoped she was all right. He reached over the seat and touched her, yes, she was warm and breathing regularly. What would he do if she wouldn't cooperate with the things he wanted to do to her? He knew for sure that he wouldn't kill her under any circumstances. He was incapable of that. So how was this going to end? He was aroused now and knew that no matter what the consequences, he had to have her. Maybe if he made love to her she would like it so much that she would become his mistress willingly and they would live happily ever after like in the story. She reminded him of a model who posed in one of his magazines. The model seemed to be offering herself in a helpless way that invited a man to do what he wished. Maybe this girl would be the same.

With that delusion in mind, he pulled the car off on a deserted side road which he knew led to a farm house recently gutted by a fire. He calmly took off his trousers and climbed into the back seat.

Gina came to abruptly in a state of pain and confusion. It took her a brief moment to fully realize what was happening. When her head had cleared sufficiently for her to know that she was being sexually assaulted, she began to scream and kick and writhe in a violent convulsive manner. In spite of her hands being cuffed behind her, she was able to buck her assailant off momentarily. He was back quickly though, and delivered a blow to her jaw which, mercifully, drove her to unconsciousness again.

Ten minutes later, sitting in the front seat alone, sucking on another can of beer, Harry Lynn was now in a completely different frame of mind than he had been in before the assault. The familiar wave of depression and guilt were engulfing him and now he was worried about how to get rid of this girl so that he could never be blamed for what he had done. It hadn't been any good anyhow — not worth the trouble. All of his fantasies were now forgotten, having been replaced by fear of disclosure. He finally decided to simply put her out of the car and leave her. If she came to she wouldn't be able to identify him. If she didn't come to, well, that would be too bad but there wasn't anything he could do about it now. It was too late to do anything except get away.

He laid her carefully outside and covered her with a soiled and smelly blanket he kept in the trunk, being careful to remove the handcuffs before leaving. He started the car and slowly drove away, hoping this would be the last he'd hear of the matter. He promised himself that he'd never do this again. It was easier to pay a whore; there was no involvement and they were far more cooperative.

The chill from the cold air and the sound of the car motor brought Gina around sufficiently for her to see the dark four door sedan with Illinois plates ILE-214. Wisely, she waited until it pulled out of sight, then sat up, trying to clear her head enough to know what to do next. After a moment she wrapped the blanket around herself and began walking. She made it to the main road in spite of the dizziness, watery eyes, and splitting headache. When she reached the road she collapsed.

CHAPTER 28

Gina woke up in a brightly lit room that smelled of antiseptic. There was a kindly looking baldheaded man in a white coat standing over her. His eyes were warm and gentle.

"Well, my dear, looks like you've had a rough time of it," he said gently, patting her on the shoulder. "Can you tell me what happened?"

She shook her head, "No."

"O.K. I understand. We'll just let you get some rest for now. You're alright and you're safe. You're at St. Elizabeth's Hospital in Farmington, Illinois. We'll talk later." With that he gently and expertly inserted a hypodermic needle into her shoulder.

"My name is Gina Oldani. Notify Dr. Edward Zarinsky of St. Louis that I'm here." Gina used her last bit of energy to say this before falling to sleep.

The next day, without knowing what was happening, Gina was transferred by ambulance to Barnes Hospital in St. Louis, where she was put under the care of Dr. Zarinsky. She slept fitfully for the next two days. Each time Zarinsky looked in on her, she was out, so he didn't wake her. Her vital signs were good so he decided to wait until she was further rested and had regained her strength before beginning a full examination.

On the morning of her fourth day at Barnes, Gina finally sat up in bed and pressed the call button for the nurse. A smiling attractive nurse appeared instantly and said, "Well, hello Gina. It's very nice to see you among the living. How do you feel?"

Still numb and slightly confused, Gina said, "I'd like to see my uncle. Has he been here?"

"I don't know. Dr. Zarinsky will be here soon to see you though. He can answer all your questions. Until then, how about some breakfast?"

"O.K." Gina wasn't up to being pleasant.

Dr. Zarinsky arrived forty-five minutes later and was unhappy to find that Gina didn't know about the death of her uncle. Unhappy because he knew he was the only one to break the news. He gave her a thorough examination to make sure that nothing was seriously wrong with her and then asked that she tell him what she has been up to for the past month.

Gina told him in complete detail about the Godfrey State Hospital fiasco, right up until the rape, a subject she found very difficult to talk about. It all seemed like it happened to someone else. It was unreal. Dr. Zarinsky was especially probing about her hallucinatory experience while at Godfrey.

"Have you had any further visions since the initial experience?," he asked.

"Yes, as a matter of fact, I've had some wild dreams since I've been here. All full of colors and noise and never making any sense. Completely unlike any dreams I've ever had before. Do you think I'm crazy?" She asked this haltingly with a worried look on her face.

"I doubt it," he smiled. "Could anyone have slipped you a drug while you were there? You have been describing the effects of an experimental drug that some people are using for kicks. It's called LSD. The flashbacks you're having are part of the after effects. Don't let them worry you, they'll go away in time."

" Hmmmm, maybe so." Gina thought about Loretta Mandeville and the funny-tasting Coke and the fact that she went "nutty" right after drinking it. "How could Loretta do such a thing? She must really despise me." Gina was not accustomed to people not liking her.

After chatting with Gina for over an hour and ascertaining that, in spite of all she had been through, she was in remarkably good condition, both physically and psychologically, Zarinsky decided to tell her about Vincent.

He knew that the time would never be right so he might as well do it while she was under his control and care. There were limits to what even the strongest person could endure and Gina was surely somewhere near that limit.

Zarinsky took Gina's hand and told her about the heart attack and how Vincent's lawyer had done everything he could to locate her. He used his best bedside manner because he genuinely liked Vincent Gambrino and his beautiful young niece as well. He wondered where in the world she got the crazy idea to admit herself to that vile state hospital. It probably contributed to Vinnie's coronary, he mused.

Gina's reaction to the news of her uncle's demise was one of shock and near hysteria. She blamed herself for worrying him and berated herself for not being there when he needed her most. "Oh, poor Uncle Vinnie, he was all I had in the world. We loved each other like father and daughter," she wailed.

Dr. Zarinsky stayed and did what he could to reassure Gina that her uncle had a very diseased heart and had lived a long and full life under the circumstances. His comforting helped. Gina needed someone to help her shoulder the grief. Just to give her more time to recuperate, he ordered a sedative on his way out. He frequently wondered if he wasn't becoming too quick to prescribe the feel-good pills these days.

CHAPTER 29

It was April Fool's Day and Gina sat up in the lookout tower of DeLassus Place and watched an unusually late snow storm. Heavy wet snows were known to fall in early to mid-March, but rarely in April. The snow that was falling this day was so heavy that Gina could not see the river below. Gina was still grieving over the loss of her uncle. She missed him very much, and his untimely death brought a renewed wave of melancholy about her mother. She fondly remembered the many good times they had spent together and she wept softly. Sometimes the thought of continuing her life with both of them gone just didn't seem possible. This very afternoon she was meeting with her uncle's lawyer to discuss his will. She dreaded it and wanted to put it off, but he was insistent.

She hadn't had any visitors since coming home twenty-six days ago and hadn't spoken to anyone except the help and Dr. Zarinsky. She realized that she couldn't live in a cocoon for the rest of her life, but her depression was like an anchor around her neck. Everything she tried to do was a chore. Nothing was interesting. She felt like she had nothing to look forward to. She realized that she was depressed and knew that someday, sooner or later, it would lift. She was almost enjoying the feelings in spite of herself, in a curious intellectual way. Sometimes she felt as though she were another person who had stepped out of her body and was viewing the whole scene from a safe, detached distance. Part of her days were now spent reading and listening to music; this was progress from her first week at home when she just sat alone doing nothing.

Lawrence K. Daniels, attorney at law, arrived promptly at eight p.m. in all his three piece splendor. He was wearing a very serious dark blue suit, gray tie and white button-down shirt complemented by those ugly wingtip shoes that were so popular among the status seeking men of the day. They were made in St. Louis and sold only by a local chain of men's stores called Boyd's. He dressed, and in fact acted, like a politician, full of smiles and compliments that would quickly fade into well considered opinions, advice and lectures. Gina wondered sarcastically if he rented an Irish Setter to round out his family portrait, as some image conscious politicians were said to do. Actually he made it clear later that he was single. He was tall, athletically-built, ruggedly handsome and highly articulate. All this was too bad because Gina was in no mood to be swept off her feet. She was in no mood to meet with Mr. Daniels at all.

After the initial amenities and his effusive condolences, he got right down to business. He explained how Vincent had left everything to Gina and described, in general, how complex some of his business dealings were. Gina listened half-heartedly. Hearing how her sweet uncle had cared enough to have this will drafted caused her to weep once again. Daniels gallantly offered his handkerchief. After a few moments she signaled him to continue.

"There is one further request that Vincent made which I think you would be wise to entertain." Daniels said, looking up from the will to Gina.

"What is that?" she asked.

"There is a man in Chicago who was a very close partner, confidante and loyal friend to your uncle for many years. Vincent has asked that you seek his advice and counsel in the event of his death. I'll leave the man's name for you. Will you contact him?"

"I don't feel like it now, but I will soon because Uncle Vinnie said to. I'm really very tired."

Daniels was sensitive enough to know he had pressed Gina as far as he should for one day so he rose, snapped his briefcase shut and said, "Gina, there are a million details we'll need to work out. Your uncle's wide spread enterprises won't run themselves for very long. In fact, it was his attention to them which insured their success. In the very near future we need to talk about some sort of management or maybe a sellout. I urge you to call the friend in Chicago as soon as you're up to it. May I call you next week to see how you're doing?"

"Of course. Maybe I'll be feeling a little better by then. Good day Mr. Daniels."

Gina was surprised at her curtness with Daniels. Her personality had always been one of utmost courtesy and respect for other people. She knew she was going to have to pull herself together. Her mother and uncle would not be proud of the way she was behaving.

Gina got out of the house for the first time on Easter morning and went to church in the huge cathedral located down the street from her high school. Being there brought back many memories. She felt peaceful and renewed.

After church Gina drove over to the old neighborhood on the Hill and parked the car for a nostalgic walk around. The weather had dramatically changed for the better. It was sunny and mild, and the jonquils had sprung from the ground as if by magic. The trees were showing early signs of budding and the air was fragrant with the smell of spring. All this was doing wonders for Gina's mood and outlook. She was beginning to shift back into her former attitude about doing something with her life that would be of value to others. She was returning to herself. Dr. Graham-Herwig had phoned on Friday and said that he was going to recommend that she receive her degree if she presented her paper by May 15th. She was evasive to him about what happened at Godfrey. Gina realized she would be a college graduate and a millionaire very soon, goals that were the dreams of most Americans. It all had an empty and hollow ring to it since she had no one to share it with. When she returned to the huge empty mansion, Gina resolved that she was going to put her blues aside and figure out something to do with her time, talent and money which would make her mother and uncle proud. Beginning Monday.

CHAPTER 30

Bernie Shaikowitz was very pleased to get the call from Vincent Gambrino's niece. He had wondered and, in fact made inquiries, about her absence from Vinnie's funeral. No one was able to tell him where she was. He knew how fond Vinnie was of her, and his inability to locate her, in addition to the recent phone call he had received from Vinnie, had made his concern acute. Hearing from her this way was a relief.

Their chat was friendly but businesslike. Gina had met Bernie before when she had accompanied her uncle to Chicago for a weekend, so they weren't strangers. Bernie suggested that he send his son to review the tangled business affairs that were best understood by Vinnie and to a lesser degree, by his lawyer. His son was experienced and could serve as good counsel. Gina readily agreed, having heard her uncle speak about the trustworthiness of the Shaikowitz family many times. The brightness of the eldest son, in particular, had been alluded to frequently.

Sam Shaikowitz had participated in the family businesses since he was fourteen years old, and now at the age of twenty-eight was well experienced. He held a bachelor's degree in business administration and accounting and had taken a master's degree in psychology from Harvard. This training gave him technical knowledge of business and people, and when added to his basic intelligence, made him a man who could compete on any level.

Sam was an average-looking guy with soft, wavy brown hair and a heavy beard which required twice-a-day shaving for him to look well groomed. At five feet eleven, he carried one hundred eighty-five pounds, which he thought was probably about ten too many. He worked out sporadically but had a keen appetite which constantly thwarted his efforts to achieve true leanness. He dressed stylishly and had clear brown eyes that always met whomever he was talking to directly. These brown eyes would be trained on Gina Oldani on April 10th at 1:00 p.m.

Sam was waiting in the parlor as Gina stepped in, smiling and holding her hand out for him to shake. He did so gladly. He was astonished at her good looks. His father had failed to mention that she was a beauty, a point he never knew to escape his father's notice before. Pleasant surprise. Sam knew that this girl's welfare was extremely important to his father. He and Vincent Gambrino were very close friends and had vowed to look after the families of one another should that become necessary. It was now necessary, and Sam's instructions from his father were to do anything and everything he could to guarantee the financial stability of Vinnie's niece. He was to take whatever amount of time necessary to do this. The importance of the mission and the importance of doing a good job were stressed. Sam had no intention of failing his father.

Sam and Gina chatted about their families, the colleges they attended, the weather and a new musical group that was becoming popular called the Beatles.

After this initial sparring Sam turned the conversation to business. There was something sad about this girl which made her all the more appealing and mysterious. He was immediately aware of his attraction to her. "What do you know about your uncle's business affairs, Gina?"

"Practically nothing," she answered innocently. "He worked when he wanted and where he wanted. I know that he started a number of restaurants and then turned them over to deserving employees. He must have been very successful because money was never a concern. He always did anything he wished and did it first class. Mr. Daniels, his lawyer, tells me that his net worth was something in the magnitude of six million dollars."

Sam thought for a moment then said, "I think I'll need to meet with him before we go any further. If he can see me this afternoon or tonight I'll set up a meeting with the three of us tomorrow. You need to be thinking about whether you want to be a businesswoman and learn to run these affairs or take another direction with your life. Whatever you decide, you're going to have a rare opportunity to live an exciting life."

Gina saw Sam to the door. The weather had turned blustery with a cutting wind and a temperature of forty-two degrees. The promise of spring was still in the air, but Mother Nature had chosen to remind people that she still giveth and taketh away. The raw weather did nothing to help Gina in her fight to become optimistic. She did, however, like Sam Shaikowitz and sincerely appreciated his coming here to give her a hand on such short notice. She told him so before he drove off to meet with Daniels.

The next day Sam, Daniels and Gina met at DeLassus Place. Daniels brought two briefcases full of papers and spread them out on the huge dining room table. When they had warned her that her uncle's affairs were complex, she underestimated their meaning. The maze of the various deals was literally mind-boggling and very hard to understand. The enterprises had been put together one at a time over the years and each one was different from the other. Vincent had tailored each package to meet the needs of the buyer so there was no pattern and, sometimes it seemed no logic, to the way he had done things. At the end of the exhaustive four-hour meeting, Lawrence Daniels summed it up, "Well, there you have it, Gina. Not a very conventional empire you've inherited, but an empire, nonetheless. I feel your options are three: you can hire a management company to run things for you, you could undertake a crash training program under the guidance of Sam here and run things yourself, or you can look for someone to buy you out. A lot depends on how you envision the future and how you see your role in that future. In other words, do you think you would be happy and effective as a business manager or would you rather sell out and pursue some other endeavor? Of the three options, I favor hiring a management person or company the least, because of the unique skills and commitment required to remain successful. It is my belief that selling or running the show yourself are the two most viable options. I'll leave you to struggle with your decision which I urge you to make as expediently as possible. If I can be of any further assistance whatsoever, don't hesitate to call."

After Daniels had gone, Gina and Sam returned to the library where they both partook of a snifter of Napoleon Brandy, and gratefully sank down in the mammoth leather chairs. The meeting had been intense and had required a lot of concentration. They were both exhausted. After a moment's respite Sam said, "Well Gina, you've got a lot to think about. But don't take it all too seriously. You'll be in good shape no matter what you do. Lawyers get paid to warn us of the possible pitfalls in life, but we're the ones who actually take the risks and make things happen. Don't forget that the longer we meet and the more obstacles he can introduce, then the more of his time he can bill you for. Sometimes it's not in a lawyer's best interest to get on with things"

"Why, Mistah Sam, how you do carry on sometimes," Gina cooed, mocking Scarlet O'Hara.

Sam appreciated the note of levity. Sometimes he was too sarcastic. "Your job right now is to try to visualize yourself in the driver's seat, doing what your uncle did. Do you like the picture? Are you comfortable with that? Sometimes it's hard to step in and live in a world created by another person. Some people are only happy when they call all of the shots; others prefer to follow the lead of another." Sam took a small sip of the brandy. "Your intelligence and potential are not a question here. You can successfully do whatever you wish. Whatever you decide, you will be taking a chance, but what the hell, so did Columbus."

Gina laughed at this sudden zanyness. Behind a day of such sobriety and talk of money and futures, it was refreshing. She liked this guy.

"Sam, I'm going to take a hot shower and then read for a while. Why don't you stay for dinner? You can have a room to freshen up."

"Miss Oldani," he said with a flourish, "I accept your gracious offer." Dinner was hearty American fare consisting of thick grilled T-bone steaks, salad, baked potatoes and lima beans. Sam ate with his usual gusto. As they were having Drambouie and coffee in the library, he remarked that her chef knew what he was doing. Coming from a restaurant man Gina figured this was high praise indeed.

The young couple, feeling at ease with one another, talked until one in the morning about anything and everything. Sam had a very lively sense of humor and a somewhat unorthodox way of looking at things. He made Gina laugh and made her think as well. It felt good to sit and free-wheel with a bright person again.

"How did you like college, Sam?"

" I got tired of it. It was a little like having someone pissing on your leg while you're standing in a large crowd. It feels kind of warm and okay at first, but then it becomes cold and stinky and you hate to call attention to your discomfort."

This kind of earthy talk reminded Gina of Karen Lee Ammonette. Where did this rich, privileged boy get it, she wondered.

They talked a lot about school and how it turns out to be what you make it. Sam said, "I believe that things work out best for those who make the best of the way things work out."

Gina asked Sam to tell her about the most outrageous character he knew at college. "I don't have to think about it for a second," he said. "It was a guy named 'Gross' Sneed. I don't even know what his real name was — maybe Bob — but everybody, teachers included, called him Gross. He was a football player and usually drunk to one degree or another and always obnoxious to the nth degree. He was loud, profane and as wrong as a boy has a right to be. One night we all had dates and were having this real nice clam bake on the beach. There was a romantic fire, guitars with everybody singing along when Gross suddenly appears. He had escaped from the local hospital where he was being treated for severe diarrhea. He was wearing one of those hospital night gowns that tie in the back, you know?"

Gina nodded.

"Gross commenced to duck walk around the campfire, a beer in one hand and his loose stool flowing out of the open gown. Needless to say the party broke up immediately. There, is that outrageous enough for you?"

Gina sat in disbelief with her eyes down as though embarrassed, shaking her head from side to side. After a moment she looked up and somberly asked, "Sam, there's one thing I don't understand."

"What's that Gina?"

"Why did they call him Gross?" They both laughed uproariously.

Sam then asked Gina to tell about the most outrageous person she encountered at Central. "Well, like you, my man comes to mind instantly. His name was "Buffy", short for Ralph Buffleston. He was somewhat older than the rest of us chronologically because he had already been in the service, but he was behind everybody in social maturity. He, too, was a football player, a guard, I think. He was about five feet eight and weighed two hundred and thirty pounds or more with a thick, black, curly hairdo that looked like a disorganized bird's nest and thick Coke-bottle eyeglasses. He was as myopic as Mr. Magoo and walked like a little Kodiak bear. Buffy, like Gross, was given to frequent excessive drinking, preferring Rosie O'Grady Wine to the more conventional beer." Gina paused and looked into the fireplace as she drew her subject into focus.

"The first year I was there the sorority I joined went over to MacMurray Hall to serenade the boys at Christmas time. We were all lined up on the front steps singing our hearts out, to the enjoyment of most of the guys, I think, when a drunk and sick Buffy sticks his head out of the third story window and vomits on us. Not a pretty sight." Sam winced.

"Buffy did have his winning ways, however. Let's not sell him short," Gina continued. "I even went out with him a few times during his 'serious period' when he ran for president of the Student Christian Organization. He won because his whole fraternity attended the meeting that night as a lark and voted him in. Buffy soon began taking the job and himself quite seriously for a while, but it was not to last. I had a Spanish class with him where he wasn't doing well at all. He absolutely needed to pass the course because it was required for graduation. I tutored him but he just couldn't, or wouldn't, concentrate. The night before the crucial final exam Buffy sat in his room. He was drinking wine and drawing childish pictures of World War II fighter planes engaging Japanese zeros in mid-air dog fights. He never did get his degree because of failing that course. I hear he drives a truck now." They both shook their heads reflectively.

After a moment Sam added that the two characters sounded a lot alike. Gina agreed and said, "It's sad looking back now and thinking about two guys, who in spite of their completely outlandish, even antisocial behavior, were well-accepted and even well-liked. In reality they were far afield from the majority of college people."

"I'm afraid the rest of us may have done a lot to encourage their behavior." They both sipped their coffee. "I'm looking forward to the tenth year class reunion. I'm very curious about what some of my old buddies are up to. How about you, Gina?"

192

"Me too," she answered with a trace of uncertainty. "I mean I would like to see a lot of old friends again ... Sam, I'm sorry but I'm terribly tired all of the sudden. How about if I give you a tour of St. Louis tomorrow?" She got up.

Sam looked at his watch and said in amazement, "Wow, I had no idea! I've been enjoying myself and didn't realize I was overstaying my welcome." He said that sincerely, not meaning to be sarcastic. Gina seemed to understand. "What time shall I be here?"

"Ten o'clock, Okay?"

"Great, see you then." He walked out wondering why he hadn't kissed her. He certainly wanted to, but he was unsure of her willingness. There was a certain, well, un-availability about Gina Oldani. He unconsciously meant to break that down if he could. He was smitten to a greater degree than he was willing to admit.

The next day brought a renewed, soft, spring-like atmos-phere to the unpredictable and capricious St. Louis weather. Sam was happy and whistling softly as he drove into the winding driveway of DeLassus place. Gina's Corvette was parked in front, clean and shiny with the top down. Sam smiled when he saw it. He had dressed carefully in a black turtleneck sweater and beige cashmere sport coat with con-trasting black slacks and soft Italian loafers. Perfect for a spring day in an open car with a beautiful girl.

Gina looked beautiful as she greeted Sam at the door with a big smile and friendly peck on the cheek. She was dressed in elegant yet sporty clothes featuring gray wool slacks, oxblood penny loafers and an expensive Irish fisher-man knit sweater topped off by a jaunty maroon tam o'shanter which she wore back on her head, cocked at just the right angle. She literally took Sam's breath away.

"Well, good morning. You look swell," he offered, some-what surprised at his awkwardness. He was always the guy who everybody said should be a lawyer because he was articulate and had the ability to think on his feet. This girl had temporarily reduced him to a tongue-tied adolescent. It didn't worry him because he knew the effect was temporary and that he would soon collect himself again and become his charming self. Sam Shaikowitz was not a man lacking in self confidence.

"Thanks, Sam. You look pretty spiffy yourself," Gina allowed. "I've prepared a picnic basket of fried chicken, apples and cheese, Italian bread and wine for our lunch." Her tiredness from the night before had evaporated. She had obviously rested well and seemed bright and happy.

"Perfect," he said heartily. "Let's go."

The weather forecast was for the temperature to reach the upper 70's, so the open car was comfortable. Gina was a careful driver but given to letting the powerful Corvette "breathe." It was fitted with fuel injection and a four speed transmission so it was, in fact, among the fastest production cars being made in America. Sam marveled at her competence with the car.

The day was as pleasant and enjoyable as both Gina and Sam had hoped it would be at its outset. They began with a tour of the beautiful and expensive homes in the suburbs of Ladue and Clayton.

"Some of these homes rival anything you will find Beverly Hills," Sam said.

Gina parked the Corvette in a lot in Forest Park where they took in the zoo and visited the planetarium before having their lunch on the high gently sloping hill in front of the Art Museum. Gina spread a blanket, and they ate lunch in the glorious, warm sunshine.

"This park and zoo are as nice as any I've ever seen," Sam said.

After lunch Gina took Sam down to "the Hill" and showed him the house where she grew up and her church. She was feeling comfortable with this likable man from Chicago who had come to offer advice and counsel but who

194

also was turning out to be a good companion in the bargain. His sense of humor was wonderful and he was very attentive and kind.

Sam's genuine interest prompted Gina to tell him about her mother and father and how she came to live with her Uncle Vinnie. After stopping to get some flowers for their graves, she took him to the cemetery where her mother and father were buried. They stood at the gravesite for several moments, not saying anything, while a wave of memories swept over Gina. Sam politely stood beside her and put his arm around her to comfort her as she began to weep softly.

As the afternoon shadows grew longer, Gina drove by her high school and pointed out the nursing home where her mother spent her last days. Seeing these two structures caused Gina to tell several stories about rigid nuns and the care, or rather the lack of it, at Sunset Meadows. She told him the story about her failure to effectively mobilize her classmates into a positive recreational program for the patients. She realized she had never told anyone that story before, probably because she wasn't proud of it. Sam seemed to really understand, however, and offered many insights about what went wrong and how it might have been approached differently. His insights made it seem not so much a failure and an impossibility but rather a faulty approach. Gina tended to forget that he was trained in psychology. He was so down-to-earth and nonacademic in the way he spoke that she lost sight of the fact that most of his illustrations about human behavior were grounded in scientific studies and theories. She found herself always agreeing with him and saying things like, "I never heard that before," or "I hadn't thought of that," or "You're exactly right." It seemed like he was always on target. When Gina said something that Sam agreed with he sometimes said, "That listens," obviously meaning that what she said was correct. She liked it.

On the way home Gina pulled into a White Castle. She told him how the "belly bomber" hamburgers sold there were famous and popular and cheap. They bought a dozen with Sam eating eight and Gina the rest. He was too kind to tell her that the White Castle chain was also located in Chicago and that his childhood and adolescent memories contained many stops and more than a little indigestion attributable to the greasy, onion laden little devils.

The pleasantly tired and wind-burned couple arrived back at DeLassus Place at sunset, just as the thermometer was starting a gradual descent from the high of eighty reached that day. It would probably go down to sixty before the night was over. As Gina garaged the car she invited Sam in for a brandy. He gladly accepted.

Once inside, they decided to build a fire and open the large windows of the library. Gina got the bottle of brandy and, on a whim, brought a package of marshmallows for roasting. They pretended they were on a wiener roast like the ones they'd enjoyed as teenagers. Sam put his marshmallow directly into the hot part of the fire and it caught fire immediately, charring it to a rich black color. Gina was more careful, preferring to slowly roast hers on a cooler part of the fire. They talked about this different style and made inferences about each other's personalities and how a relationship might exist between marshmallow roasting style and life-pattern and problem-solving style.

"If you roast hot and quick, you're impetuous and have difficulty doing things in a systematic and careful way," Sam reasoned. "If you roast slowly, you are a person who can see the consequences of your behavior and will methodically plan your moves. The slow roaster would be a good accountant and would probably take out lots of life insurance while the other guy would be inclined to racing cars and gambling. Think our paradigm will hold up under scientific, psychological scrutiny?"

Gina smiled and answered sarcastically, "Sam, I know we're just joking here but honestly, it seems to hold as much water as some of the psychiatric hokum I heard while I was at Godfrey State."

"Godfrey State, Gina?"

Gina had been suppressing the memories of the recent past and was surprised that she let slip the name of the hospital. She sat for a long moment and then decided to tell Sam the whole story, feeling that the catharsis would be good for her. She felt like she needed a close friend and confidante.

"Let me pour you another drink while I spin a rather long and bizarre tale that I have trouble believing myself. Ready?"

Sam nodded.

"It all started back in my senior year at college when I decided I wanted to do something meaningful rather than just serve out my time doing more course work."

Gina held nothing back. She told him about the pitiful Dr. Graham-Herwig and her initial meetings with Loretta Mandeville.

Sam broke in, "My God, those are two incredible characters."

"There's more," Gina said faintly.

She went on to tell about the Sheriff and his deputy, the admitting ward and the horrendous treatment everyone there received. It was at this point that her voice cracked and tears welled up in her eyes as she emotionally detailed the plight of several of the women on D1.

"It was no better for the men; in fact, it was probably worse. I never saw any of the male wards but two of the attendants who worked on D1 in the evening had been there for a number of years and had also worked on a number of the male wards. They loved to tell tales about the men. They talked about a creature named, or rather called, "Mutt" who, according to their description, was some kind of an imbecile who resembled a caveman and ate like a dog from bowls

197

placed on the floor. He never used his hands. They told of another guy named Pete Taylor who was six feet seven and extremely skinny but who had the fortune, or misfortune, to have a twelve-inch penis attached to his frame."

Sam laughed and shook his head more at Gina's forthrightness than at the story itself.

Gina continued, "The employees, when showing a new employee around, would say, 'Pete Taylor, crank up your Model T,' which he would obligingly do, revealing this legendary appendage and whirling it in a counter-clockwise direction to the delight of all onlookers. No less sad, but a somewhat cuter story, involves a little old fellow called 'Sheephead.' He was a guy who had only one passion in his life — to drink soda pop. He would do anything for the money to fulfill his addiction, occasionally running errands of the simplest kind, but mostly he would beg anyone and everyone. Constantly. One summer day, when the men were lolling around outside in the fenced bullpen area, one of the fun loving attendants told Sheephead that the lone oak tree which stood in the middle of the yard was a money tree and all he had to do to get soda money was to shake it. Sheephead, being gullible and not too bright, commenced shaking the tree while the prankster attendant threw a dime up in the branches. It came down, to the unconfined joy of Sheephead and everyone who witnessed the incident. Word of this hilarity spread, of course, and people have been throwing money into Sheephead's tree for years since. They say the old man shakes the tree every chance he gets, even today. Mostly he gets no money, but occasionally someone will play the game and reward his efforts, thereby reinforcing the behavior, probably forever. Sheephead was the only person I heard of who had something to look forward to. Doesn't it seem sad and ironic that the most therapeutic thing I heard of in my time there was a hoax played on a dimwitted old man?

Sam nodded sympathetically and said, "I gave some consideration to working in a mental hospital in my younger days. I don't know exactly why I rejected the idea, the pressure to work with my Dad, I guess, but I'm glad I didn't. You said your story was bizarre and unbelievable. So far it has lived up to that billing and more. Tell me how it felt to be locked up in a place like that." Sam asked for that information out of genuine curiosity, but he wanted Gina to continue so that he might be able to assess why a beautiful, rich girl with plenty of brain power would ever do such a nutty thing in the first place.

"Godfrey State is an abomination," Gina observed, now warming to her task. "You enter the place and what do you need? A person or persons who will understand your plight and listen to you. Right? Well, what you get is just the opposite. You're thrust into a crowded, barren environment, given a delousing cleaning and some ugly clothes smelling of lye soap. After this dehumanizing treatment I was left to my own devices. No one, except the other patients, ever explained anything to me. You are expected to simply languish. The boredom is stultifying. The only way to get attention is to act up, which I did. Only I didn't do it on purpose."

Sam frowned, "What do you mean?"

Again Gina hesitated, but only momentarily. She'd gone this far, might as well continue. Besides, she trusted Sam. She related the rest of the story including her suspicion of Loretta lacing her Coke with LSD and, most painfully of all, the runaway and rape.

Sam was stunned. He sat motionless for a moment then the blood began rising until his face was florid. He reacted with a torrent of questions. "Why haven't you notified the police?" he demanded.

"I knew you were going to disapprove and ask that," she responded evenly. "I want you to try and understand how I feel about it. I've had lots of time to think the whole matter through and I've decided to let it drop because of my own personal feelings. While a patient at Godfrey I felt enormous guilt, maybe it was shame, that I was there as a fake who had a normal life to which I could return. Some of the other women made me one of their own and told me all the very most intimate things about their lives and feelings. They would never have opened up to me like that if they had known my true identity. I decided to take my lumps, the rape and the LSD, as a way of paying my dues. As bad as what happened to me was, I'm still not even with most of those people and the injustice that has been heaped on them. I'm out now and I'm going to be O.K. I'll never forget them. They'll be with me always." Her eyes became moist.

"Gina, I hear what you're saying, but your reasoning is impossible for me to understand. You have been outlandishly wronged. The case cries out for justice. Loretta Mandeville and the rapist need to pay."

"Sam, I want you to back off. I told you how I want it and that's that. There's not going to be any retribution. Yes, I was wronged but I'm strong. I'll get over it."

"Imagine trying to prove it in court anyway. Never happen."

"What do you remember about the man?"

"There was something vaguely familiar about him that I can't put my finger on. It happened so quickly, and in the dark, but I got his license number as he drove away."

"And you remember it? Tell me."

"It was ILE-214. But I want you to forget about it. I'm trying to and I could use your help."

"O.K. Gina. Maybe justice will be done."

"What does that mean?"

"That's just a saying from back home. It means that people tend to get what's coming to them one way or another." There was a decidedly cold look in his eyes as he turned away from Gina toward the fire so that she might not see. He had already begun to think of her as family. And where he came from, family did not get treated as she had been.

The hour had grown late again, to Sam's surprise. As he walked to the door with his arm around Gina he said he would like to spend the next day with her as well. She said she'd like that, too.

"See you at ten."

"Great. Good night, Sam."

He kissed her warmly. She responded as he hoped she would.

Driving back to the hotel Sam was a mass of confusion and mixed emotions. He now knew he loved Gina and hoped he would be able to win her heart. The unfinished business with the lesbian and the owner of ILE-214 bothered him greatly. He decided to call his father that very night for advice.

Although the call got him out of bed, Bernie Shaikowitz listened carefully to his son's story and was acutely aware of the passionate feelings he expressed. He was glad. He thought his oldest son was never going to find a suitable girl. He asked only two questions throughout the half-hour conversation

"Who were the people who did these terrible things to the niece of my best friend?"

Sam explained, unaware that his father was writing down the answers.

"Do you love this girl , my son?"

"Yes, Father, very much."

"All right, Sam. Stay there as long as you want and take care of her." He paused then said tonelessly, "Maybe justice will be done.."

A chill ran down Sam's spine as he hung up the phone.

CHAPTER 31

There was no doubt in the mind of Bernie Shaikowitz what he was going to do. He had endured many face slaps and slights as a young and smallish boy growing up in the tough city of Chicago. Now that he had become rich and powerful, he no longer let anyone treat him with rudeness or disrespect. This held true for his family as well. Now the beloved niece of the man who put him on the road to success had been grievously violated, and it was Bernie's duty and responsibility to see to it that revenge be sought to uphold her honor. He had made this pledge to Vincent Gambrino and, being a man of honor, he would perform. It was an old world way of settling differences. Effective if you could get beyond the moral and legal questions.

Sam had made it clear that he couldn't understand Gina's refusal to go through the normal route of having the local authorities handle the matter. Crimes had been committed and surely the responsible people should pay. That's the way it worked in America.

The wizened Bernie, on the other hand, had great respect for the young girl's position. She wasn't doing it because of her dread of a court trial and the shame of testifying against a rapist and a clever, scheming lesbian. She had backed off because she felt guilty invading the world of the scorned, incarcerated "little people" and would like to rinse off her shame by suffering some of the humility and degradation that was a constant part of their lives. Bernie understood this perfectly. He respected her for it.

That, however, made no difference because of the code of honor which existed between him and Vincent. He said quietly under his breath, "Vincent, my friend, rest easy. I will take care of everything."

202

The next day Bernie's chauffeur drove him to a phone booth fifteen minutes from the family home. It wasn't the first time he had done so. There were times when his boss had to have absolute privacy with no fear of being overheard when he conducted his business. This was merely another one of those occasions. The chauffeur waited patiently. Knowingly.

Bernie returned to the car in less than five minutes and said coldly, "Robert, take me to the bus station."

"Yes sir, Mr. Shaikowitz," came the obedient reply as the car pulled out into the busy morning traffic and headed downtown.

Once inside the bustling terminal, Bernie strode resolutely to locker number fifty-one, opened it and inserted a small package. He walked away quickly not looking one way or the other. On the way to his office he put the matter out of his mind. He had done what an honorable man must do. His pledge to his dead friend was fulfilled.

CHAPTER 32

Twelve days after the mysterious package was delivered to the Chicago bus station there was a knock on the door of Loretta Mandeville's house. It was a rainy evening and at first she didn't hear the faint knock. She heard it the second time as it became more pronounced. She opened the door and turned on the porch light to find two hulking figures, one tall and skinny with a hat, the other of average height but stocky.

"Can I help you?" Loretta said somewhat tentatively.

"Yes'm," the tall one grinned. "Are you Loretta Mandeville?"

"Yes, I am," Loretta admitted suspiciously. These guys are creepy, she thought.

"That's too bad," the tall one said as both men lunged forward forcing their way into the house.

"What in the hell do you think you're doing?" Loretta thundered as she stood confronting the two.

The stocky man delivered a lightning quick left jab which landed squarely on the chin of Loretta Mandeville and rendered her unconscious.

Linda Griffey suddenly appeared from a rear bedroom and said, "Loretta, what's the ...Oh, my God, no!"

The heavy set man looked to the other as if for direction. The tall man nodded.

CRACK! Linda Griffey fell victim to the same left jab. She, too, was out cold.

The two women regained consciousness some time later and found themselves tied and gagged in the back of a windowless van that was on the move. They couldn't move but they could see the two sinister figures in the front of the van who were responsible for this abduction. Loretta's mind was racing. She quickly concluded that these must be two former mental patients who, somehow, in some sort of paranoid state, blamed her for their troubles. It would not be the first time that an authority figure became the focus of a deluded schizophrenic. This conclusion gave her no solace because she realized the capabilities of such people and knew that their lives were in grave danger. She tried to calm down and think rationally. She knew that it was very important not to antagonize these men and vital to get them to talk as much as possible. Hopefully she could get them to ventilate some of their hostility instead of acting it out. Talking instead of doing. It was dark in the van and she couldn't see Linda but she knew she was awake and frightened silly. She moved up against her for reassurance. Linda murmured unintelligibly through the gag. Unlike the cooler Loretta, she could think of nothing to do except to pray.

Finally, the van stopped. Loretta knew they were close to the river because she heard the sound of a tug boat. She reasoned they must be in the old, mostly abandoned, warehouse district. "Great," she thought, "nobody ever goes around there at night. Forget any outside help."

The tall man sprang energetically from the van and opened a large overhead door. He waved the van through the door into an unheated warehouse that had a concrete floor and lights. The few existing windows had been painted black and covered with rags so no clue would be given to outsiders that there was activity within.

The back doors of the van opened revealing the two terrified women, one who had a pleading look in her eyes; the other was pretending to be calmer and less intimidated.

The tall man looked at Loretta and said laughingly, "You're not scared, eh bitch? Well, we'll see about that." He took a brown bottle from his coat pocket and began pouring the liquid on a rag which he put first under Linda's nose, then Loretta's. He turned to his partner and said, "That chloroform will make them easier to work with." He received a grin and an excited nod in return for his wisdom and experience.

Gerald Louis Frazier cut a sinister figure at six foot two and one hundred and fifty pounds. He was in the habit of wearing an ill-fitting black suit and a bowler hat. He achieved his present height at age fifteen and was forced to endure the jeers of his schoolmates because he only weighed 135 pounds at that time. The cat-calls of "scarecrow" and "bag of bones" still rang in his ears at times. His gaunt, skeleton-like appearance and a curious and persistent inability to learn to read were the cause for his quitting school at an early age.

Unfortunately he found the outside world no more hospitable than the often cruel world of teenagers. By the time he was nineteen he had become involved in a life of petty crime that landed him in the state penitentiary at Jefferson City, Missouri. There too, he became the door mat of many of the men who used him at their will and ridiculed him unmercifully. On his twenty-third birthday he was sitting in his cell with one more year to serve. He was despondent and contemplated suicide. His life had become unbearable and showed no prospect whatsoever of changing. He knew he was brighter than normal people because of the way he could figure things out and understand things before others could. Why he couldn't learn to read still mystified him. It was a constant frustration. Well, the frustration would soon be over. He had stolen a spoon from the mess hall and ground it down to razor sharpness in the machine shop where he spent his prison days. He meant to take his life that night. He couldn't bear another bully abusing him and the lack of status that went with "being turned out" in the prison social hierarchy. Psychologically, he had hit rock bottom.

On what was to be his last day of fresh air in the prison yard, Gerald Louis was accosted by a huge bully who was, once again, going to use him for sport. Something snapped inside as he became enraged beyond what he thought was possible. He was not going to be humiliated on the last day of his life!

In the style of a man with nothing more to lose he deftly deposited the sharpened spoon into the liver of his tormentor who died quickly with an astonished look on his face.

The man who was killed was such a despicable trouble-maker that only a cursory investigation of the matter was done by prison officials. Gerald's life was never the same from that moment on. His fellow convicts treated him in a new way. Not only did they not "squeal," as was consistent with the prison code, but they began treating him with respect. He became a man among men. Finally, he had discovered what was required in order to live a fulfilled life. The future held promise for him. Excitement, respect, money and the freedom of never having to take any shit from anybody ever again would be his. He was to become the most deadly and reliable hit man Chicago had known in all its bloody past.

By now, at age thirty, he had "done" over thirty people. Each job performed professionally with no evidence or suspicion toward the employer was his motto. Gerald's reputation in his field had become one of excellence, and along with that his fee had now grown to $20,000 per job. Not only was he prospering financially but he had bloomed into a sadist to rival any in history. He was pensive and brooding between hits. The only time he was alive and happy was when he was planning or doing a job. He had all but abandoned conventional methods of killing people. Lately he had become a student of historical torture methods. He made his punch-drunk side-kick, Blinkey, read unbelievable accounts of sadistic torture scenes over and over to him. He often thought that he would have done his job for nothing. The fact that he made over $100,000 a year tax free was just the creme on the cookie. He also got the gratification of respect in the criminal community, respect that he craved and needed. Respect that almost made up for those many years of humiliation heaped on by unfeeling people. Now he was the one who dealt out the fear and humiliation to others. He felt more vindicated with each killing as though he was going to pay back the world , one person at a time, for the unkindness which had been shown him so many times in his past. He never considered himself sadistic, demented, or sick, just a man with a justifiable mission who happened to enjoy his work.

"C'mon Blinkey," Gerald ordered excitedly, "let's get these young lovers out of here and set up. I can't wait to see their faces when they wake up and hear what's going to happen to them."

"What is going to happen to them?" Blinkey asked. "You never tell me anything ahead of time. Just order me around," he grumbled.

Blinkey Bergston was a forty-five-year-old, has-been club fighter. Make that a never-been club fighter. He, in reality, never reached the status of a fighter good enough to be called a has-been. A third-rate pug with the necessary low IQ who got hit a few hundred times too many, he served Gerald Louis well. He never asked questions, always did what he was told and knew how to keep his mouth shut. He was afraid of Gerald Louis. He couldn't understand why they had to go to all these elaborate productions just to knock someone off though. He didn't get the kick out of it that Gerald did. He knew Gerald was sick, but the money was easy and good, so what the hell, he reasoned. Everybody had to be somewhere doing something. Right? Blinkey planned to make this his last job with Gerald. This was his third one and Gerald seemed to be getting increasingly radical in his methods. There was no need to put the hits through so much agony as far as Blinkey was concerned. Just bump 'em off and be done with it. "Yeah, this is my last job with Gerald," Blinkey silently promised himself.

208

Gerald Louis Frazier and Blinkey Bergston did agree on one thing. It would indeed be Blinkey's last job with Gerald. It would be his last job with anybody. Gerald, although convinced of Blinkey's loyalty, was concerned about the possibility of his getting too much beer in him some night and telling tales out of school. He also was becoming more hesitant to follow orders. He would have never brought him along on this run except that he needed a helper to bring off the death scene as he had envisioned it. He would kill Blinkey after this job. No one would miss him.

Gerald had vowed to himself that he would only work solo from now on. He even planned to buy a DairyQueen on the south side of Chicago to give him cover as a normal taxpaying citizen. He smiled at his own cleverness when he thought about it.

"O.K. Blinkey. Hoist her up."

Blinkey complied hastily then protested, "Gerald, I don't think I want to watch. Is all this shit necessary?"

Gerald answered coldly, "Damn it to Hell, Blinkey, you've got to be here to help when I say so. You want your money, don't you?"

"Yeah, but..."

Gerald thundered at him, "Shut up and do as I say!" It's going to be a pleasure to put this wet brain out of his misery, Gerald thought angrily.

All was in readiness. Loretta was the first to open her eyes with Linda following suit less than a minute later. They were flabbergasted to realize their predicament.

"Well, well, girls, welcome back to the land of the living, even if it is for only a brief while," Gerald said hauntingly. Blinkey hated it when he had to torment the victims with his talk.

Linda began wailing and pleading, promising the men anything if they would just let them go. Loretta, although equally aghast, was now convinced that she was dealing with a full-blown psychopath. Must try to get him talking, she thought desperately. She surveyed the scene.

Linda was tied securely onto a chair with the legs cut off and the whole bottom of the chair cut open like a toilet seat. She was naked and her bottom hung down through the seat. The whole apparatus was hung up about five or six feet in the air on a set of ropes attached to pulleys which were secured to a ceiling beam overhead. Beneath her was a sharpened steel spike about five inches in length set in a railroad tie pointing directly at her bottom. Loretta got the disgusting picture immediately although she didn't think Linda understood what was going to happen. For her own part, Loretta was sitting in a wooden chair facing Linda. She was tied very securely and couldn't move. It felt like her hair was attached to something above but she couldn't tell what.

"What are you going to do to us?" Loretta asked falteringly.

"I've been paid to come here and kill you," Gerald Louis answered matter-of-factly.

Linda began screaming and wailing. Gerald merely turned to watch. He seemed to enjoy everything about the macabre scene. His eyes glistened.

Loretta tried to calm Linda down a little, who by now was so nauseous with fear that she threw up on herself. Linda was as miserable as a person can be.

"Who paid you? Why would anyone want to kill us?" Loretta clung to the hope of talking herself out of this.

"I really don't know who wants you dead. The reasons are never known to me, just as my identity and methods are never known to them. Safer for everybody that way. Your friend there," nodding to the moaning Linda Griffey, "was not on the list. I just threw her in for kicks. Might make it look like both of you just took off when they can't find you. I can tell you that we also offed some wimpy-ass deputy sheriff as well. We had him eat his pistol so it would look like suicide. Those guys do that all the time, anyway. They usually have so much to be ashamed of. Any connection you know of?"

Loretta shook her head. "None that I can think of. Listen, how much are you getting paid to do this?"

"Twenty thousand dollars."

"I could raise that much if you'll let us go. And I promise we'll keep our mouths shut."

"Yes, oh God, yes, please!" Linda blurted.

"The old 'don't do it, I'll pay you' scene." Gerald shook his head and looked at Blinkey. "Do you know every hit I've made resorts to that—if they get the chance to talk at all. But hey, c'mon. There's professional ethics involved here. I don't know what you and the late deputy did, but it must have been pretty bad for someone to pay $20,000 to have you exterminated. I live on my reputation of always fulfilling my contracts. I have never aborted one. Never will. That's that."

Loretta's mind was frantically racing. This bad news nut was so businesslike and impersonal that she was afraid she wouldn't get through to him. Maybe the other one. He seems almost as scared as I am. Worth a try. "Well, tell me, exactly what do you plan to do with us?"

"Well now, little lady, I'd be glad to explain that. I'm going to need your full cooperation, as a matter of fact." Gerald had now begun to pace around and rub his hands together. "Your buddy up there, at the appointed signal, is going to be guided down, rapidly and violently onto that sharp, steel spike that you see glistening there. Within four minutes, I expect her to die a death from horrible convulsions since the spike will go up through her tail bone and violate her spine and central nervous system."

Loretta, although not wanting to show this sicko any weakness, gasped and looked pleadingly at the man who had earlier knocked her out. He was shaking his head in disbelief. Linda was once again wailing and pleading.

"What about me?" Loretta asked meekly in a low voice.

"Well, you're kind of an experiment too," Gerald answered eagerly. "You see, I've long held this belief that if you cut off a person's head, quickly and cleanly, well, there will still be enough blood and oxygen in the brain to sustain thought and consciousness for a period of time—maybe minutes. I don't even see any reason why the severed head couldn't see, if the eyes were open, all the optic nerves being intact and all. I got the idea one day when I watched a guy cut the head off a chicken—you know how the body continues to thrash around. So, who's to say that the other end doesn't continue to function for a while too?" He was obviously pleased with himself.

Loretta was so revolted she couldn't speak.

Gerald Louis had now worked himself into a new fever pitch of expectation.

"So you see, little woman, you're about to participate in a kind of scientific inquiry. I'm going to cut your head off with this razor sharp sword with one clean stroke from behind, and then your head is going to hang there on those lines attached to your hair. I did that so your head wouldn't hit the ground and cause more trauma or maybe a concussion. I'm then going to hold your head steady, and open your eyes if necessary, so you can witness your girl friend's demise which will follow immediately. The problem is, how are you going to let me know whether or not you're seeing and thinking after your head is cut off. Maybe I can tell by the look in your eyes as she begins to suffer the agony of her death. Will you try to give me some kind of signal?"

Loretta lost all hope of survival and launched into a screaming tirade of expletives aimed at Gerald Louis. It would be her last.

"That's right. I love it when you talk dirty." Gerald smirked as he took his position behind Loretta with the sword poised and motioned for the feckless Blinkey to proceed.

212

CHAPTER 33

It had been five years since the night Sam had called his father to tell him about Gina and her tormentors. He was so eaten up with curiosity that he had to ask his father two years later what had happened. Bernie Shaikowitz, understanding Sam's need to know that the evil perpetrators had been dealt with merely said, "Justice has been done." Sam understood that, in one way or another, the people who had caused his wife the pain had paid a price. Neither man ever knew the gruesome details or that Gerald Louis had given new meaning to the word overkill.

Sam and Gina were married in 1964 after a romantic storybook courtship. They formed a very tight relationship that was built on mutual trust and affection. They were a couple that rivaled any Hollywood had ever created. Sam was the wise and ever attentive lover and confidante, Gina, the beautiful and bubbly heiress who had brains to go with it.

Gina had periodically struggled with the events surrounding her Godfrey State stay and the untimely death of her uncle, but Sam proved not only to be a lover and her best friend; he was her therapist as well. Now, some five years later, an occasional nightmare was the only vestige of those troubling times.

Gina had acquired the stability and happiness she always knew were possible. Sam had sold the remaining restaurants and looked after the family interests so there were no business worries for her to be concerned about. She adored Sam and their three-year-old son, Orvie. Her days were filled with pleasant, family oriented things such as gardening, cooking, reading and taking care of Orvie. She had graduated from Central College when she submitted her senior thesis on time and was now taking graduate courses in social work at St. Louis University. She was happy and content with her life but had consistent feelings of being unfulfilled and a need to somehow give back to the world something for all the joy it had given her. These feelings were the only ones she had not shared with Sam. Everything else between them was based on openness and honesty. She feared that he would view these feelings as a reflection on his job as lover and husband when that was not at all the case.

It took her some time to realize that their relationship was rock solid and that he could handle her need to achieve with no problem. She scolded herself for waiting as long as she had to discuss the matter with him. Gina knew that people in love have no reason to hold anything back or to ever lie to each other about anything.

His reaction was even more positive and understanding than she imagined it would be — but then, Sam always came through for her.

"Wonderful news! I'm really glad to hear that you are going to pursue your ambitions. You have a lot to give, and it's a shame that someone as bright and capable as you is not out there contributing. What kind of endeavor had you thought about? A job?"

Gina smiled and hugged Sam and thanked him for his support, again feeling sheepish about her reluctance to tell this man anything. She took a deep breath and then continued seriously, "I hoped that we could buy and operate a nursing home."

"A nursing home?" He was unable to conceal his surprise.

Gina answered hastily, hoping to counter any objections before they were raised. "Yes, I've thought it over carefully and a nursing home meets all the criteria for what I want to do. To meet the needs of the patients and their families and weld together an effective, caring staff is a tremendous challenge. I have in mind more than running a conventional nursing home. I want to work on developing a model for the rest of the industry to emulate, something special that will demonstrate to others how it ought to be done."

Sam listened quietly and then shrugged, "Well, O.K. a nursing home it is. How can I help?"

"I can't do it alone. I'll need a partner all the way — someone with a head for business and an understanding of human psychology, a rare combination I'll admit, but I have just such a man in mind."

Sam's eyes opened wide in stunned surprise.

Gina bore down. "Think of the team we'd make. If ever anybody was perfect to make a nursing home sing, it's us." That night they made tender, passionate love and Sam promised to commit totally to the nursing home dream for at least a three-year period.

Gina pressed her naked body against him and murmured, "Beautiful. Play it again Sam."

Chapter 34

The next day Gina made an appointment to see Mr. Uriah Somes, the owner of a business which dealt in business properties but specialized in the sale of nursing homes in particular.

Somes rang the front door bell at DeLassus Place at 2:20 which made him twenty minutes late. Not a good way to start with either Gina or Sam.

"Sorry I'm late," he apologized. "Got lost. I've never been up this way before. Beautiful country and this house is magnificent."

Gina and Sam showed him into the library and took seats opposite him in front of the fireplace. They were somewhat stony as the fifty-year-old, slightly disheveled and balding man groped his way around, trying to get some kind of fix on his potential customers.

Finally, he blurted, "Why do you two want to get into the nursing home business?"

"Why shouldn't we?" Gina asked casually.

"No reason, in particular." Somes was nervous and intimidated by the wealth surrounding him and the frosty couple who seemed to be demanding that he display some expertise. O.K., he'd go for it. "It's just that the people who I've bought and sold for in the past, and I've closed a number of deals in my time, were usually of two kinds: corporate people looking for acquisitions to add to their holdings or nurses who had the right motives and intentions but little business savvy and no money. Since you seem to fit neither of those pigeonholes I need to know what you have in mind."

"That's a legitimate question," Gina said cupping her chin between her thumb and forefinger as she sometimes did when in thought. "Over the years we have had the opportunity to observe the treatment in a leading, making quotation marks with two fingers of each hand, St. Louis nursing home and a nearby state hospital. I can tell you that, in both instances, the treatment of human beings was appalling. A disgrace. We wish to acquire a facility where we can show the world that the elderly and the handicapped can be, and deserve to be, treated with dignity and respect. We want a facility within thirty miles of this house and with at least seventy-five patients. Naturally, we'd like a building in good condition, but I guess we'd be willing to renovate the right place. Sam?"

Listening intently to Gina's small speech, Sam picked up immediately, "Mr. Somes, I come from a background with training in business and psychology. I'm going to lend my entire effort to helping my wife realize her dream. I'm totally committed to the idea. While we are willing to pay the going price for a facility, we do not intend to pay the normal price for a home which is giving substandard care. That would be like giving a student an 'A' for inferior work. We won't be a party to rewarding someone for doing a bad job. So it's only fair to warn you, up front, that any offer we make will be predicated not only on the worth of the property but on its history of care. Going into this I have a negative perception about nursing homes and the people who own them. I hope, to some degree, that negative perception becomes lessened. Do you now have an idea of what we're about?"

Somes nodded and frowned thoughtfully. Gina realized that he desperately wanted to smoke a cigarette because he was fidgeting and looking around for an ashtray. He was obviously a heavy smoker. He smelled like he had spent the last two days in a smoky tavern and his teeth were badly stained. Gina wasn't about to put him at ease.

218

Hoping to get the ball back on his side of the court he asked, "What will you need in the way of financial information?"

Sam answered without hesitation, "Two profit & loss statements with a balance sheet. We'll only buy land and buildings—no corporations. The contract, if we submit one, will include a covenant that the seller will not compete within a five-mile radius and will be predicated on our ability to secure the proper licensure to operate an approved nursing home. That's about it."

Mr. Somes nodded and said, "Very good." He realized he was dealing with people who knew what they wanted and how to get it. "I have several properties in mind that I think you'll want to consider. I'll put together the financial particulars and arrange for you to tour the facilities at your convenience."

"Excellent!" Gina said, her excitement showing. "We'll be ready as soon as you can set things up."

Mr. Somes, realizing that he had met his goal for the day, a live buyer with the ability to perform, stood and prepared to take his leave. "I think we can go through a nearby hundred-bed facility tomorrow. I'll call you by ten and arrange the tour for one in the afternoon."

Gina offered her hand for a good-bye handshake and said, "Make it noon, I want to see how they feed the people."

"As you wish. A pleasure to meet you both and I look forward to seeing you tomorrow." He left hurriedly, groping for his cigarettes and lighter as he walked out the door. There was no time to lose. He had to get on the phone to see which owners he could get to set a price on their homes. He knew from experience that they were a suspicious lot who wanted to sell one day and then would change their minds. More than one deal had slipped through his fingers because of trivial, meaningless details. One thing he found to be consistent—the owners were usually squeamish about showing their income tax records along with the other financial data. Many families paid for their parents' care with cash, and this source of income, sometimes as high as 25% of the gross, was never reported. These unscrupulous people kept three different sets of books: one for the IRS, one for themselves, and one for potential buyers. It was not different from the restaurant or hotel business or any other that was able to do a portion of its business in cash. He had a vague fear that the homes he would show this young couple weren't going to meet their expectations. Maybe he would be surprised. All these excited thoughts were flowing through his mind at once.

As soon as Somes had gone Gina turned to Sam and asked, "Well, what did you think of that character?"

"Grade B sleaze bag," Sam answered tonelessly, "he's gone to hustle up a listing or two that will interest us. I had the feeling that he'll have to generate it through whatever contacts he has. He probably doesn't have one listed now. I loved the way you ignored his need to smoke. You can be a real bitch," Sam said lovingly.

"Thank you, darling. I'm glad you know about all that contract stuff. As I suspected, we're going to make a great team. I love you, Sam."

He smiled, basking in the praise.

The next day at ten Robert Somes called and told Sam that he had a good, older home for them to visit at noon. He proposed that they meet at the Salad Bowl Restaurant at eleven to go over the details before the tour. Sam agreed easily.

On the way to the restaurant Sam seemed a little off center so Gina asked, "You don't feel very good about this Somes fellow, do you?"

"No. We're meeting at a restaurant because he obviously doesn't have an office. It's hard for me to believe that he'll be able to turn up anything that we'll be interested in. I had Daniels check around, though, and surprisingly there are no other firms that deal with nursing homes. He's the only game in town. For that reason, I'm willing to give him a chance. Besides, it's bound to be a learning experience for us both. Let's relax and enjoy it."

"Oh," Gina joked, "a little of the old 'do as I say not as I do'?"

"Ouch," Sam smiled.

Somes was sitting at a small table by the window of the midtown restaurant sipping coffee and smoking a cigarette which he quickly extinguished as his clients approached. He graciously pulled out a chair for Gina while summoning the waitress. He was resplendent in a clean shirt, shined shoes and freshly pressed suit. "He's trying," Sam thought, the gravy spot on his tie and the dirty fingernails notwithstanding.

He began his pitch. "Buying a nursing home is a lot like buying a house. Most of the same rules apply. Like many house hunters you two seem to have a good idea about what you want, and I think you'll know it when you see it. 'Kay?" Gina and Sam nodded dutifully. Somes continued, happy to get a positive response and beginning to feel more at ease with these hard to read people. "I'm going to take you to a place called Pine Lawn Manor today. It's an eighty-bed intermediate care facility that's probably been in business for twenty years or so. The building was formerly a Wabash Railroad employees hospital built around the turn of the century. I've not been in it but I hear it's very nice — and has the potential to be a real money maker..."

"You mean it doesn't make money now?" Sam interrupted. "Why not?"

"Well, the business has been in the family the whole time since it started and was always successful until three years ago when the father and mother died in a car crash and the home was inherited by a, well uh, somewhat wayward son. He's let it go downhill, I'm afraid, and now he wants to sell."

"What's the price?" Sam asked.

"He's not set it yet, but I think a good deal can be worked out. Let's go take a look and see if it's the kind of place you'd like to pursue. Shall we take my car?"

Gina replied quickly, "We'll follow you in our car." She didn't want to be any closer to his vile cigarette smoke than necessary, and if his car interior mirrors his personal cleanliness, well, who needs it?

"Okay," Somes replied disappointedly.

Pine Lawn Manor was a rather attractive, large Victorian style building with two long main wings on the ground floor and a second floor which ran about half its length. It was brick which had been painted white, although not recently, and had a long, wooden front porch with lawn chairs lined up which gave the building an old time comfortable look. The front yard was dotted with pine trees which undoubtedly inspired its name.

Before they entered Somes stopped and said, "One thing before you go in. The owner isn't here, and we have to tell the nurse in charge that we want to look the place over because we're going to place a relative in a home. You understand, the owner doesn't want to excite the staff with rumors about selling. It makes them nervous and insecure."

Gina and Sam looked at each other. "I don't like the idea," Sam said.

"It's never a good idea to pretend to be something you're not. But, what the hell, we're here and I want a look. Mr. Somes, you do the talking."

The three entered the front door and were immediately stunned with the sour, fowl smell of human waste. There was a nurses' station immediately beyond the small vestibule at the entrance. There were no nurses in view, only a dozen or so dull-eyed, slack-jawed patients, all of whom were strapped and tied to their wheel chairs. None of the patients gave any noticeable reaction to the entrance of the trio. It was as though they were invisible. Nonexistent.

By and by, a middle aged lady dressed in a crisp white uniform and a nurse's cap approached them. She was grossly overweight, 300 pounds Sam guessed later, and had wispy, thinning red hair. She looked hassled and exasperated but managed a smile and said, "Hello, I'm Jane Warren, Director of Nursing. May I help you?"

"Yes, Miss Warren," Mr. Somes offered in a congenial way. "We're looking for a nursing home to place a relative in and would appreciate a tour of Pine Lawn Manor."

"Okay" she responded, "but you've come at a bad time. I'm working short handed today and it's very difficult to get everything done."

Sam stepped up and said, "We can see that you're very busy. How about if we just look around on our own and then look you up for questions and answers?"

The nurse hesitated, then allowed as how that would probably be all right.

They spent thirty-five minutes walking around and observing. Somes did some talking but Sam and Gina were silent. After they had covered the facility once, Gina and Sam split off and began to go around on their own. When they were satisfied, Gina and Sam walked out and told Somes they'd call him. Somes was left standing on the front porch feeling foolish. A salesman with no control of the situation.

As Sam headed the car for home he finally spoke, "My God, Gina. How could you possibly want to run a place like that? Everything I saw was wrong."

"That's just it honey. I don't want to run a place like that. I want to run a place properly."

"Well, I've got to have some time to recover from what I've just seen and smelled." Sam winced.

"Sam, I told you that these places can be totally repugnant. But don't be discouraged, even though it seems overwhelming. We're talking about problems and obstacles. And as you know, problems and obstacles can be solved and overcome. It merely requires people who take them one at a time with a plan. As hopeless as a place like that seems I know it can be cleaned up, and I know that good care for the patients can become a reality. Come on now, partner, don't desert me before we start." She smiled and patted him on the shoulder. He realized why he loved her so.

Sam calmed down a little and began talking about Pine Lawn Manor. "Did you notice how hot it was in there? I talked to the maintenance man, who was half drunk by the way, and he said that the thermostat doesn't work on the boiler so he has to let it run full blast on these cool nights and doesn't shut it off until he comes in at eight in the morning. By then it's ninety degrees. They have no hot water. Haven't had for over two months. When they want to bathe someone, which obviously is rarely, they have to heat some water on the stove and take it to the bath tub on one of the food carts. God, that's a hell of a way to run a train."

Gina added, "While you were chatting with the maintenance guy I had a real down home talk with the cook. Sam, she was adorable. Her name was Claire and she's seventy-two years old! But as active and spry as I am. She comes early and makes homemade pies and other special goodies for everybody. She has to use leftovers and sometimes even buys extra food out of her own pocket, but she makes sure that the people get enough to eat. She told me that when the owner gets a steer butchered for hamburger, they bring the animal's head in and boil it—eyes and all—for soup stock. Uncle Vinnie used to say that when they slaughtered pigs at the East St. Louis stockyards they used everything except the squeal, but can you believe that? Claire is a dear, sweet woman though. She said the place is always short staffed because the owner can make more money that way. He must be a real slug. The staff must really dislike him to tell strangers all this negative stuff so easily. Nobody questioned my right to be walking around and talking to people. I could have been anybody."

224

Sam looked over at Gina and asked, as though he had just considered it for the first time, "Why do families pay to have their people treated like that? I just don't get it."

"I don't know." Then sadly she said, "I let my mother stay in a place I wasn't satisfied with. But I was young and unable to deal effectively with the situation. Well, let us make a promise that no one will ever say that about out nursing home. All right?"

"It's not going to be easy, Gina."

" I know."

"Something else is bothering me. It makes sense that sometimes people must be placed in a nursing home because they can't take care of themselves and the families can't take care of them either, for one reason or another. I can understand that. But the large percentage of patients at Pine Lawn Manor really looked completely out of it. You know? They probably had nothing to say about going there and aren't able to make any decisions about their lives. So, someone makes decisions for them. They are vulnerable and without representation it seems. Aren't there government agencies that look after their welfare and protect them from the kind of poor treatment we just witnessed?"

"I was wondering the same thing. I'm going to call Governor Delmar Higgins. You remember me mentioning that I met him years ago when his mother was a patient at Sunset Meadows. He seemed like a real square shooter at the time and that reputation has followed him throughout his political career. They're talking about him as Presidential timber."

"That's probably a good idea. Politicians are always looking for a cause to champion. He might be just the guy to do the right thing — even if he does it for the wrong reason."

Gina laughed, "How can anybody with such a jaundiced view of human nature be such a sweet and honest guy?"

"It's hard to grow up in Chicago and not be cynical. But enough of this. As soon as I get you home I'm going to show you how sweet I can be."

"Eeek!" Gina shrieked in mock horror. She then slid over across the car seat and kissed him on the ear. The accelerator slammed to the floor as they looked at each other and giggled.

CHAPTER 35

For the next two weeks Somes took Gina and Sam to several area nursing homes which he said were available. Places with names like Twin Rivers, the Lola Rae and Greenview. Occasionally the home would bear the name of the family who owned it like Sherrod's or Linsin's. Usually the names had embellishments like manor, care center, village, or haven. Working the word America into the name was also popular. Naming a nursing home was, in some instances, like naming a bank or savings and loan who use words like united, first federal, national, and American to give themselves the aura of stability and respectability.

Sam had decided that Mr. Somes was of no use at all. He actually knew very little about the nursing home business, and it was plain now that anyone could walk into a home and use the old "We're looking for a place to put Aunt Tillie," as an excuse to look around. Nursing homes were like anything else. They were all for sale for the right price. Somes's contribution to the process had become nil.

The owners who ran the homes themselves all seemed to become lax and indifferent after a while. They became cold and uncaring to the patients and their families and began viewing their customers and people who worked for them with disdain. More than with disdain, they saw them as enemies and adversaries who were complicating their lives. Sam and Gina shared this observation and readily admitted that there were surely exceptions. It was just that they had yet to find one. There were other similarities which the owners shared. They all seemed to like diamond rings, Cadillac cars and talking about how much they cared for their residents.

Gina couldn't help laughing as Sam imitated one such character they had met with a big gut, a country accent, and a toothpick in his mouth. In parody he said, "Yep, this would be a damn good biness if it weren't for the damn patients and the damn help".

The more they went around visiting homes the more they realized to what a large degree the industry of nursing homes was unregulated. There were rules, to be sure, but the inspectors were spread too thin to make the rules stick in just a once or twice-a-year visit. Some of the owners talked about how each inspection cost them a hundred dollars, implying that's what it took to get the inspector to overlook violations. And the violations Sam and Gina observed were multiple and rampant. Several of the homes had more patients than they were licensed for. The extra patients would roam around in the home by day and sleep in outbuildings or in the halls by night. Their charts, if they had any, were hidden and the mattresses and other signs of their existence were stored in closets during the day. Gina wouldn't have been aware of this practice except she always felt that some of the homes were too crowded. There were people everywhere. On one of the visits she decided to count heads and compare that number with the license. Sure enough, the license read 98, yet there were 106 patients.

The economics of this fraudulent practice were immediately obvious. Start with a person who is ambulatory and easy to take care of and who has no interested family, put him up for his social security check and whatever state aid you can get, and it's all gravy. Food costs could be held down to a dollar a day without anyone grumbling and that only left the expense of washing one more person's clothes, a modest expenditure at best. This is the kind of stuff that diamond rings and Cadillacs are made of. It's also the greed that would continue to make nursing home owners generally seen as such a cold, money grubbing and despicable lot.

Sam and Gina became very proficient at evaluating nursing homes. In less than five minutes they could tell about the level of care by merely looking and smelling.

There tended to be a correlation between the cleanliness and the care. If the floors were shiny, the paint fresh and there was no odor, then the patients usually appeared to be clean and comfortable.

It's like looking at a used car for sale from an individual. If the car is clean and the seller's home is neat, tidy and in good repair, then the car had probably been properly serviced and taken care of. If the owner's home is messy and ramshackle, look out! That type of pride and care is undoubtedly linked to the used car as well.

They ran into one home where everything was clean and nice but the patients were unresponsive. They wouldn't look up and smile at visitors. This is a dead giveaway that they are not accustomed to friendly interaction with others. The tension was so thick you could cut it with a knife. Sure enough, there was a reason. The administrator turned out to be the culprit. He had an overbearing drill sergeant personality with a kind of hobnail boots mentality regarding the staff. He was a "do-it-my-way,-and-if-you-can't,-take-a-walk" kind of guy. The staff turnover at this home was much higher than normal, of course, and the care suffered as a consequence. As Sam and Gina were compiling their list of DO's and DON'T's, they added another law. If the staff has a problem with management that goes unaddressed they will pay management back. It may come in the form of theft, absenteeism or poor work, but they will retaliate somehow.

Each home they visited would bring out stories, either from the administrators, staff, or, in some instances, the patients themselves. People in the business loved to gossip about other homes. One of the most memorable stories had to do with a woman who was an LPN who owned and ran a small home in South St. Louis. It seems that in her misguided zeal to keep people alive and well—and paying—she fed a dead man for two days after he expired, ignoring the other workers' protests and admonitions. After the other horror stories they had heard, it was not surprising to learn that the woman is still there and her home is still open. It was as though no crime was great enough to get one of these deficient homes closed. In fact, in all their conversations with people in the nursing home business, not once did they hear a story about a substandard home being closed for poor care. The only reason given for closing was a fire. If they didn't burn, then they stayed open, and nobody did anything about the bad ones.

Gina made all of these feelings and observations clear in her letter to Missouri Governor Higgins. He had asked that she document her findings after she had talked to him by phone a week earlier. The skillful politician remembered her and they shared some stories about his mother, the queen of Sunset Meadows, Mrs. Harriet Wormsley. The Governor was very interested in what Gina had to say and promised her that he would give the matter his utmost attention and would carefully study the matter. As Sam had surmised, the incumbent Missouri Governor sensed political mileage surrounding this long-neglected issue. " After all", he said, "old people are kind of like kids. You don't want to kick one in the butt. Not publicly, anyhow".

The two were sitting by the pool breakfasting when their thoughts and conversation turned to nursing homes, as they frequently did these days. Sam, ever the cynic, told Gina not to hold her breath until change and nursing home reform occurred. "It depends on how politicized the issue becomes and how powerful the nursing home lobby is," he reasoned. "President Kennedy promised that this nation was going to do two things, end poverty and go to the moon. I bet I know which we actually achieve."

"Which?"

"We will be going to the lunar surface, of course," he stated matter-of-factly while taking a bite of his cantaloupe.

"It seems to me that you've slated the more difficult of the two for success," Gina said. She knew her husband was really smart and insightful and that he understood a lot about human nature but she took a more positive position about the innate goodness of mankind. She loved President Kennedy and saw no reason why both worthy goals couldn't be achieved. For her money anything that JFK had said was absolutely valid. She also didn't think it was healthy for Sam to be right all the time. A little more humility wouldn't hurt him.

"It would seem so. But you're forgetting a basic tenant that made this country what it is. When it comes to technology and getting things to work, we have no equal. Especially when the goal is as politically popular as space exploration. It can't miss, it's too American. On the other hand, although no one wants to admit it, so is poverty. American that is. America needs its niggers."

"Sam!" Gina protested.

"Easy now. When I say niggers I don't mean it in the racial slur sense. I'm talking about people at the bottom of the ladder. There's all kinds of niggers — black ones, white ones, red ones. I'm talking about the folk who have no voice, no say so, and who clean our houses, mow our lawns and yes, work in our nursing homes for a dollar or a dollar and a half an hour. I was a nigger every summer when dad got me a laborer's job. I think he wanted me to know how it feels. Well, I learned the lesson. It's boring. Just as surely as the south needed slaves to make cotton profitable, American business needs its slaves to make business work. As long as the guys with the money call the shots in this country, that's the way it's going to stay. At least that's the way my tea leaves read."

Gina thought about this troubling revelation for a minute and instinctively wanted to argue and take the other side of the issue but instead, for the moment, accepted the premise and said, "Well, if that's true, then all we have to do is pay our workers twice the going rate. Does it follow that they'll do twice as well?"

Sam smiled and shook his head no, "It's not that simple. There's some kind of law of diminishing returns at work here. Our goal will be to get the staff to do the best job of which they're capable. That will require a combination of things, We'll pay better than other homes, but only ten cents per hour better for two reasons: to keep unions out and to attract and keep the best people. But ten cents an hour alone won't do it. People need to feel involved. They need to be able to verbalize their concerns and problems and feel like they're heard and respected. We'll have regular staff meetings that will accomplish that. They also need to be complimented when they do a good job and cautioned and retrained if necessary when their work is not up to standard. This type of supervision is basic and essential but it just hasn't existed in any nursing home we've visited. The owners have to state a philosophy , how they want their home to be, and then provide the tools for the staff to make it happen." Gina was in tune now, shaking her head enthusiastically. "This type of management has been the way our family has run the restaurant business for years. Know this, baby, if you don't get the staff to do the job for you, it simply won't get done. You can't do it by yourself. I've always maintained that people are like dogs. The happier ones are well trained."

"God, Sam. Sometimes your analogies are so blatant, but I get the idea and I'm getting excited again. I saw what you're talking about at Sunset Meadows. I just didn't understand the dynamics. The administrator was a guy named Silvey who was the leader in name only. Again at Godfrey State, the little foreign doctor was just a rubber stamp for the nursing service. If you're the leader and fail to lead, then someone else will do it for you. It usually winds up being the most aggressive person around. God, that could be the cook or the janitor. Probably is in some cases."

"Yeah," Sam agreed, "our nursing home is going to reflect our personalities and our policies. We have to see to that. If we don't, then as you say, it will reflect someone else's." Gina was quiet, as though engrossed in thought. Sam continued, "Hiring the right kind of staff will be important. People can fool you in interviews, make you think they're something they're not. Their job histories, even their recommendations from former employers, can be altered. They learn to say just what you want to hear. The only way to get a solid staff is to, after reasonable supervision and training, fire the ones who don't get the job done. Some employers are hesitant to do that because of the hassle and they fear that the next employee they hire won't be any better. That doesn't have to be the case at all.. You have to always strive for excellence. If we're able to field the kind of team I'm thinking about, then people who don't measure up will stick out like a sore thumb."

"You're right," Gina said, "being a nurse or nurse's aide is like being a school teacher. If teachers don't like kids and don't believe in what they're doing, then they won't do well. They will dread going to work each day and will be grateful when the final bell rings. They probably won't last long. If they don't go into something more suitable they'll probably develop some maladaptive behavior that will hurt the kids. We need to be able to identify early the people who are loving and suited to nursing home work. How do you do that?"

"Trial and error, and make no mistake about it, we'll make some selection errors. But basically I believe that if a person can be a good mother, she can be a good nurse. Same rules apply. Good mothers do it by instinct. I don't think all the Dr. Spock 'how-to-do-it' books in the world can make a psychologically unfit mother into a good one. Might redefine her technique a little, but those books also take away people's trust in their own instincts. They are made to be reliant on a higher power rather than doing their own thinking and being responsible themselves."

"I get what you mean. If we can pick reasonably stable and normal people and make a good place for them to work, then they'll stay. There will be no revolving door where people come to work just because there is no other job available and they won't leave it as soon as they possibly can. If we get that kind of loyalty, then people will form love bonds with the patients and our job will become much easier because you just automatically take good care of someone you love."

"Right you are. I think we need to beware of a — let's call it a profile — of the type person who is most likely to be this loyal, loving employee." Sam raised his eyebrows like a college professor attempting to get a student to think. "How old will she be?"

"Older, above 40." Gina answered.

"Yes, but why?" Sam probed.

"Because, generally speaking, people know who they are and what they're good at by that time. They've sown their wild oats and are about the business of raising their families and settling down."

"Married? Black or White?"

"Doesn't matter."

"Educated — at least high school graduate?"

Gina hesitated, "Yes."

"I must respectfully disagree."

Gina sighed and shot him a tired look. "I knew you were setting me up for something. Go ahead, lets have it."

"It's just that I feel–well, it's O.K. and probably necessary that everybody be able to read and write, but I think we want people who are uneducated so they won't have the ability to go out and get better jobs."

234

"Sam, honestly. All this talk about — niggers — God that's the first time I ever said that word — and preferring uneducated people to work for us. It goes against the grain of everything I've always believed."

"I know honey," Sam acknowledged soothingly. "I also know that your instincts are excellent. I trust them as I do my own, but I'll bet you that if you took a home and ran it with $4.00 an hour high school graduates and I ran one beside it with $1.60 per hour dropouts, you wouldn't be able to tell the difference — except in the profit and loss statements."

"Mmmmm. Could be," Gina said. "Now, changing the subject, I've an announcement to make."

"Good," Sam smiled, "but you don't need to make a formal announcement that we're going inside to..."

"Yes, that too, smarty. But before that, I've decided which nursing home we're going to buy."

"The suspense is killing me. I didn't think you were interested in any of the piss pots we've looked at."

"I'm not."

"For Christ's sake. Out with it woman."

"We're going to buy Sunset Meadows."

"I didn't know it was for sale."

"Everything is. At the right price," Gina said playfully. "Now get upstairs and get those pants off."

"Yes ma'am."

CHAPTER 36

Lawrence K. Daniels was on the phone pleading with Gina to slow down and carefully consider what she was doing. "At least why don't you go work in a nursing home for a while, to get your feet wet and really understand what they're like. You might change your mind."

"Larry, I already know what they're like. They're warehouses for people who have lost their usefulness. The only thing I would learn by hanging around one is a lot of bad practices and harmful stereotypes. I don't intend to run another barely acceptable place. Don't you understand? I'm going to make this nursing home the talk of the town."

The lawyer sighed audibly, "O.K. Gina. Whatever you say. But these guys are sharks who swim on land. You won't mind if I guard your interests from a contractual standpoint, will you?"

"That's what we pay you for. Sam will be over tomorrow to discuss the details of the sales contract. When do you think it can be ready?"

"By Friday."

"Good. I'll set up a meeting with the company representatives for 1:00 Friday at your office. See you then... and Larry?"

"Yes?"

"Smile. It's going to be O.K."

"I hope you're right. See you Friday." He did smile as he hung up the telephone receiver.

Gina turned to Sam, who was reading the *Wall Street Journal* and said, "Larry's concerned that we're moving too fast. Of course he's always concerned about everything."

Sam put his paper down and said, "I think we'll be well prepared. We'll technically only buy the building, its fixtures and the land it sits on. That way we can depreciate it all and claim tax advantages. Of course they won't want to do that. They'll want to sell the corporation stock along with goodwill and stuff like that. Generally speaking, if anything is to our advantage, it's a disadvantage to them. I've met with our banker and he can guarantee a loan of up to a million and a half, so that part shouldn't be a problem. We'll be offering more than it would cost to build a new one. You know that don't you?"

"Sam, I've got something to prove and I'm becoming obsessed with it. I don't want to lose any more time than necessary. I just want to get on with it. You understand, don't you?"

"Yes."

"Even at the inflated sale price, it will at least break even money-wise, won't it?"

"No."

"No?"

"It'll make money," he grinned.

She laughed and jumped astraddle him, saying, as he smothered her neck with kisses, "One of these days I'm going to snatch you bald."

"Why, I'll swan to my days," he said mockingly, remembering an old country saying once favored by his maternal grandmother.

Friday seemed like it would never arrive. Gina barely slept the night before and envied the even breathing of the unflappable man next to her to whom she was so happily married. Lying awake she thought over the many events of her life. She dwelled on her mother, both before and after the illness, and made yet another promise to herself that she would operate Sunset Meadows in a style that would make any family happy to put a relative in her care. When she

237

could truthfully say, "I'd put my own mother there," then she'd know she had reached her goal. Thankfully, the sun finally rose. She jumped up and hurriedly ran downstairs to fix Sam the breakfast of his life.

The meeting with the three lawyers from the company which sought to sell Sunset Meadows was interesting although unpleasant. It was filled with acrimony and bickering over details and contractual language. Twice the most aggressive of the opposing lawyers (Larry, Moe, and Curly, as Gina liked to call them) threatened to end the talks and walk out, only to be soothed by a more level-headed colleague. The emotional outbursts rang untrue because the men came across as actors who were performing their prescribed roles without conviction or enthusiasm. Finally, after five hours of wrangling, the opposition said they were satisfied and believed they could support the contract as now written. Lawrence Daniels asked for a few minutes alone with his clients and led them into an adjoining office. Daniels poured coffee and turned to Sam and Gina asking, "Well, what do you think ?"

Sam reacted first, "I think you did a fine job in there Larry. I think we got everything we wanted and at $100,000 less than I thought we would."

"Thanks. Gina?" Daniels nodded.

"I agree with Sam. You more than held your own against three experienced and skilled negotiators. Though, throughout it all, I couldn't help wondering where their company keeps its machine."

"What machine?" Larry and Sam asked simultaneously.

"You know. The one they put guys like that into and later they emerge as colossal assholes."

Both men shrieked with laughter. The tension created by the lawyers was over. Everything had been put back into perspective.

CHAPTER 37

Gina kept very busy during the days between the signing of the purchase contract and the day they would assume ownership. Sam was busy also, tying up loose ends so he could devote full time to Sunset Meadows.

"The first thing we must do is change the name," Gina declared one evening after dinner. "I don't want one single thing to be the same as before. What should we call it, Sam?"

"Hmmm. Let's see. 'The Ritz Plaza'?... No... How about 'The Old Codgers Home'?... No.. How about.."

"Be serious," Gina scolded light-heartedly. "The name is important."

"You're right." As always Sam knew when to back off. "But I'm not very creative about such things. I'll trust you to give it an appropriate name." In addition to knowing when not to aggravate the woman he adored, Sam also liked to avoid such mundane chores. He actually didn't care what the place was called as long as it made Gina happy. That was his prime concern in life.

"I wouldn't bother to change the name if the home had been respectable and good under the present name. But since, in my estimation, it was not, then I feel we shouldn't fly their soiled banner any longer. It's going to be a new day."

"Right on!" Sam was mimicking a currently popular slogan of a growing number of politically left wing people in the country. A position that he did not support, he saw these fools as ludicrous and destructive—hardly in keeping with his conservative, Republican politics.

Gina and Sam arrived at their nursing home at 7 a.m. on the first of June to begin their new careers as owner/operators of the Louise Oldani Memorial Home, formerly known as Sunset Meadows. They took a quick tour through the facility and then sat down in the administrative office, which was now bare except for a desk and two chairs, and looked at each other in surprise.

Sam grinned and said jokingly, "Well, what do we do now boss?"

"Not one person in this home realized that it has been sold," Gina replied. "Isn't that incredible? Whatever else I do, I don't plan to do things secretly. That just widens the gap between staff and management and feeds the already present undercurrent of suspicion." She sat quietly for a moment then said, "Let's make a list of short- and long-term goals and begin accomplishing them this very day."

"Excellent," Sam agreed, being as compliant as possible. Some two hours later they walked out of the office with their goals all ready to be typed. Gina planned to post them on the bulletin board after discussing them with the staff. She expected to generate the same type of goal statements from the nursing, dietary, housekeeping, recreation and maintenance departments. It was important that everyone know about the priorities of management. She didn't want the progress of the home to be uncharted.

Sam had advised her to keep the goal statements to herself for a few weeks until they had time to evaluate where the home stood in all areas. He reasoned that it is hard to steer your ship to a destination until you knew from where you were departing. Gina was won over by this wisdom and declared, "Sam, you're going to have to act not only as my partner but as my advisor and counselor as well. I'm overly anxious about turning this place around. I want to do it overnight, and I need you to help me make one move at a time and not try to slay all the dragons in one day."

"I gladly accept that assignment, my dear," Sam said playfully and over-graciously. "Let me begin to make

240

recommendations to you here and now and you keep what you like and throw away that which you consider to be garbage. 'Kay?"

"Kay," Gina replied with an arched eyebrow. She knew he was putting her on somewhat but she enjoyed the game and was always a willing player.

Sam and Gina decided that for the first month they would work hand in hand with the staff. Each would serve at least one week as a worker-trainee in nursing, dietary and housekeeping so that they would not only get to know the staff and patients intimately, but would really gain the necessary familiarity with the building and see what needed to be done. They were anxious to demonstrate to everybody that they were deadly serious about making the home a first class operation and that they were willing to work harder than anyone there to make it so.

The staff was understandably suspicious at first and pulled back into a defensive posture waiting to see what these folks were really all about. They were accustomed to administrators who shuttered themselves behind office doors and relied on supervisors to make things work — or not work. It was a slow process to convince them that these new owners, beautiful and rich people with superior education, were willing to mop, scrub, and clean soiled people as they expected everyone who worked there to do. They were teaching by example, and slowly but surely the strategy began to work and pay dividends.

Within that first month the home began to take on a new shine and began to improve in every way. Gina and Sam worked six ten-hour days a week on the floor and took care of the business and paper work on the seventh.

It was necessary to discharge two nurses, four nurses' aides, two housekeepers and two cooks during that period because they simply weren't up to the task. They couldn't meet the new standard of performance. Gina and Sam made sure that they were treated fairly and given every chance to perform, but they had just been around too long and could-n't adjust to the new drumbeat that was being sounded. It was becoming a day when an employee was never asked to do anything that the owners weren't willing to do. This simple but revolutionary concept was welcomed by the bulk of the staff, and the people hired to replace the discharged workers adapted readily because they were made aware of the heightened expectations when they were trained.

The facility began taking on a kind of self policing aspect that surprised Gina. The employees took new pride in a job well done and wouldn't accept a less than dedicated effort from their peers. They found that people will accomplish more and work harder for the respect and admiration of their peers than for anything else. Sam had counted on this because he knew that the most successful high schools with the best behaved students relied, not so much on the style of the principal and the teachers, but on a student body who held poorly behaving students in low esteem. It is more important to be respected by your peers than anybody else and the scorn of those peers is intolerable. Criticism from teachers was one thing; criticism from those who you want to like you was another.

Gina and Sam, by their second month, had come to realize this and used it to their advantage. They were on the floor daily, complimenting and recognizing work well done and gently retraining errant employees where necessary. It was working just as they planned.

They were making sweeping positive adjustments on all fronts. A new, state of the art, floor polisher and buffer was purchased and a man trained to operate it. He did nothing but wax and polish floors and became one of the home's most consistently praised workers, which made him very committed to his job. And proud. New housekeeping carts were purchased and stocked with a storeroom full of equipment for proper cleaning and disinfecting. By the end of the second month the place was literally gleaming. The most sensitive nose could not detect an odor.

Sam and Gina were meeting twice weekly with the residents to discuss all matters of concern. Food and recreation were always prime topics. The patients came to have primary input into the menus and activities. The new young owners won the hearts and loyalty of the residents in a very short time because, not only were they kind and understanding, but they would respond instantly to any request made by a resident. There was a new feeling of concern. Of family.

The recreation program was dramatically upgraded because Gina considered it a vital component in the overall picture. Before, it had consisted of one part time person who wrote letters for patients and held a weekly Bingo game, without any prizes for the winners. Offering no prizes to Bingo players was like having no payoff with slot machines. It virtually guaranteed no participation.

Gina hired a young enthusiastic recreational therapist and a full time assistant, a promoted nurse's aide who possessed a wonderful and natural ability to make people feel good about participating. A small bus was purchased with a hydraulic lift so that the wheel chair-confined patients could go on the daily rides to area spots of interest and to the Dairy Queen for ice cream. Everybody now had something to look forward to. Life was becoming worth living again for many who had shrunken into a guarded depression. Gina Oldani-Shaikowitz was deliriously happy. Her dream was coming true. A large picture of her mother appeared in the dining room and not a day went by that Gina didn't find time to go by and wink. Sometimes she asked, "How am I doing, Mom?"

After the first six months of tireless dedication to the home, Sam finally convinced Gina to take a ten-day vacation to the Bahamas with their son who they both felt was being slightly neglected because of their involvement in the nursing home.

The vacation was indeed therapeutic. The tanned and rested couple returned on December first with their batteries charged and renewed commitment. They were brimming with ideas on how to make the Christmas season really special at their home.

On their first day back they were surprised to find that the home had taken a step or two backwards in their absence. Reports from certain staff and residents confirmed what their eyes and noses told them: the high level of cleanliness and care that had become the norm had not been scrupulously maintained while they were away.

Gina especially was surprised and disheartened. "What does it mean Sam?" she lamented. "I thought the staff was doing a superior job because they cared about the patients, not because we're here every day and they'll lose their jobs if they don't. What the hell's the story?"

Sam thought a moment, then responded, "Come on now. Don't take it so personally. I'm actually as surprised as you are that the place could take such a nose dive in just two weeks. And at least seventy percent of the staff continued to do a good job while we were gone. It proves something that I suspected all along."

"What's that?"

"The home has been running well, no question about that. But it has been running on the strength of our personalities and our daily supervision. Things go well because we make them go well. We're going to have to train our supervisors better. They have tended to become workers along with everybody else rather than people who are expected to see to it that everybody does what they're supposed to. Their focus has become too narrow. It proves how complex and fragile something like this place really is. We're going to have to put our heads together and do something about it. I'll begin work on the problem tonight."

"Good," Gina said glumly. After a moment of reflection she brightened up a bit and rolled up her sleeves. "Let's get

244

out there and get this place humming again." Sam smiled at her tenacity and loved her for it.

Late that night after putting Orvie to bed Gina joined Sam in the study where he had been working since early evening.

"What 'cha got there, babe?" she inquired as she served him one of his favorite snacks, a thick slice of liverwurst on rye with cheddar cheese, onion, dill pickle and hot mustard accompanied by a bottle of Budweiser.

"Thanks cutes," he replied finishing his notes. "Look at this. It appeared in the November issue of the *Journal of the American Medical Association*. It's entitled 'Aging and Caring,' by Dr. Paul E. Ruskin of Cincinnati. I'm going to use it in my in-service education series at the home. Go read it."

Gina took the small article that Sam had cut out and began.

AGING AND CARING

I was invited to present a lecture to a class of graduate nurses studying the "Psychological Aspects of Aging." I started with the following case presentation: "The patient is a white female...she neither speaks nor comprehends the spoken word. Sometimes she babbles incoherently for hours on end. She is disoriented about person, place and time. I have worked with her for six months, but she still does not recognize me."

"She shows complete disregard for her physical appearance and makes no effort whatsoever to assist in her own care. She must be fed, bathed and clothed by others; because she is edentulous, she must be changed and bathed often .... Her sleep pattern is erratic. Often she awakens in the middle of the night, and her screaming awakens others. Most of the time she is very friendly and quite happy. However, several times a day she gets quite agitated without apparent cause. Then she screams loudly until someone comes to comfort her."

I asked the nurses how they would feel about taking care of such a patient. They used words such as "frustrated," "hopeless," "depressed," and "annoyed" When I stated that I enjoyed taking care of her, and I thought they would, too, they looked at me in disbelief. I then passed around a picture of the patient — my six-month old daughter. After the laughter subsided, I asked why it was so much more difficult to care for a 90-year-old than a 6-month-old with identical symptoms.... The infant we agreed represents new life, hope and utmost potential; the demented senior citizen, on the other hand, represents the end of life, with little potential for growth. We must change our perspectives. The aged patient is just as lovable as the child. Those ending their lives in the helplessness of old age deserve the same care and attention as those beginning their lives in the helplessness of infancy.

After reading it Gina sat back and smiled broadly, "God Sam, it's wonderful. The staff will love it."

Sam nodded. "I'm planning a lot of neat stuff. In addition to the training, I'm going to institute a kind of once a week therapy session for all shifts. We'll have to pay them to come at first but it'll be worth it."

"Therapy session?"

"I studied under a very able guy at school and always wanted to try it."

Gina was interested but cautious. "What are you going to do? Psychoanalyze everybody?"

Sam laughed. "No, it will be totally non-threatening, geared to encourage everybody to talk about the things that bother them in their lives. We'll play communication games and do problem-solving tasks. All aimed at getting people to relax and reveal how they feel about themselves and their jobs and other people. We've talked about this before and I think we agreed that our staff can only give their maximum to our patients if they are feeling up to par themselves. It's tied to the 'my cup runneth over' theory, which says that you are more able to give when your own cup is full. When your cup is not full, you will be less likely to spontaneously give to others because some of your energy is being used up on your personal concerns. Talking about our feelings is one way we can relieve the stress and tension in our lives and be less hung-up. You and I do it with each other all the time." He made a steeple with his fingers attempting to look wise and pontifical. "That's why we're the most beautiful and well-adjusted human beings I know."

Gina laughed.

"Seriously though," Sam continued, "I'm excited about this idea. I think it's going to create a very healthy situation."

"Me too. I love you, Sam."

"I love you too, sweet baby."

CHAPTER 38

By early spring the Louise Oldani Memorial Home was flowering into the model that Gina had envisioned. The emphasis on making the goals of the home clear to the staff and then giving them the proper training and equipment to do the job continued. The in-service training program was a mixture of Sam's creative "therapy sessions" and his workshops where the staff role played what it must be like to be a patient in a nursing home. He required that everyone be tied up (restrained, in nursing home parlance), be fed by another person, wear glasses with foggy lenses and have stoppers put in their ears. These kinds of exercises made the point very clearly and dramatically how frustrating it is to not have your senses working properly. There was general agreement that having to be fed was one of the most humiliating of the indignities which patients had to suffer. Being tied down was absolutely intolerable for a few of the people, and having their sight or hearing diminished was bad, but there was something about having another person feed them that almost everyone found revolting. It caused everyone to be more considerate of those who couldn't feed themselves.

It wasn't long before a wealth of innovative ideas flowed from these sessions. Gina gave twenty-five dollars to anyone who came up with an idea good enough to be used. This motivator, along with the overall philosophy that everyone can contribute to a better facility, paid off like mining for gold. The following ideas were submitted by staff and rewarded in just the first three months of the program:

"Suggestions"

Sweat pants work much better than pants or slacks with patients who are difficult to dress. They are easier to put on and take off, are warm and look good. Sweat pants come in a large variety of colors and are very comfortable to wear and easy to launder.

I have noticed that persons with aphasia are able to sing entire songs with ease, while their every day speech is very limited. These patients should be encouraged to sing with perhaps the eventual aim of greater return of functional speech. Singing is excellent for the morale and allows the patient to communicate with adults who have no linguistic disturbance. As they sing together, they are all approximately on the same linguistic level. Anything that gives human beings something in common is good.

In our nursing home most patients are encouraged to get up and about every day. But there are times when a patient is ill enough so that he must remain in bed for a time. When this happens, the patient's reaching to the same side of the bed for everything causes asymmetrical use of muscles. To prevent this, either relocate the bed in the room or move the equipment from one side to the other at least once a day to encourage use of both sides of the body.

When patients cannot feed themselves, have the one who is doing the feeding seated so that he or she is surrounded on three sides by patients, or seated on the other side of a long table with three or four patients on the other side. The feeder then alternates feeding each patient from his or her individual plate or tray. This allows each patient time to swallow the food without seeming to be rushed and lets the feeder take care of three or four patients in about the same time it would take to feed one.

We should never assume that a sick or dying person cannot understand what we say, no matter what his condition. It is a good practice never to say anything in front of him that we wouldn't want him to hear. Too often people say things within hearing distance of a patient they think is unresponsive, only to learn later that what they said was fully understood.

Whenever a confused, mentally impaired older person asks you the same question many times during the day ("What day is it today?") you have to understand clearly that he really doesn't remember the many times he has asked and received this answer before. Remember, to him it's still the first time. So it's rude and pointless to argue or tell him you've already answered his question before. Patience is what's needed here. Answer the question ("It's Tuesday"). True, your clear answer this time isn't going to prevent him from asking the same question later, but neither would any other response. And remember, tomorrow you can come up with a different answer.

When a deaf person asks you a question that can be answered with a simple yes or no, there is no point in making a big production out of the answer. He's watching your lips for the answer. Give it to him quickly and add the details later, if needed.

When an older person tells us that he feels so old, it is easy for us to want to jump in with reassurances that he is not old, but this kind of quick denial tends to reinforce a negative concept of aging, implying that aging is indeed undesirable. There's a reason why this older person may feel older today. He may be tired, depressed, or any number of things, all of which could change tomorrow. The best response might be, "What do you mean?" This might lead to the reason why he feels so old, in which case you're in a better position to help.

When an older person expresses a desire to die, what he really may be saying is that he wants desperately to get relief from some current painful situation. He may feel neglected, have a terrible headache, feel unwanted or any number of things, any one of which can be temporary. It's important to find the reason. Once you do this you can get down to the specifics. Meaningless generalities, "It's a beautiful day today and you should want to see it out" or, "You'll feel better tomorrow" accomplish nothing. Before you can be truly helpful you must first find out the reason he wants to die. A troubled person needs someone to listen more than anything else.

Some of the ideas had a real flair.

Recently an employee won a handsome bonus from a large company when he solved a problem for them. It seems they were getting frequent complaints about the slowness of the elevators in their downtown office building. When timed, it was found that, indeed, the cars were moving at an unacceptably slow pace. The cost to refurbish them and to make them move faster was going to be prohibitive but it looked as though some businesses on the upper floors were going to move if something wasn't done. Management needed to act.

An elderly custodian, being a wise observer of human nature for many years, submitted his simple and inexpensive idea to the company. Very shortly, after a minimal investment, the complaint of slow elevators was never heard again.

The custodian's idea was to install mirrors on each side of every elevator on every floor. People love to look at themselves and were so taken up with it that they no longer were conscious of the time spent waiting for the slow elevators. This idea holds true for our nursing home as well. Days will be more happily spent if people are frequently able to see their reflection. It's something we never tire of.

Gina loved it when employees were overheard to say, "Miss Gina and Mr. Sam ain't too good to get down on their hands and knees and scrub floors." She knew that they had won the respect and loyalty of the majority of their employees. It was true that when she or Sam walked into the lunchroom or coffee break the conversation would change immediately and perceptibly. They would never be "one" of the workers and would never be a part of the employees' social fabric. In that regard it was still the old Massah-Slave relationship. Gina and Sam lamented this fact but understood that it was just that way. At least they were kind, understanding Massahs. The staff respected them because there was no question about their dedication to their patients and the word was getting around that something different and good was happening at the Louise Oldani Home. There was a steady stream of outstanding applicants who came to apply from other nursing homes, people whose hearts and minds were in the right place. It was becoming known as "the" place to work.

Gina's sharp mind and common sense had caused her to develop a way of relating to certain patients in a way that was unfamiliar to everyone. All the books on mental illness and the few that existed on geriatrics were advising that you follow a consistent course with patients who are disoriented, having lost touch with who they are, where they are and what day it is, and those who are experiencing memory lapses. It was also consistently recommended that people who work with patients who wish to talk about people who are dead, such as mothers and fathers, be gently reminded that they are gone and that it is now 1970 and that they are in a nursing home. "How could your folks be alive if you are 85 years old yourself?" was a frequently heard question.

In keeping with this strategy, "reality" boards are maintained throughout many nursing homes which announce the month, day and year and even the weather forecast. It was reasoned that this constant reminder of time, place and person would slow down the assault on the patient's memory and orientation.

Gina just had one problem with it all. It didn't work. The patients' memories and orientation didn't improve on a steady diet of reality. Worse than that, it seemed insulting, undignified, and unkind to tell people that their mother and dad couldn't possibly be coming to visit today—they're dead—ad nauseam. Gina discovered another way of relating to this kind of patient which was kind and made the person feel better. It also cemented the listener's relationship to the patient and guaranteed cooperation instead of the resistance and resentment that the reality system fostered. The reality game turned people off, Gina's way turned them on.

Gina stumbled on the concept one day while talking to a little ninety-year-old lady named Elizabeth McCree.

Mrs. McCree frequently yelled at the top of her lungs, wet herself regularly and was very disoriented. Each day, although unable to walk more than a few steps, she would rise from her chair and make for the door, announcing that she was going home to Nashville to visit her parents. Naturally this brought on the customary reality stuff and a tolerant "there goes Elizabeth again" reaction from the staff.

One day, early in the takeover, Gina sat down with Mrs. McCree, and when she began her unrealistic story about going to Nashville, Gina, rather than the usual reaction, said things like, "You must have loved your mother and father.

Tell me about them. Nashville must have been a wonderful place to live. "What was your house like?"

As it turned out, that was all that Mrs. McCree needed.

She ceased yelling and wetting herself which was the way she chose to vent her frustration and rage over the fact that no one would ever listen to her talk about her life. She looked forward to Gina's daily visit and no longer felt the need to try and walk to Nashville each day. Gina had made it possible for her to take the trip in her mind.

This concept was somewhat difficult for the staff to put into practice. It was easy enough to grasp the idea intellectually and everybody saw the dramatic change in Mrs. McCree, but sometimes old ways die hard. The people were unwitting victims of the way their parents had raised them — the old "shut up and do as I say" method. Just as they were raised to believe that their opinions had no value, so then did they raise their children. This style then carried over in the way they related to old people. The idea that a child or a demented person needs to be listened to, rather than corrected and instructed, simply ran counter to the learning of a lifetime. The resistance to it was illogical but nevertheless powerful and hard to overcome. Like racism. It was like trying to convince someone who believes in faith healing that it's a hoax or debunking professional wrestling to a fan who is convinced that the staged mayhem is real.

Concurrent with the implementation of all the staff-oriented improvements, a steady wave of physical changes were taking place at the home. The halls were papered in a rich mauve color that was pleasing to the eye and vastly more cheerful than the pale institutional green paint which had dominated before. A beautiful patio with water fountains, flowers and a screened-in porch were constructed. Festive picnics and barbecues were held regularly in season to the delight of all. All new furniture in the lounge, the patient rooms and dining room were provided which added a warm continuity and feeling that this place had been planned in totality and not just patched together as Rube Goldberg might have done it.

Each patient's room was decorated only after a consultation with the patient and their families. The families' positive reaction to the improvements was overwhelming. They visited more frequently, brought furniture and clothing as never before and praised Gina and Sam for the miraculous changes not only in the facility but in the attitude and behavior of their loved one. Their guilt was lessened with the feeling that excellent care was now the byword.

Gina bought and had trained two Labrador retrievers especially for the home. The dogs, Sonny and Cher, were trained as meticulously as their seeing eye counterparts and made a marvelous addition as full time mascots. Gina selected the breed because of their excellent disposition and affectionate nature. The patients and staff loved the dogs. Along with the dogs, bird cages with pairs of love birds or parakeets were put in every room where patients requested them. The popularity of this innovation grew quickly, and soon seventy per cent of the rooms had a bird cage. One day, unknown to Gina, the kitchen supervisor, Carla, walked through the home dressed like a farmer. She asked all the residents if they had seen her goat. Everyone was puzzled by her behavior. Later in the day Carla reappeared, leading a cooperative goat which stood still so the residents could pet it. It was a creative and memorable experience.

Gina also saw to it that children, preferably of elementary age, visited at least weekly. The shower of attention and affection they received from the residents was more than adequate compensation for their efforts. The positive effect they had on the old people was immeasurable. Gina always gave the children a little lecture about what to expect and how to act and then rewarded their performance with a treat after the visit. Everybody was a winner.

Gina had expected the inspections by the State Department of Social Services to be more thorough and maybe even a little constructive. They turned out to be, at least for the first two years, irregular and cursory. The inspectors found little to criticize especially after the first six months of operation, and when they did cite a deficiency, it was usually a light out or some other small trivial thing.

That's the way it went until a team of four people arrived one hot day in July to do an overdue inspection for the home's license renewal. This team was headed by a nurse named Rita Belkin who was well known in nursing home circles and a zealot for patient's rights.

Rita Belkin stood alone in an otherwise sea of apathy where nursing home inspections were concerned. Gina was aware of her reputation as a much feared and sometimes hated inspector. Each time there was a gathering of nursing home administrators her name was sure to be brought up and used in vain. She was so thorough and fanatical in her inspections that the other inspectors seemed wimpy by comparison.

Rita Belkin was a solidly built, fifty-year-old nurse who had served a stint in a large west county nursing home as director of nursing, a position she held for some eighteen months before management was forced to let her go because of her unrealistic demands on the staff and her abrasive manner. "She was unable to inspire a cooperative environment between the various disciplines necessary for harmonious functioning," was the way the management company characterized her service. People who worked with her would have phrased it somewhat differently. Something like, "She was a rigid, dictatorial bitch who only cared about one thing—getting her own way," would be the language they would have used.

The nursing home inspector job was well suited for Rita. It gave her ample opportunity to lord it over others and she could travel around to share her venomous personality with lots of people instead of confining it to a few. She would swoop down on a facility and in three days write as many as one hundred separate deficiencies ranging from minor nit-picky stuff to serious and life-threatening problems dealing with fire safety, medication and infection control. Some homes were simply unable to satisfy this hellion and the state was forced to begin license revocation proceedings, a cumbersome, costly and usually ineffective legal action which always ended up in one of two ways: the home was sold and the new owners started fresh or the facility was put on a one year probation, giving them ample time to correct the problems.

Rita Belkin would never realize what effect her crusading was having on the Missouri Nursing Home scene. Her random lambasting struck fear into the hearts of the owners who became very willing to pay officials to keep her off their backs. The officials who could control which homes she inspected assigned her to places they knew were marginal and then easily collected their payoff money to see to it that she didn't return for follow up inspections and further harassment.

The local newspapers loved the issue of poor care to the elderly, of course, and periodically wrote articles which did nothing to improve the perception of the nursing home industry in the eyes of the public. Rita Belkin felt vindicated, even saintly, and redoubled her efforts to single-handedly whip the industry into shape. She did find it curious that she was constantly moved around to new homes while the other inspectors tended to have more stable assignments allowing them to work with homes on a long term basis. Her supervisor easily explained her apprehension away by confidentially sharing an upper-management strategy that utilized her as a trouble shooter on a white stallion. This was easy for her to swallow since it was exactly how she perceived herself anyway. The guys who were recipients of the graft watched her antics with amusement and did all they could to make the threat of being "Belkinized" a real and frightening possibility for all nursing home owners. After being terrorized by Rita the owners were only too happy to come to terms and gratefully accept a different and "more understanding" inspector in her stead.

It was with this background that Rita Belkin strode into the Louise Oldani Memorial Home and asked to see the administrator. Gina was summoned over the intercom but didn't respond immediately because she was in the middle of a session with a group of residents —not a good way to start with Rita Belkin, whose sense of self importance was never lacking in the first place, but had now swelled to gargantuan proportions.

Rita cooled her heels in the waiting room outside Gina's office for a full thirty-five minutes before Gina finally rushed in, profusely offering her apologies. She explained that she had a rule that nothing short of a dire emergency could interrupt her sessions with patients.

I've heard that line before, Rita thought. The patients are the most important priority in my life stuff. We'll see. She had been consistently disappointed, not in what administrators said, which was always good, but in what they did. She had yet to meet one who didn't do the "I'm-for-good-care" song and dance. Then she would find multiple and sometimes serious infractions of the rules in the homes. She always found it very satisfying to humble that kind and bring them to their knees. This pretty young thing with the expensive designer clothes might prove to be the best yet.

Gina could feel the disdain, or was it down right hostility, oozing from Rita's pores as she stood there in her K-Mart clothes and a run in her left stocking. Rita was no slave to fashion.

Gina had heard of the notorious Rita Belkin, but she was naturally ignorant of the game that Rita's bosses were playing. She wasn't yet aware of the compulsive nature of this insecure women who sought to find identity in her shallow personal life through the domination of others. She was careful to hide under the cloak of being the way she was for the good of old people; this gave her all the license and respectability she needed. No one could argue with such a noble purpose.

Gina sensed that this woman was not to be trifled with, so, rather than becoming friendly and helpful, she became businesslike and somewhat brusque. She hoped to put this seedy pain in the neck out of her life as quickly as possible. Gina wondered silently if Rita had undergone surgery to have her charisma gland removed. Rita had that effect on people.

With that rather chilly beginning, Rita methodically began her task. She first made a quick tour through the whole facility to get a feeling for the place. She then went room to room with her large legal pad, making notes as she went. A thorough review of all charts, a monitoring of two medicine passes and a evaluation of the dietary and house-keeping departments followed. She was seen poking under beds with a flashlight looking for dust and sticking thermometers under hot water faucets and into food to insure that both were the proper temperature. She checked staff schedules and demanded to look at the time cards and the payroll for the past six months to insure that a proper staffing level had been maintained. She examined the finger-nails, hair and even the feet of over half the patients. She talked to each of them about how they were being cared for, how they liked the food and what was the thing they liked least about the facility. Gina had to admit that she was a little intimidated by all this. Sam attempted to help her deal with the apprehension by saying that it would be unnatural not to feel anxiety when you're put under such scrutiny. He had a way of making everything so clinical.

At the end of the third full day of inspecting, Rita announced that she would meet with Gina and Sam at 3:30 that afternoon for an exit interview. At that time she would make a preliminary review of her findings.

Sam begged off, claiming that he had a pressing prior commitment that he couldn't ignore. Actually, he was aware that his dislike for Rita Belkin was so intense that he and the nursing home would be better off if he avoided her altogether. He knew that Gina was far more adroit at handling difficult people. She had a gentle way about her that made it very difficult for others to beat up on her. Sam, on the other hand, tended to become aggressive when battle lines were drawn. His decision to not participate in the exit interview was a good one. Gina understood.

Promptly as agreed, Rita appeared at Gina's office door and was politely invited in where tea and oatmeal cookies awaited. No need to not be civilized.

Rita Belkin's personality had undergone a change. She was now smiling and friendly rather than cold and officious as she had been for the last three days. Gina was puzzled but preferred what she was getting now to what had gone before. The reason for Rita's metamorphosis was soon to be disclosed.

"Well, Gina," she began, "you've done an outstanding job here. I gave this place as thorough an inspection as I could and I'm not able to find anything that is seriously amiss. I must admit that I went overboard looking for problems." She let that soak in for a minute then continued, "I've never said that to an administrator before. I usually find many things wrong because it's nearly impossible to keep a nursing home completely trouble free. Usually I don't have to look for problems very long because disgruntled employees are always happy to lead me directly to them. I must say that you have an unusually loyal and dedicated staff. They all seem to like you. If I were to inspect and grade hospitals the way I do nursing homes they'd all be shut down. Hospitals make more mistakes, and I'm talking about life-threatening mistakes, in medication errors and contamination than nursing homes. But surprisingly they don't have the same high degree of government regulation that nursing homes have to live with. And you haven't seen the last of it. Soon there will be a bill drafted by the state that will call for new, higher standards of care and a timely process for

261

closing homes that don't measure up. I'm very happy about it."

Gina smiled and responded genuinely, "I have no doubt about your commitment to good care for the elderly, Rita."

While mouthing these platitudes Gina was aware of her feelings of irritation at this self-righteous, pompous woman who obviously enjoyed her position of power. Maybe it was partly due to her frumpish appearance. No, Gina thought, it would be no different if she were personally impeccable. Probably worse in fact. I'd like to pop into her house by surprise some morning and inspect it thoroughly. Gina was amused at the prospect. It was a little like pretending that someone who intimidates you is dressed only in their underwear. Gina actually appreciated a diligent inspector but couldn't shake the uneasy feeling that comes from being evaluated by an outside agency—even if she was doing a good job.

Rita smiled with gratitude and said, "Thank you, Gina. It is not very often that I have a decent, friendly conversation with an administrator. I'm usually backed into an adversary relationship with them. You wouldn't believe some of the conditions that are being tolerated."

Gina nodded affirmatively and added, "Yes, I would. Sam and I visited a number of homes in the area before buying this one. I wholeheartedly agree that something massive needs to be done. You can't do it on your own."

Rita was pleased to find this oasis of understanding.

"Yes, I realize that, but I'm not going to give up trying. I get threatening phone calls now and I meet with hostility almost everywhere I go. All of that bothers me, but old people deserve a better shake than they're getting, and by God, I'm going to do all I can to see that they get it." She hit her fist on the desk for emphasis.

The two of them talked until seven o'clock that night exchanging war stories and sharing idealistic views on how the nursing home industry needs to change. They parted,

262

feeling refreshed and promising to keep in close touch. Each believed that she had found an ally this day. Gina was relieved to see that this nemesis of nursing home owners was a human being. Her motives, which may be overzealous and self-serving, were nevertheless preferable to those who turned their backs on the rampant abuses which she knew existed in nursing homes.

CHAPTER 39

Sam was glad to hear that their home had received such rave reviews from Rita Belkin. He knew that if anybody could expose her human side it would be Gina. She was so honest herself that she usually brought out the best in others. His decision to stay clear of Rita Belkin was correct. His presence would have kept the exit interview stiff and formal because he couldn't have disguised his impatience with the woman. Bureaucrats of any kind gave him heartburn. But more than that, he was becoming bored with the nursing home. He had enjoyed the early days when it was a mighty challenge, and he liked working side by side with Gina, but now the challenge had dimmed somewhat as the home was running smoothly. It was now a matter of maintenance of effort and he was a man who flourished on a fast track with lots of competition rather than settling down in a groove. He knew that Gina would understand his need to continue his own interests, but at the same time he wasn't anxious to tell her. He was waiting for the right time. His delay meant that he knew it would be a disappointment for her. He did have one more project that he wanted to instigate and then he planned to hire and train a social worker or psychologist to carry on his work. He outlined his idea to Gina over lunch the next day.

Between bites of tuna salad, Sam launched into his program. "You know how we've struggled with offsetting the guilt that the adult children feel about putting their parents in a nursing home?"

Gina nodded, "It's a problem with every admission. Usually it gets better when they see how well we treat their parents, but it creates a barrier. I believe the parents twist

264

the guilt knife even though they know that their children have to go on with their own lives."

"Exactly," Sam agreed. "People don't easily come to the point where they realize that they are powerless to change the fact that aging carries with it losses—losses in physical and mental abilities, as well as feelings of worthlessness and the depression that goes along with it. We simply can't bring back youth to our aging parents, as much as we'd like to. We can't recapture their lost health and vitality or reverse a memory loss or bring back others in the family who have died or moved away. Children must learn to recognize the emotional feelings which result from these losses and let their parents know they understand and care about their well being. You and I have been moved many times by the anguish, frustration, pity, anger, and remorse that people feel as they try to do the right thing for their parents. Well, we can't change the facts of aging. We can only address the consequences of it with understanding and sympathy. That's my strategy. We've now started groups with employees and with patients and, even if I do say so myself, they've been enormously beneficial."

Gina agreed enthusiastically, "Our nursing home wouldn't be nearly so successful without the work you've done." She hoped she didn't sound condes- cending.

Sam didn't take it that way as he continued, "I'm going to organize three groups of people who have relatives in our home and do the same kind of thing. They need the opportunity to empty their hearts and unpack their guilt baggage. When they do, they'll not only feel better but they'll be better with their loved ones. It all seems so simple to me."

Gina responded by leaning over and touching his hand. "Well, it's not simple. It requires someone like you who has the training and understanding to think of it. Your special skill at facilitating the groups is what makes it work."

Sam smiled and merely said, "Thanks, baby."

Gina knew that Sam was getting restless. He was just too creative and ambitious to be satisfied with his current role for very long. The time for his breaking out was near.

She prayed for the strength to let him go with no guilt whatsoever. An old saying came to mind. "If you have a bird in a cage and you love it, let it go. If it truly loves you, it will be back."

CHAPTER 40

It was the Tuesday before Thanksgiving. Bernie Shaikowitz had flown to St. Louis to pick up Orvie and then the two of them would return to Chicago to be joined by Gina and Sam for a joyous holiday. Sam and Gina planned to drive up early Thursday morning so they could be at the nursing home for the Thanksgiving program which would be held on Wednesday. Everybody was in a good mood and an early snow was predicted to add to the festive atmosphere.

After Orvie was in bed, Bernie joined his son and daughter-in-law for brandy. He smiled and said proudly, "That boy is smart as a whip, and so well behaved and respectful. Not at all like his father."

They all laughed.

The conversation eventually gravitated to nursing homes, as it always seemed to do when Sam and Gina were present.

Bernie said how happy he was that they were having success at it and how appropriate it was for husband and wife to be involved in business together. He joked, "You're saving me a room aren't you?"

Sam answered, slightly more serious, "Is that what you would want?"

Bernie thought for a brief moment. "No, I don't think so. If I lose my health, or my mind, just put me in a plastic bag and leave me out front for Mr. Deeters, the garbage man."

"I'm serious, Dad."

"Well, O.K. Hell no, I don't want to go to a nursing home, not even a good one like yours. Besides, I don't have to worry about it. I've got the money for private nurses." Everyone was silent until Bernie turned the question to Sam and Gina. "Do you guys want to go to a nursing home when your time comes?"

Sam answered, "Yeah, if I'm confused and messing my pants. It's best for all concerned."

"Gina?"

"Well, I wouldn't put it quite that way. I'd like a long and productive life like everyone else. But I'd never want to require that Sam or Orvie take care of me if I was incapacitated. I've thought a lot about the subject and I want their love, but I want it now, while I can return it. They don't need to prove it to me later by devoting and ruining their lives taking care of a sick old lady. That's like the mistaken notion that families have to bankrupt themselves to buy an expensive funeral to prove how much they loved the dearly departed. It doesn't do anybody any good except the flower shop and the undertaker. So yes, it's a nursing home for me. You boys come visit when you can."

"I'll remember that," Sam chided.

Thanksgiving Eve dawned gray and foreboding. It looked like snow in the forecast was going to prove accurate although the temperature was still in the forties as the day began.

Everyone in the household arose early because it was going to be a busy day. The Ozark Airline flight 543 left at 9:20, so they would have to leave for the airport no later than 8:00. Everyone was cheerful at breakfast and enjoyed the excitement of Orvie as his adoring grandfather kept up a constant stream of good-natured chatter with the boy.

The group arrived at the airport on time and because of Gina's insistence, and over Sam's objection they walked the Chicago-bound pair to the boarding site. Hugs and kisses all around. As they quickly disappeared behind a closed door Gina felt a tug of anxiety.

"Let's watch the plane take off," she said.

"O.K.," Sam said patiently, "Is something the matter?"

"No, it's silly," she shook her head.

"Come on, now," Sam coaxed, knowing there was something bothering her.

"I was just wrestling over the possibility of never seeing them again," she finally admitted.

Sam laughed and hugged his wife. "No chance of that. I've written our life story and that kind of stuff isn't included."

"Glad to hear it," Gina tossed off sarcastically as she wiped away a tear. "Let's go Sam. I want to be up and cheerful for the people today."

"As you always are."

The Louise Oldani Memorial Home was heavily decorated from the driveway to the rear door as it was at any holiday time. The decorations were largely made by the residents who, under the guidance of the recreation director, had been working for weeks on pilgrims, turkeys, cornucopias and other traditional trappings. They took pride in their accomplishment and beamed as visitors and staff laid on the compliments. Maybe too syrupy for some, but you couldn't tell it. Everyone was in a fine mood and dressed in his or her best clothes. The staff dressed in their "Sunday-go-to-meetin's" as well, to make it seem as much like a family affair as possible. The feeling of family was there.

Gina was everywhere, touching, joking, and being generally delightful. Residents excitedly introduced her to out-of-town relatives the way anxious school kids introduce a favorite teacher to their parents.

By 3 o'clock the party was over. The food had been plentiful and delicious—this was the one day that Gina let the diabetics cheat—and the entertainment program had met with roaring approval. All the visitors had gone by now, and the home slipped back into its routine as the evening shift came on and many of the residents took a nap.

Even Gina seemed tired as she and Sam took four o'clock tea in her office as they watched the beginning of the promised snow fall. "Sam?"

"Yaaas?" he drawled.

"Let's leave for Chicago now. We'll be there by midnight if we do and then we can relax all day tomorrow. What say?"

"I am but a slave to your every whim."

"There's not another man like you," she declared.

"True," he agreed modestly.

By the time they got packed and on the road it was 8 o'clock and dark. The snow was coming down steadily but was not yet sticking to the road because of the warm temperature which had now begun to inch its way down.

The Mercedes Benz sedan seemed comfortable and stable at fifty-five miles per hour, and both Gina and Sam began to relax, chatting easily about the day's events.

After thirty minutes or so on the road Gina became drowsy and couldn't stifle repeated yawns.

"Crawl into the back seat and take a nap, sweetie. You're over-tired and I want you well rested and relaxed for tomorrow."

"'Kay," Gina purred and did as he said without a whimper. "I love you," she said as she curled up in her mink coat. She fell asleep immediately.

CHAPTER 41

The next conscious thought Gina would have occurred four weeks later as she opened her eyes in total numbness and confusion. Her first awareness was the faint sound of music. Christmas music. Where was she? She caught a glimpse of something and rolled her eyes in the direction of the light to recognize a small Christmas tree on a table with a white sheet under it. She wanted to turn her head for a better look but was unable to. It struck her as odd that she had just woken up from a night's sleep but didn't feel the usual need to go to the bathroom. That was always a first thing with her. As she lay there silently, trying to collect herself and to figure out what was going on, she became aware that she was unable to move. She tried her toes. Nothing. Her fingers. Nothing. Her brain systematically instructed every part of her body to move. To do something. But there was no movement. No feeling, No feedback of any kind. She felt a momentary flush of relief as she thought that this was a return of the bad dreams she used to have. It was not unlike them. You pinch yourself in a bad dream to wake up. Right? She could think the thought but couldn't do the deed. Someone was coming into the room. They're looking at me she thought. They're dressed in white. Nurses! Maybe I'm at the nursing home. Where is Sam?

"Look. Her eyes are open. She's awake! I'll call the doctor. STAT. He said to notify him immediately. I never thought she would ever come out of it. Glory be."

That person left. The other stayed and wiped Gina's forehead and face with a cloth. She then pulled the sheet down and did something with Gina's body. She couldn't tell what. She couldn't feel anything and she was unable to talk. She tried again. Impossible. She could see. She could hear.

But nothing else seemed to work. She became frightened, panic set in. She lost consciousness.

She awoke again, sometime later, but had no way of telling how much time had gone by. This time she was aware of voices. A familiar man's voice. Bend over so I can see you. When he did, she recognized Dr. Edward Zarinsky.

If she were able to speak she might have said, "Hi, Doc. Haven't we already done this?" But his manner didn't suggest that he was in the mood for jokes. He was wearing his most concerned look.

"Well Gina, I'm very happy to see your eyes open. Can you hear me?" He directed a small flashlight into each pupil. "Very good," he said to no one in particular. "They react normally." Dr. Zarinsky went on with some further testing of reflexes and made some of the customary grunts and murmurs that everyone expects a doctor or a car mechanic to make.

Finally he bent over so that his face was inches from Gina's and told her, "Gina, honey, if you can hear me and understand what I'm saying, blink your eyes once." She did so, without hesitation, still sure that this was another bad dream.

"Great!" he said heartily with a big smile. "O.K., now we can communicate. One blink means yes, two blinks means no, three blinks mean I don't understand or I don't know. Got it?"

Gina blinked once.

"Good girl." Zarinsky seemed mildly excited, as was the nurse who stood in the background clearly admiring the handsome MD. He continued working with this helpless woman for whom he obviously had great affection.

"Let me start by filling you in on some things of which you are undoubtedly unaware. First of all, you were in a serious head-on collision with a truck on Thanksgiving Eve. It is now December 23rd. You have been in a coma since the

272

accident. Only because you were in the back seat was your life spared. You're now at Barnes where I've been looking after you. Did you realize any of this?" Blink-Blink.

"Gina," Zarinsky now measured his words most carefully, "I've always admired your courage and resourcefulness. Your ability to roll with life's punches and to make even very negative situations become positive has always impressed me greatly." He paused, dreading what he had to say. Maybe because of that dread he decided to tell Gina only about Sam's death and nothing more about her hopeless condition until she had time to deal with his loss. How much can one human being take?.

Zarinsky left her room stoop-shouldered and spent. Psychologically drained. He went straight to his Jaguar and headed for his sumptuous, suburban home where he proceeded to get outrageously, commode-hugging drunk. He knew that he would kill several thousand brain cells and damage his liver slightly and end up with a thundering hangover, but all of that was nothing compared to the hell which lay ahead for Gina Oldani Shaikowitz.

CHAPTER 42

Dr. Zarinsky called in several specialists to examine Gina in order to confirm his diagnosis. They all were in agreement. She had suffered a vertebral vascular infarction which causes occlusion of the vessels in the mid-brain stem. The condition is referred to as the lock out syndrome. The eyes can open and are seeing but there is no movement possible below the nose. Eye movement and blinking are the only possible functions. Prognosis: poor. Nobody knew how long she would live. Maybe a long time. Maybe not.

Bernie visited frequently, flying down at least three times a week. He asked Zarinsky if he could be present when the news of her condition was revealed to Gina. He wanted to comfort her as much as possible, although he dreaded it.

Zarinsky summoned as much strength and kindness as he could as he took on the dreaded job of informing Gina. Bernie was there holding her hand. When the physician had finished, Gina merely closed her eyes. Naturally, there could be no display of emotion or questions. Her cards had been dealt. There was nothing else anybody could do.

Bernie sat with Gina all day long for five straight days. During that time he talked almost constantly. He was beside himself with grief over his son's death and Gina's tragic fate. He told her every single detail he could think of about Sam's childhood and his life. He assured her that Orvie would be raised by him and his wife and that naturally he would have the best of everything.

Bernie wasn't sure of the best way to handle some subjects. How often should he bring Orvie to visit? Should he tell her about how he was handling the estate? He definitely decided against telling the story of the retribution he had exacted on Loretta Mandeville and the rapist. That story would give her no comfort. During the times when he could think of nothing to say, he read the newspaper aloud, hoping to give her any pleasure he could. He left out the distressing stories about the Viet Nam war. Only the soft stuff.

Bernie Shaikowitz had been doing a lot of thinking and soul searching. He pondered the nature of man. What kind of man could order and pay for the deaths of other human beings and yet be so moved and caring about those he loved? He decided that the two seemingly contradictory behaviors were linked. He was a man who would do whatever was necessary to take care of his own. A simple answer to a very complex question, but it served him well. It let him off the hook.

Bernie realized that he was making himself sick agonizing over this beautiful, wasted life lying in the bed with tubes feeding her and tubes draining her. Cruelly, they believed that her brain was still working but there was no avenue for expression of feeling or thought. Sometimes she even refused to play the blinking game. That was the only way she could control her environment.

Bernie was drinking himself to sleep every night, something he had never done before. He was sallow and losing weight. Sometimes, without warning, his body was wracked with sobs. He was hollow. Bewildered. He felt he couldn't hold up much longer. He had to have relief from the most acute discomfort he had ever felt in his life. He could only see one way to try and salvage his sanity. By taking care of his own in the best way he could.

Gina had been in the hospital for over five weeks and Dr. Zarinsky was telling Bernie that there was nothing further that they could do. It was time to move her. Bernie had already decided that he wanted Gina to decide where she would go. It seemed to him the choices were three. She could stay in a hospital. Any hospital. She could come home with him and have excellent around-the-clock care or she could go to her nursing home. Bernie recalled their conversation on the morning of the accident when she voiced a preference for a nursing home if infirmity should come. He thought she was serious and that she should be offered this option.

In his heart he hoped she would go to the nursing home. He couldn't stand to see her like this much longer. To him, it would be the best answer for a problem which was without a good solution. He was without hope. Shattered.

As Bernie hoped, Gina blinked yes to the nursing home. She did so instantly, without the slightest hesitation. Bernie knew she had already thought it through and he was grateful that she had made this decision.

He had one final agonizing task. He had to have Gina's assets legally put into a trust for her son with him as executor until Orvie was twenty-one. It was complicated, but Lawrence Daniels prevailed upon a local judge to visit Gina. The judge was persuaded that those were her wishes. Done.

Two days later Gina was in a private room in her nursing home. Bernie had gone back to Chicago to try to regain his mental health. His visits to St. Louis would be infrequent from this point on. She was essentially alone, a prisoner in a body that wouldn't work. She silently prayed for God to take her.

Her thought process had become fuzzy, partly because of the insult her brain had suffered and partly because of the sedating medication she was given. In her lucid periods she had thoughts that were indescribable. She couldn't vent her emotions. She couldn't cry, laugh, rant and rave or kick something. Everything stayed bottled up. There was no way to excise the grief. In some of her dreams she had feelings so strong that they took shape and she believed she could touch them. They were tangible, somewhat like the feeling that amputees must get when they believe their severed limb is aching. It was the brain's effort to try and make you as you were before.

Gina was in a private room with a special nurse assigned to her care twenty four hours a day. She got good care. A daily sponge bath, regular cleaning of her diaper and proper care of her urine catheter, and monitoring of her intake and output were some of the duties performed. She was turned frequently so that bed sores wouldn't develop, and her limbs were exercised so that her circulation was maintained and so that her muscles wouldn't atrophy too much. In spite of this, she was losing weight, wasting away.

Her private duty nurses read to her and the TV set was on at all times, more for the nurses than for Gina. All the girls, especially on the day and evening shifts, made sure they went in and spoke to her each day. They were closer than the night shift because Gina had worked side by side with them. She had met with the night shift frequently but that bond that forms between people who stand shoulder to shoulder wasn't there.

As the weeks and months went by, the attempts by the workers to cheer Gina up waned. Gina overheard more than one of them say, "She's given up the will to live."

Eight months dragged by. Gina knew she was giving in. They were right; she had lost the will to live. This was a struggle she couldn't win; she was ready to go.

Gina overheard that the home had been sold three months earlier to a rapidly expanding corporation based in New Orleans. Changes were taking place — economizing, staff cuts, everything imaginable to enhance the company's profit margin. In a matter of a few months the home had completely reverted to the condition it was in before Sam and Gina bought it. Maybe worse. The staff was unhappy and poor care was resultant. Most of the good employees were leaving.

One bright, sunny morning in May a frumpy woman walked into Gina's room with a clipboard. This authoritative lady told the nurse to take a break so she could speak privately with Gina. The nurse quickly and quietly left.

"Hi Gina. I'm told you can blink yes and no. Remember me?"

Two blink answer.

"No? I'm Rita Belkin, Inspector with the Division of Aging. Now do you?" Blink.

Rita tried to disguise her shock at the appearance of the once-beautiful lady who was now gaunt and chalky.

"Good. I hoped you would. I'm here to inspect the home for licensure. It's in trouble again."

"Everything, and I mean, everything, has gone to pot. If they don't do something about it, I'm going to recommend that their license be taken away, although that's easier said than done."

Gina didn't care any longer. She'd suffered enough. Her strength was gone. She wished this woman would leave and let her be.

Oblivious to this, Rita continued, "I already have twenty-six pages of deficiencies and more to come." She must have thought this would be good news to Gina. It wasn't. Now, everything she cared about was down the drain. Rita kept rattling for another ten minutes or so but Gina heard none of it. She went into a fetal position soon after Rita left and died a week later at the age of 32.

CHAPTER 43

December 3, 1983

The day shift at LaSalle Gardens Nursing Home was congregated in the dining room to celebrate the retirement of Hattie Mae McReynolds, LPN. Miss Hattie, as she preferred to be known, had worked at the home since it opened in 1955. She had begun as a nurses' aide, was promoted to medical technician and then was granted a one year leave of absence in 1970 to take training for her practical license.

The affection displayed at this ceremony was genuine.

She was, indeed, held in the highest esteem possible by one and all. She was a model of the kind hearted, concerned and competent person that all employers look for. The nursing home administrator, Mrs. Charlotte Jeebs, extolled her many virtues in a prepared speech before her fellow employees. Among other laudatory statements, she said that Miss Hattie was not only good at her job but was extremely loyal and dependable. She was presented with a dozen roses and a silver chafing dish from the management.

When asked if she would like to say a few words, those who knew her were surprised that she rose to do so. She was normally a shy lady who let her deeds do her talking for her. A hush of anticipation fell over the people gathered.

She began softly, wiping a traitorous tear from her eye. "I've been here since the place was built. Seen a lot of changes. Lot of changes." People in the group, feeling the mounting tension, began to respond as though it were a church meeting, saying "Yes, Lord" or, "Yes, indeed."

One younger lady, who obviously was full of admiration, kept saying "Teach, Miss Hattie, teach." Miss Hattie seemed to swell up to twice her size. "Back in '55, when they first opened, patients got cursed at, kicked at and treated like dogs. Treated like dogs."

She was testifying now, whipping the people up. "Yes, Lord."

"Teach, Miss Hattie."

She continued, "It wasn't until Miss Gina and Mr. Sam came that this place began to really take care of folks like you should. Like they deserves."

"I heard that."

"Tell it like it is, Miss Hattie."

"Those people cared. They made us all care. I was proud to work for them. Proud to be a woman who could do for others. And, in the name of Jesus, I always did the very best I could. Everyday." She threw both hands up and looked upward as though looking for a response from above. This ignited the room. Everybody stood up, whooping, hugging and making joyful noises.

The people calmed down. Miss Hattie had more to say. "I've learned this in my life: Love is the most important thing in this world. Only if you give love will it come back to you. That is the rule of God and the universe. Don't be lookin' to no man or possession to make you happy and take care of you. Only by giving love will it come back—no other way." The crowd remained quiet, respectful of the wisdom. "I believe that Jesus is watching all of us. When we do good He smiles and when Jesus is smiling about your life, it will be good and you will know happiness. Yes, love will come to you."

Miss Hattie's lower lip was quivering now but she was determined to continue. A brave, honest woman. "After Miss Gina and Mr. Sam passed, the place went down again." Murmurs of agreement. "And I know Miss Gina didn't rest easy knowing that. But praise the Lord she can rest easy at last because we've put the home back where it should be. I'm leaving you today with this solemn promise. If you dare let things slip back to what they were I'm going to come back and mess over all of you." With that she threw her hands in the air and said "Thank you, Jesus!" The people went foolish.

EPILOGUE

Miss Hattie's emotional, historical review of The LaSalle Gardens Nursing Home, a.k.a., The Louise Oldani Memorial Home, a.k.a., Sunset Meadows Nursing Home, a.k.a., McIlvane Manor was more or less right on target. The home had real ups and downs after Sam and Gina died until it was sold to a St. Louis family operation that knew how to run a quality home.

This company held the employees in high esteem as Sam and Gina did. They bought into the philosophy that the employees must be satisfied before they can give top flight care. To make the lives of some of the employees easier, the company added on a 40' X 40' room that was used as a daycare center for the children of employees. This lifted an intolerable burden of expense and worry from the backs of nearly half the employees.

While the home probably could never again be run with the imagination and energy that Sam and Gina provided, it had risen to a very respectable and acceptable level. It was clean and safe and had a number of caring employees. You would put a relative there.

The state of Missouri passed a sweeping, comprehensive, omnibus nursing home bill in 1982 that requires a new and higher level of care. The state department of aging has hired and trained adequate staff to see that these standards are maintained. Many homes in the state simply couldn't measure up. More homes were closed in a recent two-year period in Missouri than in any other state. But the ones that stood the test are proper. The bad ones are gone.

Nursing homes are now the second highest regulated entity in existence, second only to nuclear power plants. They're beginning to show it.

There will probably be other tragic nursing home fires. Occasionally, there will be people laying in their own waste for longer than necessary. And some elderly person, somewhere, is probably being neglected or even abused as you read this. But by and large, the industry has progressed the past thirty years. There is room for more improvement, but the system has worked. Our elderly are now being treated with the respect that they deserve.

As Miss Hattie would say, "Thank you, Jesus."

12337294R00154

Made in the USA
Charleston, SC
28 April 2012